The enormity of what she was doing hit Bridie like a blow. She was disposing of the babies' lives—as best she could, she reminded herself. Pegeen would understand that. She had begged her to look to their future. But she would never have seen their future like this.

'Wait now,' she said. 'Wait. Have—have you told him about the money?' Her mouth was dry, her tongue stuck to its roof.

Alphonse nodded. 'He is shocked to the very heart to hear that you want to sell the boys. He can't understand anyone putting a price on their own flesh and blood.'

She coloured to the roots of her hair, went hot and cold with shame. Yes, she was selling her own flesh and blood, or trying to. How dared this Alphonse be so pious and pompous about it? He wasn't poor, dirty, tired and alone in the world, and hungry most of the time. He and his brother had everything, she nothing. She needed money. They didn't. They wouldn't even miss it.

'I need the money,' she insisted. 'I'm alone. All alone.' She opened her hands in a gesture of entreaty.

If he was moved at all, it didn't show. 'How much is the blood-money? Thirty pieces of silver?'

Her fingers itched to scratch him, to mark the other side of his face as she had marked the first. She wondered how he had explained that to his brother. She held back, ready to burst into tears. The price of betrayal —that was what he meant! But it wasn't that, she told herself. She had found a home for the boys. Pegeen wouldn't begrudge her something for herself, alone and penniless in an alien land. 'Twenty-five dollars would do,' she whispered, 'to give me a start, like.' She knew it was an enormous sum as he looked at her with his brown eyes . . .

Barbara Cooper was born in Montreal, Canada, the second of five children. She was educated there and earned an Arts Degree from the University of Montreal. She met her first husband working at the Canadian Atomic Energy Project at Chalk River. They made their home in Oxfordshire and later in Lancashire. When he died she turned her hand to part-time work to have time to bring up her three children. Now married again, she writes romantic fiction.

Barbara Cooper's three other Masquerade Historicals are *The Choosing*, *Fortune's Kiss* and *Pale Moon Rising*. She has also written a longer novel, set in Canada in 1922, called *Beyond Paradise*.

THE PENNY ROAD

Barbara Cooper

MILLS & BOON LIMITED
ETON HOUSE 18–24 PARADISE ROAD
RICHMOND SURREY TW9 1SR

First published in Great Britain 1987
by Mills & Boon Limited

© Barbara Cooper 1987

Australian copyright 1987
Philippine copyright 1987

ISBN 0 263 75882 6

Set in 10 on 10½ pt Linotron Times
04–1087–82,050

Photoset by Rowland Phototypesetting Limited
Bury St Edmunds, Suffolk
Made and printed in Great Britain by
Cox & Wyman Limited, Reading

PROLOGUE

'Ah, Pegeen, there'll never be another like you!' Hugh Prendergast ran his hand through her luxurious red hair spread over the hay. 'You get in a man's blood, drive him mad with desire.' He tugged at a handful of her hair, pulling her face towards his.

'Ouch!' she cried, 'That hurts! Why can't you be gentle, Hughie?'

'Would you be liking me better if I were?' His lips closed on hers, demanding, claiming them as his right. His fingers were hard on her breasts. 'You're mine, whatever happens, remember it.'

'It's wrong, It's wrong what we're doing. I'm promised to Maling.' She shivered but did not move away from him. She didn't want to—she couldn't, and him so powerful and her body wanting him so. 'It'll never come right for us.'

'It's right for us now. Maling'll never know. Keep your warnings and your tremblings for some other time. This afternoon is our own. No one'll disturb us. No one comes near the place.'

'It was clever of you to think of it,' she murmured. 'You've always been the crafty one, thinking of places where we could be with each other. This one's the best of all.' Her hands were busy, playing a tune upon his back. It started down the length of his spine, over the twin humps of his taut buttocks, then back to his shoulders. The words of the nuns and the priest were just a faint whisper in the afternoon sunlight—words said on a Sunday in a packed church. What did they have to do with what Hugh and she shared? She could put them out of her mind when he touched her.

His lips were a fire, moving from her nipples to her hips, to the inside of her legs. There was no softness in him today, no softness at all. He was all male, her true partner. She bit at his shoulder, clawed at his neck. Ah, she could match flame with fire. Talking could wait. He'd said they had to talk. There had been precious little talking between them. Where was the need of it, when body spoke to body as it was doing now?

She cried out when he took her—a song of pleasure and of triumph. He was hers . . . all the beauty of him and the strength. He poured himself into her, and she gloried in the act. She forgot the hardness of the dirt floor, the prickliness of the hay under her, the desolation of the hut, abandoned with the failure of the potato crop and the exodus of its owners to America to salvage what they could of their lives.

She slept in his arms, warm, satisfied. He kissed her awake. She stirred and ran a finger down his cheek, still pressed to him. This was the time she liked best, when she lay with him, teasing him, tantalising him. The second time was better than the first. At any rate it was for her, because the fierceness had gone from him. All the fire was in her.

Today there was no second time. He tossed her clothes to her. He was putting on his shirt.

'Get dressed.'

The terse command shocked her. 'There's no hurry. I've the whole afternoon.' Her hand lay on her dress, but she made no move to slip it on. Nakedness had never frightened her.

If she thought to tempt him into renewed passion, she was mistaken. He stood looking down at her, pulling his belt tight around his lean waist.

'Cover yourself.'

There was something about the words and the way he said them which frightened her. He was looking at her as if he didn't like what he saw. She blushed, the colour hot in her cheeks. Why was he making her feel ashamed? She pulled the dress against her body, shielding herself from his gaze.

'Put it on. We have to talk.'

'Turn round, then.' She didn't know why she said it. She had never felt she had to keep herself hidden from him. He shrugged and turned away, waiting for her. She dressed herself. 'Shall we sit by the fire? I'm glad you thought of lighting one, Hugh.'

'It's only a few sticks. No one will notice the wee trail of smoke—not here.'

Pegeen put her shawl round her shoulders, and sat on the stool near the hearth. There was a bit of sunlight coming through the chinks of the wall, but it was a sad-looking place, bleak and deserted, and it was cold, cold with a December chill. Strange she had not noticed it before. But she never noticed where she was with Hugh. When he was there she was warm, be it in barn or lonely cottage.

'Sit beside me.' She patted the other stool placed close beside hers. Hugh didn't sit. He stood over her. She couldn't read the expression on his face, but she shivered. He looked remote, as icy as the fear spreading round her heart. 'What is it?' she whispered.

'It's ended. It's over.'

She heard the words, but could not believe them. She was numb, dumb, and could only look at him.

'Don't you understand what I'm after saying?' He didn't move, didn't touch her.

'I heard you,' she mumbled. 'It can't be over! You can't be finished loving me—not after what we just did.'

'I never spoke about love. What's love, anyway? A kiss in the dark, a quick fumble in the hay.' He was a dark shadow beside her, straight and tall—and distant.

She put out her hand and touched his leg. 'It's not you saying these things. Tell me it's not you! It's the truth we never said anything about loving, but wasn't it there in every embrace, in every kiss you burned on me? Wasn't it there?' Her fingers gripped his knee.

He reached down and pushed them away. 'There's no use hanging on to me. I've told you it's done.'

'But why? Why?' she pleaded. 'You said I was in your blood. You can't be casting me off!'

'You're a witch—I'll not deny that! You've pleased me better than any girl I've ever had. It's the bright hair of you and the paleness of your skin acts like a charm on a man.' His hand rested for a moment on her hair falling about her shoulders, gleaming even in the dim light. 'Ah, let's not be quarrelling, Pegeen. We both knew it couldn't go on. You're promised to Maling.'

'Promises can be broken.' She clasped both his knees. 'Why should I marry Maling when it's you that I want?'

'Because you can't go back on your promise. Because Maling's my brother.'

'The true reason, Hugh? I deserve that, at least.' She took her hands from his legs and stood up to face him.

'It's just like I said,' he blustered. 'We knew it would end. Let's walk away friends. We've both enjoyed it; nay, you needn't deny it.' He held her by the shoulders away from him.

She looked into his set face. 'There's never friendship between a man and a woman. How can there be? Hugh, Hugh, why are you pretending I meant nothing to you?'

'I'm pretending nothing. I'm telling you it's over.' At her sharp intake of breath, he went on. 'There's no need to take on. I've told you you're more satisfying than any woman I've ever had. Isn't that enough for you?' He shook her.

'No, it's not! How can it be?' Her hand came up from her side, and before he could stop her she had clawed his face. Four great scratches drew blood from one cheek.

'You devil!' he cried, and captured her hand, twisting it cruelly, forcing it behind her back and pushing her to the wall. He held her there while she tried to escape. Her foot tried to kick him. She would have kneed him if she had been able, but he held her too close, off balance.

His lips descended on hers in a brutal kiss—a kiss she found herself returning as his tongue entered her mouth. Then he shoved her aside so that she fell to the floor like a rag doll thrown from its owner.

She lay where she had fallen, and listened to him speaking to her from a distance.

'You're magnificent when you're angry, and there's no denying that I'll miss the excitement of mastering you! But marry you—and that's what you seem to expect suddenly—no, never! You've nothing to bring to the marriage bed but yourself, and I've savoured that anyway. I intend to be a rich man with a wife who'll bring me some cash! Marry you, and I'd be like the rest of them here, saddled with babbies every year and never enough to go round. Nay, it's not for me. Not for Hugh Prendergast! I've seen what love does for people . . . It shackles them for ever.'

Pegeen couldn't rise to her feet. All her will, all her pride in herself, had gone out of her. She put her hands over her ears to keep out the sound of his voice.

'Get up,' he growled, and his foot pushed at her. He pulled her hands from her head.

'Why should I?' she snarled at him, and managed to grab at his leg and trip him so that he fell beside her. Even then, she couldn't believe what he'd said. Her fingers seized his jacket. 'Hugh, you've enough wealth already. You've a crop of wheat that'll keep you all winter—and didn't *I* get the seeds for you from the place where I work?'

He sat up, not touching her but brushing at himself as if to remove the stain of her fingers. 'I wonder what you had to do to get them? How many times did you go with O'Malley?'

She slapped at him, would have marked him again, but he slid himself out of her reach. 'I never went with O'Malley! I can't help it if he thought that I would. I did what you asked, got you what you wanted. You've the luck of old Nick himself—you and your mother! I suppose she's behind all this. She's the one who tells you what to do—and you do it. She's the man of the house!' Pegeen's scornful laugh echoed in the hut.

'The old woman has a head on her shoulders. You can't say No to that.'

'She's never liked me. She's the meanest old woman in all Kilkenny, and she has you under her thumb. She's never ruled Maling the way she's ruled you.' Pegeen rose to her feet, dusting herself.

'Ah, has she not? It was herself put Maling out—put him working on the Penny Road. She knew the only way for him to make any sort of living at all was away from the place. She promised the Da the place wouldn't be divided up again when he went. She couldn't help it he died in his prime.'

'And left all to her, beggaring you both!' Pegeen clasped her hands together, wanting to make him see he had to fight his mother.

'I'll have it all when she dies. I've only to wait. Wasn't she right then about planting wheat instead of potatoes?' Hugh rose, and kicked a piece of peat towards the centre of the fire. He stood near its warmth, warily keeping himself out of Pegeen's reach.

'She saved you from the potato blight. All the fields round you are black with the perished crops, and most of your neighbours dead or gone from here to try their fortunes in the Americas. Does she plan to buy up their land—with a rich wife for you?' Pegeen faltered on the last words and leaned on the wall away from the fire. The spirit had gone out of her. She had always known there was no winning over old Mrs Prendergast.

'What if she does?'

There it was—the confirmation of the old woman's plans. Pegeen for the first time admitted to herself that Hugh was lost to her. She began to cry, turning her face to the wall. 'Go away, I hate you! You're a worm, not a man. You'll be sorry all the days of your life that you pushed me away.' She struck at the crumbling plaster with one hand and then the other. 'What am I to do? I'm disgraced. Maling'll not have me now.'

'Of course he will!' He took a step towards her, and another, and seized her hands in his own. 'Maling's the one for you. He doesn't need to know anything about us. He's the most trusting soul on earth. He thinks you're a saint dropped straight down from Heaven. He's working himself to the bone on the Penny Road, starving himself to put a little by so you two can marry. The old woman was cruel hard on him, turning him out because he wanted you so.'

That only made Pegeen cry the harder. She had betrayed Maling, who truly loved her, for this brother of his; trapped by his kisses, his wicked embraces. She loathed herself in that moment. Maling, with the dark good looks of him so different from Hugh, who was fair and light complexioned. The people of the district always said it was a marvel two brothers could be so unalike, and both so handsome it would break your heart.

Hugh's blue eyes were close to her own. She shivered uncontrollably and snatched her hands from his grasp. How could she have been taken in by him? Even this afternoon he had possessed her again. That was black treachery! And if what she suspected were true, she was doomed, damned. He'd betrayed her. And she'd betrayed Maling! Good, decent Maling, who never complained about the back-breaking hardness of digging a road that went from nowhere to nowhere so that the politicians in Dublin and London could say they were doing everything possible to keep men alive. A penny a day. That's what they paid him and all those other scarecrows of men who laboured for themselves and their families to keep them alive on a penny a day. You'd think it was their fault somehow that the potatoes had rotted in the fields, that they had nothing to eat. Pegeen wept for them all—and she wept for herself. What was she to do?

She tore herself away from Hugh, from the hut, and ran into the December afternoon now turned colder and misty. She hated Hugh. She hated herself. She could not bear to stay in the same place with him. She ran, her breath coming in great gasps, over the blackened field, through the hedge into the next desolate spot. She heard Hugh in the distance, calling to her, trying to find her. She sank to the ground and wept till she was utterly spent. The rotting potatoes of 1846 were her only companions. They were as black as her treachery, as black as Hugh Prendergast, and he the only smallholder in the area who was not completely ruined.

When she rose to her feet, her mind was made up. She wasn't going to stay here, to go on working where she worked and have Hugh marry someone else. There was but one thing she could do. She would go to America, and she knew the only way to get the passage money. The old woman would pay. She'd make her! She had the power. But she wouldn't go to her now. No, not as she was. She'd go dressed in her best at a time when she knew Hugh was out of the way. She'd best her! There was no other way out. Hugh had meant what he'd said; she realised that. She was ready to accept that he was a black-hearted villain. Her long cold vigil in the potato-field had changed her—changed her for ever.

Old Mrs Prendergast sat by a cheerful fire the Sunday morning when Pegeen called.

Pegeen had prepared well for the outing. She wore her best black skirt of good wool, and a heavy green shawl wrapped over a white blouse with lace on its collar. It had been her mother's. No matter, her mother was dead—gone like the others, starving and fevered. Only Patrick and Michael and young Bridie were left out of ten Langtons who had lived next door to the Prendergasts all the years of their lives. And they'd all died this very year, like so many others in Ireland.

Old Mrs Prendergast wasn't all that old—in her forties, Pegeen reckoned. She was still a fine figure of a woman but small with it, with snapping blue eyes. That was where Hugh got his looks. She, too, had been fair, but now her hair was white and she wore it in a bun on the top of her head. She waved Pegeen to a low stool beside her.

Pegeen, her red mane in two careful plaits wound round her face, pushed the stool aside and chose a wooden chair with a back.

'Help yourself to a mug of herb tea,' said Mrs Prendergast, 'since you seem to be quick to help yourself to a good chair.'

Pegeen ignored the suggestion. She sat very straight, her back not touching the wood. At least, this way, she could look down at her hostess, which would have been impossible if she had taken the stool. There was no use beating about the bush with this one—she might as well wade straight in.

'Is it the Widow O'Shaughnessy you've picked out for Hugh?' She managed to keep her voice soft, her heart hard.

'What makes you think that?' Mrs Prendergast was watching her closely.

'She has more money than most. She'd make a good catch! The best one around.' Pegeen marvelled at herself. She might have been talking about the weather or the time of day—not Hugh's future. She put him out of her mind.

'You haven't come here to tell me that.'

Pegeen nodded. 'Then it is herself you've settled on. Mind, she's a will of her own and is a good pious girl. Very religious she is, always running to the priest. She wouldn't marry anyone with the hint of a scandal about him, not when she has the pick of the country around —and her with more money than she knows what to do with. Ah, her husband was the wise one. Like you, he grew wheat. A pity his money couldn't save him from the fever, but he was never a robust sort—not like your Hugh and Maling.' Pegeen sat back.

Mrs Prendergast rose to the bait. 'There's no scandal about either of my boys!'

'No, of course not,' Pegeen agreed, very sociable. 'But there might be.'

'What do you mean?'

'Why, nothing. Nothing at all.' Pegeen rose to her feet. This had to be handled carefully. She was fighting for her life and must not show any weakness. 'I think I will have that tea, after all.' She went to the fire and poured herself some from the pot resting there close to the smouldering peat. 'I've always been friendly with Maureen O'Shaughnessy. We could have a grand crack about all the poor men who're wooing her now she's a widow. Why, my brother Michael fancies she favours him, and a nice little dowry she'd bring him. It'd put the place back on its feet.'

'Your brother Michael won't win her! She'll be looking for someone with cash to match her own.'

'Someone like Hugh.' There was the barest tremble in Pegeen's voice. So it was true! She'd known it ever since that terrible day when Hugh had told her he'd finished with her. She steeled herself to go on. 'Isn't it a pity Hugh spoiled it for himself?' She sat down and sipped slowly at her cup. It was bitter, so bitter she nearly spat it out.

Mrs Prendergast's eyes narrowed. 'Hope to have him for yourself, do you? You never will. I'll tell you that now. Don't think I don't know what's been going on —and my poor Maling betrayed!' She put a handkerchief to her face.

'Save your tears for someone who'll believe them,' Pegeen advised her. 'We both know you put him out.'

Mrs Prendergast put her handkerchief back in her pocket. 'I only did it to bring him to his senses. He needs to marry well—not to a penniless girl he's grown up with.'

'It's Hugh we're talking about,' Pegeen reminded her. 'It's Hugh's the father of my baby.'

Mrs Prendergast choked on her tea. 'What baby? Are you sure?'

'It's not something I'm likely to mistake! I'm sure.' Pegeen might have been talking of someone else, some unfortunate girl. All her feeling for Hugh had dissolved in the chilling cold of his denial of her, in the time she'd spent weeping among the blackened potatoes. The only thing which mattered now was besting this old besom. 'I wouldn't want to be telling Maureen O'Shaughnessy about it, and her running to the priest—and that mother of hers, the biggest gossip in all of Kilkenny!'

'You'll not marry Hugh! Never! I won't have it,' the older woman hissed at her.

'I don't want to marry Hugh!' Pegeen found it was true as she told it. 'I couldn't stand living here with you.' She began to laugh. 'I'd be dead in a year, with you ordering me to do this and do that and never a minute's rest or respite. Nay, I'll marry Maling, and you'll never see your grandchild—Hugh's firstborn. We'll be over the sea.'

'Hugh'll have others—ones born in wedlock!'

'Maybe he will and maybe he won't. Maureen O'Shaughnessy never had any to her first man.' Pegeen shrugged.

'That's as may be. But he was a weakling—you said so yourself. Besides, madam cocky, who's to pay for you going over the sea?'

'You are.' Pegeen clenched her hands together. It would never do for them to shake, and her to see it.

'*I?*' Mrs Prendergast sputtered with rage. 'Never! As long as I live, there'll never be a penny from me—not for your sin! I'll tell Maling, and he'll throw you aside.'

'After he's killed Hugh,' Pegeen said the words softly. 'You'll remember the fights they've had before this. Maling's the stronger, and he'd be glad of the excuse to wring his brother's neck. Where would you be then, with neither of them at your bidding?'

Mrs Prendergast sat as if turned to stone. Her face had paled.

Pegeen pressed home her advantage. 'Maling's slow to anger but his rage can be terrible.' She shivered. If Maling found out . . . He mustn't find out!

The older woman echoed that thought with a cackle of harsh laughter. 'I wouldn't be in your shoes for all the world when Maling finds out! How far along are you?'

'I've missed just the twice. The first time I hoped against hope, but now I know it.'

'Ay.' Mrs Prendergast looked her up and down. 'Stand up and walk in front of me,' she commanded.

Pegeen did as she was bid.

'You've that look to you,' Hugh's mother grudgingly admitted. 'It's in the face most of all, a tightness round the mouth, but you'll carry it well.'

Pegeen did not like being examined like a cow or a horse, but she bore the scrutiny as well as she could.

'It's January now,' the old woman mused. 'How soon can you be away?'

Pegeen let out her breath in a long sigh. She had won! She had not thought she would after that mention of sin, but Mrs Prendergast was shrewd. She could see where her own interests lay. She had pinned all her hopes on Hugh, and when Pegeen had said she didn't want to marry him, that had tipped the balance—that, and Maling's temper. Pegeen shivered again at the very thought of it. It would all be directed at her when the baby arrived early. Pray God, she would be able to convince him then! But that was in the future.

The present was to drive her advantage home, to haggle with the old woman about fares to New York. She had set her mind on America. Let others go on the boats to Canada; she wanted to go to New York. There was still more to arrange with the old harridan. She must make the offer to Maling, and appear to be sorry that he hadn't been treated fairly. The old woman wouldn't like eating humble pie, but Pegeen herself must not be seen to have any part in this reconciliation between mother and son.

It took the better part of the morning to settle all the details, and by the time it was finished, Pegeen had a sneaking admiration for her future mother-in-law. She was hard as nails, but she had a mind on her.

It was agreed between them that Maling and Pegeen would marry as soon as the priest should call the banns, and that they would take passage on the first available ship from Waterford or Cobh. Mrs Prendergast would find the money somehow. Hugh should not know about the baby until after they had arrived safely on the other side of the world—if then. Pegeen had to agree to that, and indeed saw the sense of it. If Maling found out, that was her own lookout. There'd be no help for her if he did!

Everything went as the two of them planned. Maling and Pegeen were married in the first week of February, and started their married life with her twin brothers Patrick and Michael. They kept her on till the end of the month at the farm where she worked, and she and Maling booked a passage for the middle of March, straight to New York. She went through it all as though it were happening to someone else. She seemed to have stopped feeling anything, to have almost stopped living. She didn't look like a bride. She cried a lot when no one was looking.

Maling had to go to Waterford to arrange about their ship. When he came back, he was worried about her, she was so white and so listless. He asked Patrick and Michael what was ailing her. They said there was nothing, nothing at all, save homesickness at the prospect of leaving. Pegeen had always been very attached to the old place and to them. She sorrowed to leave. He asked Pegeen herself.

'Ay,' she agreed. 'It's like tearing something out of myself. I'll be all right when I'm there. We'll be together, but I miss my Mam and my sisters. It's like they only died yesterday. I know it was six months ago and more, but it's just hit me now.' She cried on his shoulder.

Maling talked to Patrick and Michael, and to Bridie. Bridie was Pegeen's only sister left. She worked at the big house of the English gentry, in the kitchens. He went up to see her. She was only nineteen, but she might help. She was fond of Pegeen.

Bridie, too, was sorrowing. 'Half the servants have been told to go. I'm among them,' she told him. 'The master's been that generous. He's been feeding the hungry. Now he can't do it any more, he says. He hasn't even enough for himself. He's letting us go. What shall I do? My brothers can't help me; they've little enough of their own.'

Maling had seen enough of despair and hunger and death. He had heard enough stories of want, working on the Penny Road, of whole families dying of starvation. He had seen some of them, too, and the sight had sickened him even more than the horror of the black, desolate, ruined fields of potatoes.

The Langtons were his family now, and he'd not see this girl want. Why, she was only a slip of a thing, all eyes and dark hair—hair as dark as his own. She was nothing like Pegeen, but she was her sister.

'Come with us, Bridie. It's the answer for all of us.'

'I haven't the passage money,' she wailed, 'or I would. There's nothing to stay for. No work, nothing to eat.'

He did not hesitate. 'I know how it can be done. We'll change our passages.'

'How?'

'We'll go to Canada instead. It's cheaper. Mind, we don't need to let on to anyone here—just leave it to me. We'll have some money in hand. It's a fine joke on the old woman!'

He hushed all Bridie's protests and found he had to hush some of Pegeen's as well. But when she heard that her sister was coming with them her whole face lit up, and she was more than grateful to him. She looked happy for the first time in weeks.

So it was that at the end of March 1847 all three of them sailed from Cobh for Montreal.

Maling was well satisfied. He was married to Pegeen, the girl he had always loved from a tiny thing. They had a passage to the New World, a place where he could make his own way and not be always in the shadow of his brother. All life was before him. He hugged Pegeen and he hugged Bridie. It had been a grand idea taking her along. Pegeen had brightened up a treat, and the old woman had even provided them with food for the trip. She had almost made him think she'd miss him. He wondered about that, because they had never got along well. Maybe she didn't want to be remembered as hard.

Well, he would never see her again. He was off to a new life, a better life, he and Pegeen.

It all lay before them, just for the taking. He laughed in exultation. The future was theirs, he told the two girls, and they laughed with him, Pegeen throwing back her head, her lovely red hair escaping from its pins. She looked so alive that he bent to kiss her lips, and she clung to him. Strange, she seemed bulkier, somehow. She couldn't be plumper, could she? It was only to be expected, he supposed. She was a married woman now. He kissed her again.

CHAPTER ONE

BRIDGET LANGTON SHOOK with fright. It was bad enough to be alone in the world and to have to make decisions for others, but now she was trapped. She was a prisoner —held firmly by this man she had never seen before.

He half pushed, half dragged her from the bedroom, marched her along the corridor to a sitting-room, and shook her once he had the door closed.

'Who are you?' What were you doing in Madame Duvalier's room? Don't you know she's not to be disturbed? Didn't anyone tell you?' He punctuated each question with another shake.

Bridie sagged in his grip. 'Stop, stop!' she pleaded. 'I've done nothing wrong. I work in the kitchen.' She kicked out at him. Even if she was a servant here, that gave him no right to abuse her. For good measure, she scratched at his face and was horrified when her long raking claw drew blood, spoiling his dark, handsome countenance.

It gained her her freedom. As his hand rose to assess the damage, she ran to the furthest part of the room, panting, 'Whatever you mean to do to me, I'll fight you! If I had a knife, I'd use it on you. I've done nothing wrong. Ask her—ask that woman whose room you've just snatched me from!' She pointed a trembling finger towards the wall. 'Why am I being treated like a criminal when I've given Madame Duvalier her heart's desire, and that twice over?' She glared at her captor, aware of his dark eyes on her, aware too that he paid little attention to her words but paced warily towards her, lean and big and ferocious. Why had she ever thought it a good idea to substitute Pegeen's twins for Madame Duvalier's dead baby?

In one swift bound he thrust aside the chair behind

which she sheltered and had clasped her in both arms.
Her struggles were to no avail. This time she was truly
his prisoner. Strength draining from her, she managed to
stutter, 'Who are you to treat a poor girl so?'

His laugh was scornful. 'I am Monsieur Duvalier's
brother. He asked me to hold you here until he can
speak to you.' He made no move to release her.

Bridie was very conscious of his body, she was pressed
so close to him. He was warm and strong, and the
masculine smell of him filled her nostrils. She had wondered often what it was like to be held in a man's firm
hold. Now she knew. In spite of what the nuns had said
back in the village she came from, and the way the priest
had thundered about the sins of the body, wasn't there
something about a man—about this man—which made
her legs go weak and her head swim with the nearness of
him? She slumped against him, shamed, astonished.

Something Pegeen had once said slipped unbidden
into her mind. It was last winter, the terrible winter of
1846, she had said it when so many of them were dying,
and Pegeen had somehow seemed not daunted at all but
had worn a look of shining wonder that Bridie had found
no reason for. 'Sure, there's a kind of terrible sorcery in
the blood; a bit of witchcraft, I'd be calling it.' She had
crossed herself at the words. 'When people are dying,
that's when some are most alive. It's a kind of disease,
and it's got hold of me. Pray it never gets you in its grip,
for nothing matters but the day itself and the living of it.
The others are so many shadows.'

Bridie had stared at her sister and crossed herself in
her turn, but now she knew the meaning of the words
—and it was all this man's fault! Tears began to flow
from her eyes. She could barely see his face for them, but
she knew what it looked like. Handsome as the devil
himself he was, with his deep dark eyes as well lashed as
a girl's, and his brown hair to match falling into waves
above a high forehead. Her scratch was a livid mark
down one cheek, his mouth under the moustache was
full, his lips pink, and there was a dimple just by their

edge. Why did he have to be looking at her and smiling?

It was a grim enough smile, she told herself as he released her and threw her none too gently on to one of the straight-backed chairs. She could see his chest heaving as he stared down at her.

'Tears won't do you any good, *ma fille*! Nor will trying to run away. I mean to have the whole story from you. My brother will be in later and decide what to do, but I'll help him to make up his mind.'

Her tears dried on her cheeks. She licked her lips and looked up at him. 'I'll wait till he comes. He looks kinder than you. I'll tell him how it came about.' She closed her lips firmly and folded her arms.

'You'll tell *me*—and now!'

Bridie shivered in spite of herself. He was so big and threatening. 'I'll not!' Her voice quivered in spite of her efforts to control it.

He laughed at her—a laugh which rumbled in his chest as if he was truly amused. 'What a wild thing you are.' He fingered his cheek. 'You'll pay dear for this, and you'll tell me the whole story. You work in the kitchen, so what were you doing up here?' Pulling another chair near hers, he sat down, and took both her hands in his own. 'I'll be safer this way!'

His grip was very firm. Bridie wanted to pull away. She was angry still, but there was something about his closeness, about his touch, which pulled the anger out of her. She said nothing.

'Whose babies are they?' he asked gently. 'Why did you put them there? Are they yours?'

She shook her head. 'No, not mine. They're my sister's.' Her hands still fluttered in his, although she could have removed them. 'They're my sister Pegeen's. Pegeen Prendergast.'

'Did she let you take them away? What are the pair of you after? Money?'

Bridie shook her head. Her throat was choked. 'Pegeen's not after anything,' she mumbled, forcing the words out. 'She's dead. She died last night, birthing them. She'd never give up her babies. It was my idea, not hers.'

'I'm sorry about your sister,' he said stiffly. 'What's your name?'

'Bridget—Bridget Langton.' It was all very well for him to say he was sorry about her sister; he had never known her. It would never be the same for Bridie without her. 'I wanted her babies to have a home— to be cared for. Madame lost her baby. They said in the kitchen that she'd been taking on so much that the doctor had put her to sleep.'

The man looked at her closely. 'So you played God. What do you do in the kitchen?'

'I'm skivvy here.' If her hand had been free, she'd have crossed herself.

'It's nothing to be ashamed of, starting at the bottom. You'll soon be something better if you work hard.'

Bridie felt like slapping the condescension from his face. 'In Ireland,' she was stung into retorting, 'I was under-cook at a great house.'

'Were you?' Again she was subjected to his searching scrutiny. 'I suppose you kept yourself tidier then.'

'You'd find it hard keeping tidy if you had to work as I do.' Bridie's hand, had it not been held, would have flown to her hair, which she knew was hanging about her face.

'Why haven't you done better for yourself in Montreal?'

'I did the best I could. How were we to be knowing that most folk speak the devil's own tongue here? That French jabber is strange to our ears, and stranger still to our mouths. There's no getting on with it.' This time she managed to remove her hands, and didn't they want to go back to his? She tucked them firmly together.

'There are English people in Montreal—some with houses grander than my brother's. Didn't you apply to them?'

'When I did, they looked down their noses at me, just the way you're doing.'

'I'm not surprised,' he told her, 'if you looked at them and talked to them as you're doing to me!'

Bridie sat up straighter in her chair, and gave him a look of loathing. He thought he could treat her like dirt. First he mauled her, then he looked down at her. 'I'm as good as any of them! Why should they, or you, be looking at me as if I was some kind of worm? You've cash and enough to eat—that's all the difference. I had to leave Ireland because there was naught to eat. Everyone said this was a land of plenty. Well, I could tell them the rich have plenty, and the rest of us go hungry here, too. We have to sell our babies, poor little innocents. I'm only doing it because Pegeen was after begging me to do something for them, and there was nothing at all I could do for them myself. I couldn't feed them; I couldn't keep them warm and clean. There was only clothes for one, and that was because I made them. Pegeen seemed to have no interest at all in preparing. She kept saying there was plenty of time, but there wasn't. She was so big towards the end that I should have guessed it might be twins. They run in the family. Patrick and Michael are twins—that's why they've both come in for the place, though it's too small for the two of them.'

Bridie didn't know why she was telling him so much when only a few minutes since she had sworn to say nothing. Now she felt like talking to him, pouring it all out, the worries she had had with her sister, the wrench she still felt at leaving her home, the loneliness of being in a strange land where things were so different. She only paused to take breath.

But his next words took that breath right out of her body. 'We come to it now, do we? You want payment for the babies. Why should my brother pay you anything?'

Her head came up. How could she have let her tongue run away with itself? It was talking to him that had done it. He had cast some sort of spell over her just by being near. If she had waited till his brother had come, he would have been grateful. He would have offered her something. She'd not have mentioned it—just smiled and accepted. She rounded on the man sitting so calm and composed beside her.

'Did you see the way Madame in there looked at the babes? No, of course you didn't. You weren't there. You were only called in afterwards. Had you seen the look on her face, you'd not be questioning me. You'd be down on your knees thanking me—and your brother beside you!'

'Somehow, that doesn't sound like François,' was his forthright comment. 'What made you think such a scheme was going to work? Is anyone else in this with you?'

'Why shouldn't it work?' she countered, her brogue more pronounced in her excitement. 'Madame Duvalier's baby died. Pegeen's two lived, and need a mother. The whole grand idea came to me sudden. Wasn't Nurse O'Rourke swilling tea in the kitchen with cook and the others while I was cleaning the pots? She said the poor little mite was dead and Madame was drugged, not yet knowing it. 'Twas the doctor had done it to her, to hide her grief from herself till she'd slept and got the strength to be facing it. Hasn't the poor woman lost two others before, and the doctor now saying she mustn't ever try again?' Bridie's hand flew to her mouth that she should be saying such things to a man—and him not even a relative.

He did not appear to take it amiss, but put his head on his hand. 'Poor Marie-Rose, poor François—all their hopes dashed once again.' His expression was sombre.

Bridie felt encouraged to continue. 'Said I to myself, it needn't be a sad day for this house. Weren't Pegeen's babies sent for a reason? None of them were paying any heed to me scrubbing away at the pots. And wasn't it a strange thing that Nurse O'Rourke spoke out in English and all of them knew what she was saying, and when I tried to talk to them they only *parleyed français.*'

'Yes,' he interrupted. 'What did you do?'

'Took my hands from the water and my shawl from the

hook by the door and slipped out quick as I could. I ran all the way to Mrs Delaney's—her that was minding the babes till things could be settled. I snatched them up, and brought them straight here.'

'Didn't she try to stop you?'

'No, why should she? She had no claim on them, didn't want them. Poor soul, she has six of her own! Glad to see them go, she was, helped me wrap them up warm against the cold air.'

'Cold air? It's July.'

Bridie ignored that. Everyone knew babies shouldn't be taken outside—not so soon after they had arrived, even if it was a hot summer. 'I didn't know how I should get them upstairs once I'd got back, but didn't it all go easy at first? The blessed babes didn't make a sound, and I was able to creep past the kitchen door and up the back steps and found Madame Duvalier's bedroom, for I knew it was just at the head of the front stairs.' She paused, and found his dark eyes regarding hers with something that might have been admiration in their depths.

'Go on,' he commanded. 'What then? Wasn't my brother in the room? Didn't he stop you, or speak to you?'

'I'm coming to that! How was I to know that he was there, asleep in a chair to one side of the bed? He didn't stir, and I didn't see him. I crept, quiet, to the bed. Madame Duvalier was lying there. There wasn't much light, for the shutters were shut. Just one bar of sunshine was lying on the blanket, and it touching her hand from the high window on the left side.' Bridie brushed her long black hair, which had come out of its tidy bun with the exertions of the morning, out of her face and raised blue eyes fringed with dark lashes to Monsieur Duvalier's brother. She didn't even know his name, but wasn't he a grand listener?'

'Pale she was,' Bridie continued. 'Her hand fluttered at me like she was reaching out for the babies. I knew it would be all right. I sat with her, and I tucked the twins one under each of her arms, so that when she woke, whichever way she looked she'd have them beside her. It was then I was overcome with what I was doing. I whispered to the twins that I wanted to keep them, that they mustn't ever forget me or Pegeen . . .' She raised her eyes to the man facing her. 'I knew it was foolish. I should have left straight away, but I wanted a sign from her—a sign that she'd keep them.'

'What sort of a sign were you hoping for?' His expression had lightened.

'I don't know.' Bridie's bow wrinkled. 'I didn't want her to find me there, else she wouldn't be thinking the babies were hers. I felt tired, I felt drained. Hadn't I been up all the night? I just sat there, quiet—when all of a sudden I was pulled from the bed. I didn't know it then, but of course it was Monsieur Duvalier. He'd wakened in his chair and saw me by his wife.'

'You must have given him quite a fright!'

'No more than what he gave me! I don't know what he would have done—shouted down the house, maybe —but Madame awoke and called out to him. She called him "François" and he let me go, sprawled on the floor. I didn't know what to do—whether to run from the room or stay where I was.'

'I take it you stayed. What happened then?'

'One of the babies began to cry. Just a thin wail it was, but Madame cried out something in French and I saw her hand go to the babe. Oh, the joy on her face as she gathered him to her! "*Mon fils, mon petit fils*"—that's what she said.'

'My son, my little son,' he translated. There was no softness in his voice or his face. 'So you'd won. She accepted him as her own. You had your sign.'

Bridie looked at his stony countenance and would have put her hand on his, had she dared. 'I wasn't thinking of that. Sure there's enough grief in the world to go round, and more. I just sat on the floor and felt pure delight in her happiness. Don't you see? It made Pegeen's death somehow easier to be borne?'

He didn't answer. She didn't know whether he understood how she had felt. It didn't matter.

'Then the other twin let out such a yell that Madame turned to him with such a comical look to her face. She laughed, and she held him up, and—would you believe it—he wet all over her hand! I couldn't stop laughing —that was my undoing. I think he'd forgotten I was there. Madame Duvalier didn't even give me a glance, she was so wrapped up in the twins. She kept calling out to them, and to him too. Every minute she was saying, "*Regarde, François*", and following it with all sorts of French. I wasn't sure if she had noticed the things the babies wore, as they weren't the things she had made ready. Maybe she explained it to herself and to him, for he didn't have the chance to get in a word. But he didn't tell her they weren't her own boys. That I do know.'

'That was when you thought the babies might be put to good use; that you might sell them?'

Bridie was stunned by the venom in his voice. 'No!' she protested. 'It wasn't like that, not like that at all. I couldn't move away. I kept watching her, even when Monsieur Duvalier went to the door and called you to the room. It was like warming myself at a fire on a cruel winter's day. It was only after you dragged me away, pushing and pulling at me, that I began to think I had nothing, that Monsieur Duvalier might be generous . . . After all, I'd given him two fine sons.' She softened her voice.

'And people have to pay for what they want, is that it?' His brown eyes were full of scorn.

Bridie shrank back in her chair. 'You make it sound like I only thought of dollars! It's not so, but I'm on me own—I've nothing, nothing at all.'

'You gave them to her. I don't know that François will let her keep them.' He leaned forward. 'They're probably sickly—as close to death as her own baby was. The only difference is that hers didn't live at all.'

'Poor little soul,' Bridie crossed herself. 'I don't suppose there was more than a few hours between the two birthings, and that poor lady in there with all the world's goods, and Pegeen with none. Madame Duvalier's baby didn't have the will to live, but Sean and Sennen have, even without their Mam. There's no accounting for the odd ways of the Lord—no disrespect intended.'

'As you say, there's no accounting.' He shrugged and sat back. 'Sean and Sennen? That's the babies?' He seemed to have trouble getting his tongue round the names. 'What kind of names are those?'

'Irish names,' Bridie answered proudly. 'At the last, Pegeen knew she was going, and the priest was with her and he christened them right on the spot . . . It seemed to comfort her, the sound of those names, almost like she was back home. Sure, didn't Father Mulcahey do it because he thought they'd not much chance without her? He's a good man is Father Mulcahey. Do you know him, then?'

'*Mais certainement*, everyone knows Father Mulcahey. He's always collecting clothes and money for the poor Irish who come off the boats with nothing—and never seem to have anything months later.'

'What chance do they have of getting anything together?' He had caught Bridie on the raw again. 'Everyone else was here before them, and they don't want them to get ahead.'

He shook his head. 'Is that the way of it? Why don't you admit that they're lazy—every last one of them. And if they get any more, they spend it on drink! They'll never better themselves. Like you, they take a skivvy's job instead of holding out for something better.'

Bridie rose to her feet. 'I'll not stay here and be insulted by the likes of you!'

'Sit down!' he thundered. 'You're not going anywhere until my brother deals with you, and then François will put you out of this house.'

Bridie glowered at him, but she sat down. Whatever he said, she couldn't leave till the twins' future was settled.

He got to his feet and perched on a table some

distance from her. He lit a cigar, blowing the smoke away. It wafted in the girl's direction as he spoke. 'I've had Irishmen working for me. They talk well, but when it comes to real work I'd rather have a German or even an Italian.'

Bridie knew nothing about Germans or Italians, but she was not prepared to have him rubbish her country-men. 'Irish people work as hard as anyone! Had anyone here said I've not done my work properly—not slaved as hard as any?'

He smiled at her. 'Skivvies don't come into the con-versation very often, *ma fille.*'

She seethed at the callousness of that remark, and was trying to think of an equally cutting retort when he asked, 'Live in here, do you?'

She nodded, wary of the gentleness of his tone.

'Yet you were with your sister when she died. Did you have permission to leave the house?'

She did not even try to lie to him. 'Sure, if I waited for that, I'd never get out! I was worried. I'd done it before. I slipped out, like.' She rubbed her hand across her eyes. Why was he keeping on at her? She was tired. She stifled a yawn. She had been up half the night with Pegeen, and hadn't been able to sleep for her concern about the babes and what'd become of them. Mrs Delaney next door had given a hand with them, but only because Father Mulcahey had asked. Bridie knew the woman would soon shift them. How could she do other? She had six of her own in the one room.

'Have you ever slipped out before?' Bridie was brought back to the present.

'Now and then,' she admitted. 'Pegeen needed me, don't you see? She had no one else.'

'How often would now and then be?'

She sighed. She might as well tell him the truth. He had said she wasn't to go on working here. 'Every second night, except when it was raining too hard. I've been here a month, and it wasn't long before I found a drainpipe down from the attic window. I'd shin down that when the others were sleeping, and stay with Pegeen. Then when it was light, back I'd come and slip into the kitchen as soon as the door was open.'

'And you were never caught—and stopped?' The expression on his face was unreadable.

She shrugged. 'Never. But there were times I just scraped from it, and times I was tired and slept a little too late, but the Mother of God looks after her own. She knew it was for Pegeen's sake I did it. It was for Pegeen I took the job, too. I'd been working in a little eating-place—waiting on table, doing dishes and the like—and getting my meals and some for Pegeen. But it wasn't enough; she was going hungry. We worked it between us, and I talked the people in the café into letting Pegeen do the pots and some cooking, just for her food. At first they weren't best pleased, but sure Pegeen could charm an angel if she put her mind to it!'

Another cloud of cigar-smoke hovered over Bridie's head. 'Where's her husband? You said she was married.'

Bridget yawned again. What did he want to know all this for? She felt his eyes on her, and it was as if his hand touched her again—like fire all over her—fire that tingled without burning. Where did such thoughts come from? Better to keep talking and not let them take hold.

'So she was, but didn't he die on the way over? He was buried with all the others who died on the ship, when we touched shore.' She raised dry eyes to her questioner, and her voice was low. 'Why are they after calling them coffin-ships, those ships from Ireland, when none of those buried had coffins? They were just put in a big hole in the ground and the earth filled in on top of them. Not a flower, hardly a prayer to see them off. Pegeen and I watched. They promised to put some sort of cross on the grave but we never knew if they did. Is that any way to treat the dead? And Maling Prendergast the best-looking boy and the sweetest in all of Kilkenny? There were some said his brother Hugh was the handsomer, but Hugh had sharp eyes and a hard mouth. Thin-lipped, not like yours.' She had not meant to say that last bit. It just slipped out, and she saw his hand go to his mouth and trace the outline of his lips. It was almost as though her own fingers did it, so warm did they feel.

She hurried on with her recital as his eyes held hers. 'Pegeen never cried—never cried at all. I sometimes wondered how she felt about Maling; if she'd stopped loving him—if she ever loved him at all. He was mad about her—took her from his brother, he did. Why do women follow their men—do what they say? Answer me that.'

'Do they?' His gaze still fastened on her.

'Sure you must know that they do—more fools they! I'll not follow that road. I'll live by myself when I've got enough cash. Go back to Ireland and have me own little place with a wee Irish girl to wait on me, and tempt me to eat.'

This time he laughed at her words, a full round laugh with merriment in it.

She almost laughed with him, so infectious was the sound, but what was she doing laughing with Pegeen scarcely cold? She straightened her face. This man had the power to turn her thoughts upside-down. She longed with all her heart to go back. She told him so, and added for good measure, 'Wouldn't it have been better for the pair of them—Pegeen and her Maling—to die at home? Pegeen had said it'd kill her to leave the old place. It's killed the both of them, so it has.'

'Sean and Sennen are left,' he pointed out. 'Yet you'd give them away—sell them, in fact!' His eyes were accusing.

'It's their only chance, don't you see? When I got back here and heard about the mistress and her little lost baby I could only think of one thing—sure, it was the answer to prayer. And it was. Didn't I see her face?'

'So you went back and fetched them.' He didn't answer her question. 'What if my brother comes in here with one on each arm and gives them back to you?'

'He'll not! He's a kinder man than you. Besides, he'll

see he has a bargain, whatever he pays for them. She'll never have any more, will she?'

'So you tell me. That's what Nurse O'Rourke has said to the servants. The doctor may tell a different story.' He rose to his feet and towered above her so that she had to put her head back to look at him properly. 'François won't keep the twins if there's anything wrong with them.'

'There's nothing wrong with them!' Bridie had never even considered the possibility. 'They're a little small, but that's only because they're twins.' Her head was still in that unnatural position and she wondered why that should be so—and what his name was. His brother's name was François. What might be his? No, she would not ask him!

She rushed into words again. 'Father Mulcahey said they were perfect. He said they'd a fierce hold on life.'

'They'll need it. Traipsed through the streets not a day old. The doctor'll be examining them now. I expect that's what's taking so long.' He began to pace up and down. 'I know he's been sent for.'

Bridie watched him in silence. For all her brave words, she felt a pang of anxiety. What if the doctor should find something wrong with one or the other of the boys? Sennen was smaller than Sean, and paler. Mother of God, let them be fine! Only a little boiled water had they had since their birth.

'What's your name, girl?' he shot at her, coming to a halt over her again. 'What did you say what your name was?'

'Bridget—Bridie,' she stammered. 'Bridget Langton.'

'That's not an Irish name—Langton. They're all O's and Mc's, O'Brien, McMahan.'

'What do you know about it? There've been Langtons in Waterford and the country round for generations, so there have.'

'If you say so.' He draped himself on the desk again. 'If you had some money, Bridget Langton, what would you do with it?'

'Start me own business.'

'What kind of business?'

'A potato business.'

'What sort of business is that? I'd have thought you'd have nothing to do with the potato. It chased you out of Ireland, didn't it?'

'That was the blight. Sure it wasn't the potatoes' fault. It was the rain made them rot in the ground. But the potatoes here are grand fellows—big and round and white fleshed. I've peeled enough of them downstairs to know!'

For the first time he looked friendly. 'So you'd grow potatoes. You'd need land for that.'

'No, I'd not.'

'Don't be silly, girl! You'd need land.'

'I wouldn't be growing potatoes.'

He ran his hand through his hair. 'But you said you planned a potato business.'

'Ay, I'd cook 'em and sell 'em—cheap, you know. Maybe through the streets, maybe in me own little shop.' She rubbed her eyes, wondering why she was confiding her dreams to this man. She didn't like him. He certainly didn't like her. 'Baked potatoes,' she said dreamily. 'Colcannon, fried potatoes, potatoes to eat in the hand—ah, the smell of them'd bring in the custom, so it would.'

'You think they'd take on? Would there be enough people to buy them and make you a profit?'

'I'd make a go of it, certain I would.'

'You're very sure of yourself. Can you read? Can you write? Can you keep accounts?'

'I can sign me own name, if that's what you mean —and I know well what a penny'll buy.'

'A cent,' he corrected her. 'It's dollars and cents here.'

'I was forgetting.' Why did everything go out of her head just because he was looking at her?

'I wonder . . .' he began, but she wasn't to find out what he was wondering, for the door was flung open and his brother François strode in.

Before Bridie had even a chance to say a word to him, to appeal to him, his brother seized his arm and took him straight out of the room. She was left to herself.

She ran to the door. Even as she did so, she heard the key turn in the lock. She cried out, and rattled the knob.

'*Sois tranquille,*' his voice hissed through the door. 'Be quiet! We must talk, my brother and I. I'll be back later.'

Bridie gave up pulling at the handle. She knew it was no use. She heard the voices move away. A prisoner, that was what he had made her. The terrible devilry of the man, practising witchcraft on her so that she told him all her inner thinkings. It was because he'd touched her and listened to her, and she'd been taken in by his ways. Let it be a lesson to her!

She sank to the floor, weeping. He had made her his prisoner and there was nothing she could do about it, nothing at all. Only wait, like he'd said.

CHAPTER TWO

'WELL, ALPHONSE, what do you make of the girl?'
François Duvalier pulled his brother into an adjoining
empty bedroom and stretched out on the bed.

'She seems a decent sort. Her name's Bridget
Langton. She's Irish, a victim of the famine. The babies
are her sister's. She died having them, and they're less
than a day old. What does Dr Bourassa say of them?'
Alphonse thought his brother looked tired as he sagged
against the cushions on the bed. He offered him a cigar.

'Not in here!' snapped François. 'Well, perhaps I will.'
He put out his hand, and took it.

Alphonse lit it for him and draped himself in the easy
chair, handing his brother an ashtray. 'What's to do,
mon frère?'

'Marie-Rose is convinced they're hers. Is there any
way we can maintain that fiction?' François took a deep
drag on his cigar, then put it down on the table beside
him. 'Oh, they're fine healthy babies.' He gestured with
one hand. 'Incredible, isn't it, that a woman who's had
all sorts of hardships manages to produce such a lusty
pair, and poor Marie-Rose has a dead baby—and no
hope of having any more.'

'Yes, François.' Exactly what the little girl had said
—in different words, of course. A strange little thing.
Alphonse watched the spiral of smoke ascending from
the discarded cigar. 'She has the most beautiful blue
eyes.'

His brother made a sound which was halfway between
a sigh and an exclamation of disgust. 'Hm-mph! You're
usually more fastidious than that. She didn't look any
too clean to me.'

'Honest muck!' Alphonse smiled, not a bit put out.
'I've no designs on her.'

'I should hope not! What does she want?'

'Money to start a little business of her own.'

'How much?'

'We didn't get that far.'

'Hmph. You were with her long enough to get her life story.'

Alphonse smiled again. Just like François to be so prickly! He was always like that when he was worried—and plainly he was worried now.

'How much do you think, to buy her silence?'

'Twenty-five—fifty-dollars.' Alphonse shrugged. If he knew his brother, the sum would stagger him.

'Fifty dollars! What does she suppose I'm made of?'

Alphonse crossed his legs and straightened a little in his chair. François was so predictable—and so careful! 'She looks around,' he said lazily, not sure why he was taking the girl's part, 'and she sees the things money can buy.' He gestured towards the furnishings of the room.

'Necessities—the lot of them. A man's family can't live in a pigsty.'

'Quite! And a fine business pays for the luxuries, does it not?'

'I don't know why you're getting at me. You could have been part of that business. You let me buy out your share to set up on your own.'

'I'm not complaining, François. I'm doing very nicely in property, and I enjoy it. Making furniture was never in my line. But let's get back to the problem in hand. You'll have to buy off the midwife, too.'

'I'll let Bourassa handle that. He'll keep his mouth shut—he owes me a favour or two. Five or ten dollars for goodwill will take care of her, particularly if we spread the story around that a mistake was made.'

'What sort of mistake?' Alphonse raised one eyebrow enquiringly. He was beginning to enjoy watching his brother solve things.

'I would have thought it was obvious! There were three babies. The first one never lived, but the other two—whose late arrival surprised everyone—were fine husky specimens. A little small, of course.'

'A stroke of genius, brother! I applaud it. And if the midwife has anything to say, it was her mistake not to have thought of more than one.'

'Exactly.' François permitted himself a deprecating laugh. 'I fancy it's what Bourassa will tell her.'

'Particularly if you instruct him to do so.'

'Tell me, did anyone see the girl bring in the twins? Did she confide in anyone?'

'I fancy not. It seems all to have been done on the spur of the moment. In any case she doesn't speak French, and that's all most of the servants spoke to her.'

'They're all French.' François raised his cigar from its resting-place and took an appreciative puff. 'What else would they speak?'

'Not all of them. Your little skivvy, Bridget, speaks only English.'

'My little skivvy? Does she work here, then?'

'*Certainement.*'

'We must put an end to that.'

'Yes, naturally.'

'We'll need some sort of document from her—her signature or her mark—something to threaten her with if she tries to make trouble later on.'

'She tells me she can write; enough to sign her name, at any rate.'

François took another puff and then put down the cigar in some agitation. 'I think it would be wiser—yes, definitely wiser—to find her a job in some other town. Say Quebec, where we can keep an eye on her. Better to take the long view and avoid trouble.'

'Rather harsh on a girl who speaks no French.' Alphonse did not know why he was defending Bridget. 'Just suppose the story ever got out—I know it won't, but suppose the worst—it wouldn't present you in a very good light. Banishing a girl who'd done you such a favour to a place where no one spoke her language.'

'She'd soon learn it.' He regarded his brother with a

frown. 'I'm the one who's doing her a favour. How would she rear twins? And you needn't raise that supercilious eyebrow at me! Oh all right, it's true it wouldn't look well. Why not send her to La Beaupré? She has an endless succession of nieces she schools for service. Your Irish girl won't even be noticed among them. She'll learn some French and get training for something better.'

Alphonse considered the proposition, his fingers together and held at his lips. 'It's not such a bad idea, *mon frère*. I imagine you'll want to investigate her story, make sure she did have a sister who died in childbirth. Then there's the sister to bury. There's no money there.'

'*Tiens*, does it never end? Where do I start investigating?'

'With Father Mulcahey. You can arrange the funeral with him as well.' Alphonse was watching Françoise closely to see how he took this suggestion.

Somewhat to his surprise, his brother's face lightened. 'I'll pay for the funeral. Nothing fancy, you understand, but it's the least I can do.'

'That has a pious smack to it.' Alphonse's mind was working rapidly. Why was his brother volunteering to pay for an unknown woman's funeral? He supposed it might be a way of softening Bridget. 'Will you put a marker on the grave?'

'Something simple. The woman's name—and baby, we could add—just to keep the record more or less straight.'

Light began to dawn. 'Your own little one?' Alphonse felt stirrings of sympathy for his brother. So it had meant something to him, after all. He had thought all the emotion had been on Marie-Rose's part. François must have wanted this child, this son.

'He can't have a proper ceremony. He never lived . . .' François' voice was even but very low. 'But I would like to think there'd be prayers said over him, a woman to hold him.'

Alphonse was silent. François must be deeply moved,

for he was not given to extravagant gestures. Marie-Rose must have humanised him considerably. The power of a good woman! He marvelled at it. To break the silence, more than anything else, Alphonse said gently, 'And the child—your own boy—where is he?'

'Over there.' François gestured with one hand towards a chair in the corner of the room. On it rested what Alphonse had assumed was a blanket. François sighed. 'You'll take care of the girl for me? Attend to all that? I'd be very grateful if you would.'

Alphonse did not want to agree, or to be involved with the Irish girl and her disposal to suitable employment, because he knew that was what his brother meant. But he was touched by the way François looked towards the blanket and its hidden burden, and then looked away. '*Bien*,' he said. 'I'll do what I can. How far are you prepared to go in actual cash?'

'I should think a few dollars would be enough to satisfy her? That, and the funeral paid for.' François stubbed out his cigar as there was a knock at the door.

'Monsieur Duvalier! Monsieur Duvalier! You're wanted at once.'

He rose to his feet and handed the key of the room to Alphonse. 'I'm needed. Go back to the girl. I expect you'll want to think over what you're going to say to her, but lock up here when you've decided.'

Alphonse took the key and watched his brother leave. Yes, he needed to think. He began to stride about the room. What was the best attitude to take? Just tell her she was going out in the country for a few days, and that his brother was thinking about what to do? In that way she would be in a more amenable frame of mind when he finally dealt with her. It was the sensible way. Why, then, did he feel so unwilling to set about what his own head told him was the right way to do what François wanted? The girl was nothing to him—just a pair of beautiful eyes. *Sacrebleu!* How she'd fought him! His lips curved into a smile at the memory. He fingered the scratch, grateful that his brother had made no comment on it.

He found his steps had halted by the little bundle on the chair. His hand reached out of its own volition to raise the cover. After all, this was his nephew, even if he had not lived. François wouldn't mind him looking. It wasn't ghoulishness—it was family interest. He decided there was not enough light to see clearly, and took a few steps to the window, pulling the curtains open; then he went back to the chair.

The little face looking up at him was the image of Marie-Rose. As he gazed, the blanket, disturbed, rolled away from the body. He drew in his breath sharply. There was something wrong with the feet. The little body was perfect, but the boy had club feet.

Alphonse drew in his breath sharply. No wonder they hadn't allowed his mother to see him, but had drugged her into a deep sleep immediately. Poor Marie-Rose, and *pauvre petit enfant*! Better that he had never properly come into the world, never uttered a single cry. He wanted to turn away, to repudiate what he saw. Why had he looked? No wonder the door was locked! No wonder François wanted this poor little mite buried with Pegeen. With shaking fingers, he rewrapped the tiny creature.

Wasn't François fortunate to have two healthy babies substituted for this damaged one? He couldn't begrudge him his luck. He walked over to the other chair and sat down. All he could think of was Bridget Langton's clear eyes as she had said her sister was dead. She deserved more than a few dollars. She deserved François' undying gratitude. But it wasn't his brother who was dealing with her—it was himself. He had been given a free hand, and had a choice about what to do.

Bridie woke, Monsieur Duvalier's brother sitting watching her. She sat up, struggling against the layers of sleep pressing her down. What was she doing here? What was this man doing looking at her? 'What's your name?' she demanded. 'Who are you?'

'You know who I am, my girl. I am Alphonse Duvalier, and I've brought you something to eat.' He pointed to a heaped plate on a nearby table. 'And something to drink.' He rose and poured two glasses of wine from a decanter. The one he gave her he had half filled with water. 'Put something in your stomach first.' He drew a small table nearer her chair and set the full plate on it with a fork and a knife.

Bridie didn't bother with either. She saw there was bread as well, and helped herself to a thick piece. On it she laid a slice of meat with her fingers, and bit into the whole before he might change his mind. She was starving! A second slice followed the first, and she devoured a tomato as well and some lettuce before she looked up. It was disturbing to find him watching her, and she fidgeted, taking her glass in one hand and finishing the wine in one gulp. That made her cough and then splutter.

Alphonse got up and thumped her on the back. 'Steady, Mademoiselle! No one will take it from you.' He poured her another glass, and went to stand at the window looking out, as if sensing she did not welcome his gaze.

Bridie would have liked to show him dainty table manners, but he wasn't looking. She finished the third slice of meat to find there was no more bread, and then took up the knife to cut the rest of the meat into more manageable portions and to eat the potato salad that accompanied it. The second glass of wine mixed with water she treated more carefully, but she finished it as well and sat back, satisfied and ready to do battle. She nearly disgraced herself by belching.

'When's your brother to see me, Monsieur Alphonse?' She stifled a giggle over his name. That such a handsome, well-set-up man should bear the name 'Alphonse' struck her as amusing. She much preferred the sound of François. It was much more manly.

'What's so funny?' he was quick to ask.

'Nothing! Sure it's nothing at all.'

'*Bien.*' He came over and sat down in a chair opposite her. 'We'll talk some more.'

'Wait now,' she waggled her finger at him. 'It's not you I should be talking to—it's your brother. He's the one with the twins.'

'I'm acting for him.'

His eyes were on hers, stirring her up and fine he knew it, Bridie told herself. She didn't want to talk to him. He could get a girl turned inside out. Why had she let herself drink the wine? It only made matters worse, but she had been very thirsty.

'Why should you act for him? Are you his man of business?'

He laughed aloud at that. 'Not usually, but he's asked me to deal with you.'

'Why would he be doing that?'

'Because he doesn't speak much English.'

Bridie told herself that was reasonable. Alphonse had no troubles with English, or none that she could hear. 'Well then,' she held out her hand. 'Tell me what he said to you, and I'll be off, back to work.'

Alphonse ignored her outstretched hand. 'You're not going back to work! Not here. François won't allow it. He doesn't want you near the babies.'

'Why not?' Bridie had never considered that possibility in spite of what he'd said before. 'I'll do them no harm.'

'He means to claim them as his own. His wife says they look like him. That's shaken him a bit.'

Bridie's heart sang. He meant to keep the boys. Praise be! She had known all along that he would. Jesus, Mary and Joseph, weren't they grand boys now? She smiled in triumph. 'Sure, didn't I say that he would?'

'I don't think you quite understand. François is a careful man. He means to keep the boys to himself. You're to have nothing to do with them.'

'Nothing,' she echoed. 'Nothing at all,' and found her words had come out in a whisper.

'You must agree never to see the boys again.'

Bridie opened her mouth and nothing came out—not a squeak. Never to see Pegeen's sons again—her own nephews!

'Another thing,' Alphonse went on, his voice calm as though he hadn't destroyed her world. 'You must sign a paper giving up any rights you might think you have. That's after he's seen Father Mulcahey, and made sure you're telling the truth about them.'

She stared at him. 'I am telling the truth.'

'If he takes them—and he says *if*, make no mistake about that—his wife will name them Jean and Jacques. They'll take the name of Duvalier, of course, and be brought up in the true faith and as his sons. They'll speak French as their mother tongue, but he'll see that they learn English too. He's a good business man after all, and knows the value of a second language, even if he's never learned it himself.'

'Yes,' said Bridget. French or English—what did it matter? They'd never speak their own tongue, never have the Gaelic; still, they would have the faith. Father Mulcahey would approve of that. The enormity of what she was doing hit her like a blow. She was disposing of Sean's and Sennen's lives—as best she could, she reminded herself. Pegeen would understand that. She had begged her to look to their future. But she would never have seen their future like this.

'Wait now,' she said. 'Wait. Have—have you told him about the money?' Her mouth was dry, her tongue stuck to its roof.

Alphonse nodded. 'He is shocked to the very heart to hear that you want to sell the boys. He can't understand anyone putting a price on their own flesh and blood.'

She coloured to the roots of her hair, went hot and cold with shame. Yes, she was selling her own flesh and blood, or trying to. How dared this Alphonse be so pious and pompous about it? He wasn't poor, dirty, tired and alone in the world, and hungry most of the time. He and his brother had everything, she nothing. She needed money. They didn't. They wouldn't even miss it.

'I need the money,' she insisted. 'I'm alone. All alone.' She opened her hands in a gesture of entreaty.

If he was moved at all, it didn't show. 'How much is the blood-money? Thirty pieces of silver?'

Her fingers itched to scratch him, to mark the other side of his face as she had marked the first. She wondered how he had explained that to his brother. She held back, ready to burst into tears. The price of betrayal —that was what he meant! But it wasn't that, she told herself. She had found a home for the boys. Pegeen wouldn't begrudge her something for herself, alone and penniless in an alien land. 'Twenty-five dollars would do,' she whispered, 'to give me a start, like.' She knew it was an enormous sum as he looked at her with his brown eyes.

Alphonse's eyebrows rose. 'That's a tidy sum! Would you expect it all in one payment, or would you, having been paid, demand more and more till you became a stone about my brother's neck, an ever-open hand grasping at his wealth?'

Bridie gasped. However mixed his similies, she knew very well what he was driving at. 'Just give me what I ask,' she said. 'He'll never see me again. Except once a year his man of business—that'll be you, will it not? —must prove to me that the boys are in good health and are happy.' If he could impose conditions, she told herself, looking at the livid scratch on his cheek and remembering the feel of him as he had held her—well, so could she!

This time she saw she had scored. Alphonse was taken aback. 'He'll never agree to it, and I'm not sure that I will.'

'Suit yourself!' she retorted. 'I've no wish to see you.' She almost believed it! 'But if not you, then Father Mulcahey—I'd be taking his word.'

'I'll put it to my brother.'

'Right. Is it now you'll be doing it?' She gestured towards the door.

He made no move to leave but took her hand in his.

'All in good time. First we must settle where you're going. You can't go back to your sister's place.'

'What do you mean?' She struggled to free her hand. 'I'm not going anywhere—especially with you, if that's what you mean! I'll not leave this house.'

'I meant nothing of the sort!' He took his hand away as though he had been stung. 'I like my women considerably softer and plumper than you—and considerably cleaner, too, and without claws.' His hand went to his cheek, and he smiled.

His amusement stung her into angry retort. 'There's some as have found me attractive, and you needn't laugh! Why, Hugh Prendergast said I had eyes the colour of a lake with the sunlight on it reflecting the blue blue skies—and he the one all the girls were after setting their caps for. Even Pegeen, I sometimes thought.' She would have liked to kick his shins, to wipe the scorn from his face, but she didn't touch him again, just raised her blue eyes to his dark ones. He was right about not going back to Pegeen. The very thought made her shiver.

He looked down at her, the corners of his mouth twitching. 'Yes, the eyes are good. How old are you, Bridget Langton?'

She felt uncomfortable under his scrutiny. 'Nineteen,' she replied, trying to draw herself to her full five feet of height. Since she was seated, the effort was wasted.

'Not very big for your age,' was his verdict. 'That can't be helped, I suppose. How long since you've had enough to eat?'

'I don't know. We never had enough to eat all the last year. The weight just fell away from us—all except Pegeen. She managed to stay as she was—not that she was ever fat, but she looked better than the rest—until we went on the boat. Then Maling and I had to make her eat.'

'Gave her some of your share, did you?'

'Yes, for with the babies coming, what else would we do? We were luckier than most. We had some food.

Maling's mother saw to that. I don't know why Pegeen never had a good word to say for her.'

'Spare me your recollections,' he advised. 'I've decided where you'll go. I'll ring for the carriage.' He pulled the bell-rope hanging by the fireplace.

'I'll fetch my things,' Bridie offered. 'My nightie and such-like.' It was a grand relief to have decisions out of her hands.

'You won't need anything,' she was informed. 'You'll come as you are—and don't start complaining! You'll be safe and comfortable with enough to eat and a bed to sleep in. I'm taking you to my old nurse. She's a respectable woman and will treat you kindly. In a few days I'll come to see you. If all goes well, I'll even bring Father Mulcahey.'

'Does that mean you'll speak to your brother?' Suddenly, she was uncertain that she liked any of this. It was all very well of him to take her to his old nurse, but who was to say how his nurse would feel about having her dumped there. Where was it, anyway?

'I'll speak to him, but you'll have to wait for his word.'

There was a discreet rap on the door, and Alphonse went through and stood outside in the corridor to give directions to the servant who stood there. He came back to her.

'There, that's settled! In five minutes we'll go down the stairs and out of the front door. The carriage will be waiting. You're to speak to no one—if anyone should be around. Is that understood?'

'Yes, but . . .' she began.

He interrupted. 'Do you want my help or not?'

'Of course I want it! But *why* are you helping me?'

'I'm doing it for Marie-Rose, for Madame Duvalier.'

'I see,' said Bridie. 'She's a fine woman. Everyone says so.' It gave her considerable comfort to think that the twins had found a real mother. Not that it was settled yet, but with him taking charge, and Pegeen watching over her boys . . . It suddenly struck her. She'd forgotten all about Pegeen and her heart sank. 'I can't go!

You know I can't. Pegeen's to be buried, and there's no one but me to see to it.'

'Don't worry, girl. My brother has said he'll see to it,' Alphonse told her. 'One or the other of us will go to Father Mulcahey, and everything will be attended to.'

'That's very good of you, but it wouldn't be right.'

'Why wouldn't it? Is there anything you can do for her now?'

Bridie shook her head. The only thing she could do for Pegeen now was to ensure the twins' future. Why not let him take charge of everything? She was tired out, and he had offered to help her. 'Mother of God, I've no money to pay!' The admission was wrung out of her. 'But there's wages to come. Promise me it won't be like Maling, just thrown in a heap with all the others.'

'You have my word. Father Mulcahey will say what's right. It's settled.' He took her arm and led her from the room. A great burden seemed to fall from Bridie's shoulders. Just the same, he must not be allowed to think he could have it all his own way. 'I'll come behind you.' She detached her arm from his; she didn't want him so close. 'It wouldn't look right for us to go down the stairs hooked together, and through the front door.'

With a sharp sigh he pushed her in front of him. 'You go first then, girl. And mind, not a word out of you!'

Bridie held her tongue and went down. She wondered why he never used her name but only called her 'girl'. She prayed all the way that she could trust him, that he truly meant to help her. In her exhausted, bemused state she was never quite sure if she heard right. It seemed to her that he spoke under his breath as he followed. At first his words made little sense to her, nor could she understand afterwards why, if he had said them, he'd say them in English.

'Blue—I've never seen such a blue, more like the colour of flowers than of any lake. *Sacrebleu!* Am I a boy, to be bowled over by a pair of blue eyes?'

Startled, she turned round to look at him, but she must have been mistaken. He was looking straight ahead and frowning. He motioned her to go on. Bridie did as she was bid, and went out of the front door, down the outside stairs to the waiting carriage.

CHAPTER THREE

'MONSIEUR ALPHONSE, *qu'est-ce que c'est?*' was the greeting Mademoiselle Beaupré directed at the pair as they descended from the carriage in front of her cottage.

Bridie had only time to note that it was a wooden structure with a long porch running along the front and a few straight-backed chairs standing sentinel halfway along it. So this was the village of Notre-Dame de Grâce, their destination. It was out in the country—but not in a rural setting that was in any way familiar to her. The lovely green of her own land didn't clothe the fields. Instead, there were strangely shaped patches of cultivated land before other houses, all of them with verandas of some sort, and largely unpainted.

She was bundled indoors before she could investigate what was growing in the garden. It was hot. Indeed, the heat of the July day, combined with the shock and exhaustion of the previous one, had lulled Bridie into a dazed, half-awake state and the journey had been accomplished in almost total silence. Monsieur Alphonse at first had tried to point out a few places of interest on the way, but as drowsiness had drifted over the girl he had become quiet. The only things she really remembered were the name of the place they travelled to, and that he had said her hostess was a splendid cook.

They went into a parlour; a small room, but solidly furnished with a polished floor and rag rugs. Mademoiselle Beaupré indicated a chair to her, though she and Monsieur Alphonse both remained standing. Bridie was glad to sit while a long conversation in French took place. The chair she had been directed to was a big wooden rocking-chair, and she found it surprisingly comfortable.

Though she could not understand a word of what was going on, it was clear that Mademoiselle was delighted to see Monsieur Alphonse. She asked him questions, wanted him to stay, called in a little blond girl, who looked about thirteen. She poured him a glass of wine and curtsied as she gave it to him, then crept out of the room with only the slightest of glances at Bridie.

Mademoiselle Beaupré was a very tall erect woman with a lined face and white hair. Bridie had ample time to study her as the conversation progressed. She walked with the aid of a cane, and gestured with it, too. It was a lovely piece of dark wood with a ferocious dog's head carved for the handle. It was not long before Mademoiselle's eyes turned towards the seated girl.

'Stand up,' said Alphonse. 'She wishes to have a proper look at you.'

Feeling rather like a horse or cow that had been led, protesting, to market, Bridie stood. Two pairs of eyes examining her made her uneasy. 'Sure, what does she expect to find?' she asked angrily.

'Be quiet, Bridget! She thinks something might be made of you, once you've been scrubbed down and are in clean clothes.'

That was too much. Far from receiving this in silence, Bridie sputtered in rage. 'It isn't everyone who has servants to fetch water for them so they can bathe and dress in their finery!' She ignored the fact that he had called her by name for the first time.

Alphonse laughed at her, but Mademoiselle was not amused. She looked the girl up and down and made some biting comments—at any rate, Bridie was sure they were biting. He appeared to have some difficulty in calming Mademoiselle. He drew her to one corner of the room, leaving the hapless Bridie standing in the centre. She saw him reach in his pocket and put some money into the woman's hand. He folded her hand over it, and she gave him a nod of agreement and a smile.

'*Pour vous*, Monsieur Alphonse. *Seulement pour vous*,' were the words Bridie heard.

Alphonse came over to her. 'She says she's doing it for me, so keep that in mind.'

'What's she doing?'

'Keeping you here, girl. Surely you understand that?'

'For how long?'

'As long as needs be.' There was impatience in his voice. 'Till everything's arranged, just be patient. Mademoiselle will take care of you.'

'I'd rather just have the money and get started on my shop!' Bridie didn't care if she sounded ungrateful.

'Would you, Bridget?' His eyes held hers, and she was lost in their depths. 'Where would you go? Have you anyone to stay with? Besides, my brother hasn't agreed yet to giving you anything.'

'But he will. Surely he will?' Her hand reached out to him.

He held it for a brief instant and again shivers went up her whole arm. 'You're not a prisoner here, but there are arrangements to make. In any case, your precious twins are safe. Isn't that enough for the present?'

Bridie hung her head. 'Yes,' she muttered. Suddenly she didn't want to part from him. He was the only one she knew in this household. 'Does she speak any English?' She turned her face towards her hostess.

'Not much,' he admitted.

'How can I talk to her?'

'I'm sure you'll manage. You'll pick up French in no time. She's a good, kind woman. She'll feed you and clothe you—and teach you a few manners.'

Bridie stared at him, affronted. 'What's she going to clothe me in?' She crossed her arms over her breast as if daring him to snatch her clothes from her.

'Something suitable. I've left her something to provide for you.'

This statement did nothing to still her doubts. 'I suppose you'll take that off the money from your brother.'

'*Bon Dieu*, is there no satisfying you? You find fault with everything!' He threw his hands in the air in a

gesture which was both angry and totally French. 'You'll
be all right here. I won't forget you.'

Bridie gulped. Did he really mean that promise? It
somehow made her feel better, but she didn't want to let
him see she was so easily quieted. 'Who's the young
girl?' she asked. 'The one who poured the wine?'

'One of her nieces she's training for service. She takes
all her nieces in hand and finds them jobs in grand
houses.'

She felt a stab of fear. 'Is that what she's going to do
with me?'

Alphonse didn't answer that directly. 'She'd have her
work cut out, wouldn't she?' His eyes were hard and
bright.

Bridie almost stuck out her tongue at him. The nerve
of the creature! She was just to be left here with no one
to talk to, and it had taken nearly an hour's drive to
reach this place. How would she ever make her way back
if it wasn't to her liking? But, devil take him, she would if
she had to. She felt like sitting down and crying. Tears
came to her eyes.

Again he took her hand. 'The fresh air and good food
will work wonders with you in a day or two. And you can
use the time to reflect on your future and pray for the
repose of your sister's soul.'

Bridie was forcibly reminded of Pegeen, and the fact
that this man had promised a proper burial for her. She
had no recourse save to trust him. In any case, there was
no more time to protest. He took his leave of both of
them, and she was left facing Mademoiselle Beaupré
and her frown.

Immediately, she was whisked out of the parlour into
the kitchen and sat in a small chair while water was
heated on the black stove in the corner. It was like no
other piece of kitchen equipment that Bridie had ever
seen. It was round and pot-bellied, and made the kitchen
so warm that she was sweating with the heat. The little
girl fed it with wood logs.

Bridie tried to talk to both Mademoiselle and the little

girl, but the extent of her efforts was to learn that the child's name was Anita, a name foreign to her tongue but easily enough said.

When the water was bubbling, a wooden bath was carried in and filled. With Mademoiselle pointing and Anita gleefully miming getting undressed, Bridie realised with a feeling close to horror that the bath was meant for her. She took off her clothes, feeling that, if she didn't, they would be torn from her. She dropped her dress and her chemise on the floor and got into the warm water as quickly as she could, arms clasped over her breasts.

At a terse command from Mademoiselle, Anita whipped her things away and then began to rub Bridie's back and arms with soap which might better have been used for the laundry. Mademoiselle herself washed her long black hair, and even gave her a nod of approval at its thickness and lack of lice. 'Sure, it hasn't been easy to keep it so nice,' Bridie told her, not caring whether she understood or not. She was beginning to feel quite left out as they chattered to each other in French over her head. For good measure she added, 'I've never had a bath before with two complete strangers. Pegeen used to scrub my back, if I asked her.' Anita giggled to hear her speaking and rubbed at her legs. Bridie managed to get the soap from her then, with a muttered, 'I'm quite able to do that for myself!'

By the time she emerged glowing and refreshed from the water, she had lost all feelings of modesty and was wrapped dripping wet in a towel. With the heat of the kitchen it was not long before even her hair was dry. Mademoiselle produced a blue and white checked gingham dress, and this was slipped over her head. What had happened to her old clothes she had no inkling, but the new dress, though short, fitted tolerably well. It was loose in bust and waist, and Anita made signs of a swelling bosom which made all of them laugh.

So great was Bridie's pleasure that she threw her arms round Anita and tried to teach her to jig. 'Begob,' she declared, smiling and breathless and barefooted, 'you've the makings of a fine Irish dancer! Just lift your skirts a little, and show your ankles.'

Mademoiselle produced a pair of slippers, and the two girls were shooed outside to a small porch that looked over a field, and Anita brushed Bridie's hair—not too easy a task, since it was thick and long and wavy. She looked almost glad to be called in.

The afternoon sun was still warm, and Bridie sat on, her back against the steps, her head resting against a pillar. She schooled her mind to thoughts of Pegeen, but Alphonse Duvalier's face kept intruding. Ah, he was handsome, but there was arrogance in the tilt of his head, in the lean body of him. Now hadn't that been a fine suit he'd been wearing—grey worsted, and cut to fit snug. She sighed. Why was she wasting her time mooning over the likes of him? He'd never be giving her the time of day, but for the twins. 'Forgive me, Pegeen,' she murmured, all alone by herself in the sunshine. 'You'll have to watch over them two from wherever you are.' She found nothing strange in sending such a message to her dead sister. Hadn't she and Pegeen almost known what the other thought all the time—at least until the past year. Wait now, wasn't it always that way between sisters, when one of them found her man? Would she ever find a man and follow him to the ends of the earth the way Pegeen had done? No, she told herself. She was going to get some money together, and sail back to Ireland.

Her musings were interrupted by Anita calling her to come in. Bridie was motioned to a table with benches set in an alcove of the kitchen away from the stove. She and Mademoiselle ate in some style, with Anita waiting on them. Her eyes had nearly popped out of her head at the quantity and quality of the food served at that first meal. Hot onion soup with cheese sprinkled on it was set before her. It was accompanied by dark bread, very fresh and surprisingly light. Then there were vegetables from the garden: green peas, butter beans, lettuce and tomatoes, and some slices of cold brawn.

Bridie's only trouble was that she could not finish everything on her plate. Her stomach must have shrunk, after all it had been through. She looked longingly at the food, and tried to explain to her hostess how it was with her. Mademoiselle directed the removal of the remains, and Anita, with a wink, produced a bowl of strawberries and cream.

'There's no resisting such a dish!' Bridie smiled at them both and took up her spoon. 'Just to sample it, like . . .' She surprised herself by finishing the whole.

After that, though she wasn't quite sure what was expected of her in this household, she followed Anita and washed the pots quite willingly, in spite of the girl's protests. Mademoiselle went to sit out on the front veranda, so the girls had the kitchen to themselves. Anita was silent, but not Bridie. She couldn't stop her tongue running on.

'I see fine how it is,' she told her. 'You're frightened of your auntie. You have to do what she tells you, and you're such a little thing.' She took her hands out of the washing-up and gave Anita a quick hug. Her words poured out, the brogue strong since she was mainly talking to herself. 'I'm a bit in awe of her, too. When we were doing the jigging before, her face wore such a frown, but she wasn't angry, exactly—more stern, like she felt she had to be. You must listen to her,' she admonished the child. 'I know well how it is, servants have to learn to keep their place. A fine struggle I always had at the big house, but I was somebody—under-cook has more leeway than a maid of all work.' She sighed, and held up a plate to make sure it was clean. 'You put me in mind of my young sister Nora. But she's gone now. Dead and gone with Da and me Mam, Daniel and Maeve—she was the little one. Still, there's no use going over that. I'm alive, and Patrick and Michael left behind at the old place, and the two of them struggling against the hunger and the blight. Think of the living—that's what my Da said. He was right. Did I think of the others, there'd be no life left in me. Ah, but 'tis hard, fierce hard, to forget.' For good measure, she hugged Anita again. The girl hugged her back, and began to point to things and tell her their names in French.

It was a game they played until it began to grow dark and they were sent off to bed by Mademoiselle, and a long pink cotton nightie, not new but still with lots of wear in it, was provided for Bridie. She and the girl shared a double bed in a tiny room whose ceiling sloped down to the floor. Even before Anita blew out the candle and crept in beside her, Bridie was asleep.

She woke early with cock-crow and shook Anita awake. 'You shall learn English, and I shall learn French,' she informed her. 'For every child needs to be educated—that was me Da's way. He made us all go to the hedgerow school whether it was rain or it was shine. Just thank your stars you aren't after sitting under a hedge with the rain down your back! To speak or teach the Gaelic was officially forbidden, see, so the priest had to hold the school in secret. I tell meself that if I could master the Gaelic and the English, I can surely pick up a smattering of the French. Wait, now,' she exclaimed as Anita yawned and rubbed her eyes. 'Say after me: The top of the morning to yer honour. That's the way to greet a fine Englishman when you bring a cup of tea to rouse him up.'

The girl repeated the words after her, and was delighted when she praised her. The two of them went down to face the day. Anita took her in hand and they did the chores together, learning and laughing, the pair of them friends.

Mademoiselle Beaupré supervised the cooking herself. Indeed, she did the greater part of it, with Anita allowed only the most menial of tasks. At first, Bridie was relegated to this role as well, but she felt bound to prove herself as the first day flowed into the second and there was no sign of release.

'I'll make you an Irish stew,' she tried to tell Mademoiselle. She was shooed away, but would not accept her dismissal. She took the knife Mademoiselle was using to cut pieces of meat into cubes, and by signs, showed her she meant to make a dish. Mademoiselle shrugged and stood back, very watchful, only directing Anita not to interfere. Bridie went ahead, adding onions, parsley, potatoes and carrots. She stirred it and cooked it, and offered the first taste to her hostess.

'*Bien,*' was the verdict, but Mademoiselle added a spoonful of honey and a sprinkling of herbs. French Irish stew, Bridget said to herself with a grin. After that, she was entrusted not only with picking the vegetables from the garden but also with cooking some of them and watching the preparation of sauces.

It was on the third day that Father Mulcahey came in a black buggy drawn by a fat spotted horse. Mademoiselle must have expected him, for she welcomed him and invited him in. Even though the summer day was warm, Anita was summoned to the parlour and directed to bring hot chocolate and slices of fruit cake. It was some time before Bridget was summoned.

Father Mulcahey greeted her with warmth and news. 'You're a lucky girl, Bridget. Mr Duvalier has taken a hand in your future, and Miss Beaupré reports herself well pleased with you. Neither of the brothers Duvalier could come today.' Father Mulcahey sat down again, and Mademoiselle waved Bridie to a chair with her stick. 'I've come with the news. I'm delighted to tell you the babies are thriving. Jean and Jacques—that's what they're calling them. They're so pleased with them, they might be their own flesh and blood. Your poor sister, God rest her soul, will be looking down and smiling all over her face—if you understand my meaning.'

'Yes, Father. I'm terrible glad, father, about the babes.' Bridie was delighted the boys had found a home. Monsieur Alphonse had been as good as his word.

'I've the paper for you to sign.' Father Mulcahey took a document from the pocket of his well-worn soutane. He fished out pen and ink as well. 'All you've to do is sign at the bottom.' He held out the paper to her.

Bridie took it. 'Yes, Father. Thank you, Father. Will you be reading it to me, then—so I've the sense of it?'

'I'll tell you what it says,' he offered. 'You should never put your cross to anything you don't understand. It says you're willing to give up all claims to the boys in consideration of their being given a good home and brought up as François and Marie-Rose Duvalier's own. It's a fine thing they're doing, Bridget, a grand fine thing.'

'Yes, Father, it is. Sean and Sennen'll be grateful to them all their lives.'

Father Mulcahey proffered the document again. 'Just sign it, Bridget. There's ink in the pen, and I'll inscribe your name underneath.'

'I can write my own name, Father.'

'That's good, my child. Just be doing it, then.'

'Yes, Father.' Bridie made no move to take the pen. 'Is that all it says? Just that about giving them a home?'

'What more should there be?' The priest put the ink-bottle down on a small table near his elbow. 'If that isn't just like me! I'm forgetting.' He struck his knee with his hand. 'I'm to keep an eye on the lads. See them once a year to make sure all's well with them.'

'I can ask you about them, then—how they're looking —if they favour Pegeen or their Da.' Bridie sat on the edge of her chair. So it wasn't Alphonse who'd do the telling.

'Yes. I never knew their Da, of course, but I'll do my best to give you the news of them. Only, Bridget, my child, wouldn't it be wiser to put them out of your mind and not dwell on them? You've your own way to make.'

'Forget them, you mean?' Bridie bit her lip. It wasn't like her to question a priest, but she had to make it clear that she had not given them up lightly. 'I don't think I could, forgiving your reverence. They're Pegeen's own.'

'Your sentiments do you credit, child. It's very hard for you, but best for the boys.' He offered her the pen again. 'Time will heal your aching heart, Bridget. Pray for its coming. Now, if you'll just place your mark.'

'Yes, Father.' Bridget's voice was meek, and she took the pen. 'Is there nothing else written there? Nothing else at all? Nothing about me?' She got the words out with difficulty. She didn't want Father Mulcahey thinking ill of her, but she had to know.

'There's nothing else at all in it,' Father Mulcahey assured her. 'Just write your name, child.'

Bridie signed the document. It was betrayal, wasn't it? Had Alphonse Duvalier ever meant to help her with her little shop? She bit her lip so hard that she tasted the salt of her own blood. She should have known that the rich did precious little for the poor—save for keeping them in their place. But the twins—ah, the twins would grow up among the rich. They were safe. 'What happens now, Father? Will I be going with you, back to the town, you know?'

'You're to stay here, Bridget, and be a good girl. Learn the French and be obedient to Mademoiselle Beaupré.' The priest's long solemn face twinkled into a smile. He eased his tall frame out of the chair, pocketing his possessions.

Bridie immediately rose to her feet, as did Mademoiselle Beaupré. The priest shook the old woman's hand, murmuring over it in her own language. She walked with him to the door. Bridie tugged at his cassock. 'But, Father, how long am I to stay here? Did they tell you?'

He shrugged. 'As long as needs be. You're comfortable here—and happy. Don't fret yourself over it. The Duvaliers have said they'll help you. That's what they're doing. I shouldn't wonder if they didn't find you a situation cooking for some grand family in Quebec or Three Rivers, for it wouldn't be seemly for you to stay here in Montreal, now would it?'

'Why wouldn't it?' Bridie blurted out. 'I'm here now. Pegeen's buried here—she is buried, isn't she?—and I've never even seen her lowered into the ground. Not that it matters. I've seen half the folk I used to know covered up in winding-sheets and the earth mounded over them. They might have let me go to her funeral.'

She was sobbing with the intensity of her emotions.

Father Mulcahey put his hand on her shoulder. 'Child, child, the funeral's tomorrow, and a carriage is to be sent for you. I've explained all that to Mademoiselle Beaupré.'

'What good's that?' Bridie sobbed harder. 'When I have no French and she has no English.'

Mademoiselle put her arm round the girl, and she cried as if her heart would break, murmuring, 'Pegeen's my sister, don't you see?'

Father Mulcahey patted her on the shoulder again. 'It's a woman's sympathy you're needing now. That's why I left it to her to comfort you. Mind, the carriage'll be here at eight.' He climbed into the buggy and picked up the reins.

The old woman led Bridie back into the house, straight to the kitchen, and Anita was charged with making her a hot drink. Over the tisane of herbs, a conversation of sorts took place.

Bridie said she would need something black to wear. Anita burst into tears to hear about her sister. Mademoiselle was the only practical one. She sent her niece up to her room to fetch a black dress and a hat-box, and Bridie had to try on the dress. It was too long for her, and loose as well. Mademoiselle clucked her tongue and waved her hand for needle and thread, and the three of them got to work. The two girls hemmed, and Mademoiselle put in tucks, and when next Bridie tried it the fit was considerably better. Then the hat-box was opened.

The black hat it contained drew a gasp of admiration from both girls. Anita touched with a reverent hand the black feathers that cascaded from its brim. Bridie was fascinated by the yards of fine veiling. That she would wear such a delightful piece of millinery to Pegeen's funeral was surely to give her honour! She could almost hear her sister's throaty laugh in the very room as Mademoiselle set the confection upon her head and arranged the net about her face.

Anita ran for a mirror and held it up so that she might

gaze on herself. And gaze, Bridie did. Why, she looked a
fine lady! The good food of the last few days and the time
spent gardening had given a glow to her cheeks and a
look of health that had been missing for months. Her
black-lashed blue eyes looked enormous, the bones of
her face too prominent, but still the effect of the hat was
surprising.

'*Belle, belle!*' Anita exclaimed, and danced round her,
in her excitement forgetting her aunt's strictures about
deportment. '*C'est magnifique, n'est-ce pas?*'

'*Bien.*' Mademoiselle's assessment was cooler, but she
looked pleased. '*Pas si mal.*'

It was no use asking where the hat had come from.
Bridie supposed it must have come from some grand
household as a cast-off. It didn't really matter. It was
hers to wear.

She wondered if Mademoiselle or perhaps Anita
would go with her in the morning, but when she finally
succeeded in making herself understood, her hostess
shook her head decidedly and gave her a long speech
about Monsieur Alphonse, and sent her off to bed to get
her rest. Bridie was left wondering if she was to travel
alone in the carriage, or if he meant to come for her.

She dreamed about her sister, horrible dreams in
which a fierce Pegeen stood over her, demanding what
she'd done with her babies, why she was to be buried
with someone else's child. Where were her own? Bridie
woke moaning in the dark of the night. Anita's arms
slipped round her, and she cried out her heart.

'Why should my own sister be angry with me?' she
begged of the girl. 'Sure I've done all I could.' She found
herself addressing her sister, so vivid was the dream still.
'Only wait now—the wake, is that the way of it? Pegeen,
you never had a proper wake with all the relatives there,
and they talking and wishing you well. Oh, Pegeen,
don't you see, there was only me. Jesus, Mary and
Joseph, I couldn't have borne it alone! Monsieur
Alphonse said I must look to myself—that's what Da
would have said, too. Don't haunt me, Pegeen! I'll

always love your boys, even if I can't see them and hug them and tell them about you.'

Anita only exclaimed, '*Sois tranquille*, Bridget. It was *un cauchemar*.' She held her tight.

It was as if Nora held her, Nora the little sister who had been just about this girl's age when she had gone. Bridie grew calmer. Of course it was a nightmare, just as she said. She had felt Pegeen's death heavy in her mind, and she had not let herself think on it. Sorrow had to be faced; it was no use pretending it wasn't there. It never went away—just got lighter as the days passed. She only wished they'd pass quicker. When tomorrow was gone, Pegeen was certain to fade, never forgotten, but no longer there.

Bridie was dressed in her finery and ready long before eight in the morning. She had had a small breakfast —just bread and milk. It was all she could manage. She sat on the front veranda, and Mademoiselle clucked her tongue and told Anita to pick some daisies and roses for a bouquet. The girl ran to obey, and tied them with a bit of string. Mademoiselle found a short length of black ribbon and was retying the offering when a carriage drove up.

A woman Bridie had never seen got out of it. Mademoiselle received this visitor without any of the ceremony she had accorded the priest yesterday. She simply handed over the Irish girl to her and waved them both away.

Bridie clutched the flowers in her lap as the woman introduced herself in careful English.

'I am Mademoiselle Charette, one of Madame Duvalier's household. I take you to church.'

'Madame Duvalier?' Bridie repeated, jolted out of herself. Did Alphonse Duvalier have a wife? This woman didn't work for François! Bridie knew all the faces there.

'Madame Duvalier invites you to take tea with her, *après*—after—*l'enterrement*.'

Mademoiselle Beaupré had said that word often enough for Bridie to know she meant the funeral. Why should Alphonse's wife want to see her? He hadn't said anything about a wife. Why would he? There was no reason for her to feel worse than she already did, she told herself. It was nothing to her if Alphonse had a wife and two or three little ones. He was nothing to her. It was just foolishness, her foolishness, that kept him in her head. The sooner she gave him his dismissal, the better. She would be finished with him today, but why did the very idea make her feel sadder than ever?

CHAPTER FOUR

ALPHONSE WAITED ON the church steps for Bridie and her companion to alight from the carriage. François immediately took charge of Mademoiselle Charette, as they had agreed between them. He tipped his hat, and left.

Tucking his arm into Bridie's, Alphonse led her away. 'We shall have a little stroll first.' She was so pale that he wished there was somewhere to walk other than the graveyard, which stretched to one side and to the back. No wonder the girl tried to pull away, but he kept a firm hold. François wanted the matter settled today.

'Is your brother not going to speak to me?' She raised those lovely blue eyes to his.

'I'm acting as his agent.'

They skirted a large headstone, and the early morning sun struck her face where the veil was swept back by the breeze.

'Does your brother think the same as you? He must trust you.'

'I have my brother's full authority to act for him.' Even to his own ears, his words sounded pompous.

The girl halted on the path. 'Right, then, let's learn what you have to say, for there isn't much time.'

'There's more than enough.' Why did she look at him so trustingly? It unnerved him. 'I'm glad to see you're looking so well. Are you happy with Mademoiselle Beaupré?'

'She's a grand woman, and the little niece Anita is teaching me French. I'm very grateful to you for placing me there, but now I can manage for myself.' She raised her eyes to meet his, standing stock still to do so. 'Is that what you're going to tell me? That all's settled, that you'll give me what I asked?' She smiled at him.

'My brother isn't sure that to give you what you asked would be wise,' Alphonse began.

'Why not?' Bridie interrupted. 'He has the twins —they're all right, aren't they?' She caught at his sleeve.

'They're fine; they look fatter already.' He brushed her hand aside. She had a habit of reaching out to him. It was endearing, and it was dangerous. She was a very pretty girl. He had known she would be, but he could never have guessed what a difference a few days would have made.

'I signed the paper,' she reminded him. 'It didn't say anything about the money, but you're going to tell me that your brother agreed?'

'Can't we sit down and talk this over?'

Her eyes were flashing now. 'Where shall we sit?' she demanded. 'On that fine black gravestone over there? Is it as black as your heart?' It was as though she guessed he was going to deny her the money.

'Damnation!' Alphonse muttered under his breath. He couldn't blame the girl for being angry. How had he let François talk him into this absurd situation? Why could he not just pay her and be done with it? If that wasn't just like François to be so tight about a few dollars. He had declared that it was enough he was paying for the sister to be buried. He had the twins to support now, and the girl should be grateful, not grasping.

'I'm not proposing to sit on any gravestone, whatever its colour!' he snapped back. When she looked at him with those lovely blue eyes, he wanted to give her whatever she asked. What a change in her whole appearance after only a few days. Wherever had Mademoiselle Beaupré found that hat? It might have been made for this girl. With it on her head, she carried herself like a queen.

'Then what are you proposing? You said we should sit—while you're standing there with your mouth hanging open ready to spin me some fine tale about hardship, well, I'm sitting—and waiting . . .' Bridie plumped herself down on a granite headstone, her skirt obscuring most of its lettering.

The only carved words that met Alphonse's eye were, 'Bring truth to light.' He regarded them sourly. What was it about this girl that made him hesitate to do as François had instructed? He couldn't bring himself to turn her off with five dollars. She was too defenceless —and too pretty. François was a tight-fisted devil!

While he was still searching to find the right words, Bridie spoke again. 'And another thing . . . You needn't try to fob me off with seeing your wife. Whatever you've to say—say it now. I'll hear it from you, not from her.'

'I have no wife.' Where had she got hold of that idea?

'Haven't you so? Then who's this Madame Duvalier who wants to see me after the service? Mademoiselle Charette said she'd asked me to come—ordered, more likely! Wait now, I know what fine gentlefolk are like. They pass you from one to the other till your poor head is swimming and there's nothing at all in your hand. I'll not see your wife, whether you have one or not.'

'I'm not married.' Alphonse wondered why he was bothering with the girl. It was no concern of hers if he had a wife.

'Who's Madame Duvalier? The lady who brought me here said I was to see Madame Duvalier. Does she mean your brother's wife?'

'No, it can't be her.' He was puzzled. Marie-Rose could have no desire to see this girl. She didn't know she existed. His brain cleared suddenly. 'It's my mother!' he exclaimed. 'I didn't know she'd asked you to call.' What could his mother want of her?

'Does she know about me—and the twins?' He was happy to note that her voice seemed calmer, less angry.

'François must have told her.'

'Didn't you know he was going to?'

Alphonse shook his head. Trust his mother to get the truth out of François! Perhaps if the girl saw her, she would be easier to manage. Yes, he would say no more for the present. Let his mother handle it—she would know exactly what to say, how to deal with her—she might be prepared to do something for the girl: help her to another job, make things easier for her. It wouldn't do any harm at all for him to have a talk with his mother too. Then Bridie could go back to Mademoiselle for a few days more while they sorted something out between them. He smiled at the girl. 'Why not go and see my mother? It can't do any harm, can it? Listen to what she says, at least. She'll be sympathetic to you, know what a sacrifice you have made.'

He saw Bridie hesitate. He saw her grip the flowers she held as though she might find some answer from them. He heard her exclamation as one of the thorns caught her finger, saw the drop of blood as she held up her hand. He sprang forward with a clean handkerchief, and wrapped it round the finger.

She seemed nervous when he touched her, and her voice was high as she murmured, 'Sure, you'd think they could make roses without thorns.'

He held the handkerchief in place until the bleeding stopped. 'Promise me you'll see my mother?' He smiled again, very conscious of her nearness and smallness, and the way her dark lashes fell on her cheek.

'I—I promise,' said Bridie. She sighed as she said it, and looked up at him.

'*Bon!* Let's get back to the church.' He held out his hand to her, and found that it had gone straight to her waist. His other hand joined it there to lift her down. Her lightness surprised him. Why, the girl was skin and bone. She needed taking care of, good food and some ease.

He set her promptly on her feet. Why did she have this strange effect on him? Why did he want to protect her, to help her? She was, after all, only a poor Irish country girl. It was those eyes of hers which weakened him. Resolutely he turned his own eyes away from them, and without touching her, escorted her to the church.

Bridie found she could not quite control her breathing as she went up the aisle with Alphonse. It had nothing to do with him, of course—it was the occasion. But still, when his hands had closed about her waist she had felt shivers of what—pleasure? excitement?—she couldn't name the multitude of sensations deep inside her. Best not try. Best put it straight out of her mind. This was Pegeen's day—poor, lovely Pegeen, going to join those others, Da and Mam, and Nora and Maeve and Danny.

They slipped into the front pew, and she was gratified to see there was a sprinkling of congregation. Mrs Delaney was several rows back with three or four of her brood and there were one or two others—neighbours and such.

After a first, hasty glance, she tried to keep her eyes away from the casket—a plain wood box. She was grateful to the Duvaliers who had provided it, and wondered if it was one of the things Alphonse had meant to speak of.

Father Mulcahey intoned the Latin of the Mass; he said the prayers for the dead over Pegeen, and all the time Bridie was dry-eyed. She who had wept buckets for Maling had none left for her sister.

Later, at the open grave, she shed no tears. If she had wept at all, it would have been for herself and not for her sister. Pegeen had left all this behind her. She was safe. It would be wrong to cry for herself. She had more pride than that. But her control nearly broke when the earth began to fall on the box. She'd never see Pegeen again, never laugh with her, not see her boys grow into lads —into men. She threw the flowers she still held into the grave, and turned away. It was over.

She managed to say whatever was necessary to Father Mulcahey, to the neighbours. A few brief thank yous, and she was escorted to the carriage. A different carriage this time; the other had gone. Well, no matter. It was time to meet Madame Duvalier. She sank down on the seat, Mademoiselle Charette beside her, Alphonse facing her.

Alphonse directed a few questions to Mademoiselle Charette. She answered with a glance at the Irish girl, and wrapped a blanket from under the seat round her, rubbing her hands and clicking her tongue.

'You'll feel better when you've had a hot drink,' Alphonse said, and directed the driver to hurry.

In the same dazed state, Bridie allowed herself to be led from the carriage, up the front steps, into a house she had never seen before, a fine big house on the top of a hill. She was taken not to the parlour, or even to the kitchen, but to a small sitting-room with bright chintz curtains and big chairs.

A woman with white hair and snapping brown eyes rose from a rocking-chair. 'Come, sit down.' She seated her in a companion rocker with a fine cushion at its back and one on the seat.

'My mother speaks good English,' said Alphonse. 'I'll ring for tea, *ma mère*.' He strode to the bell-pull. 'No, no, I'll not have anything. I'll leave her to you.' He held his mother's hand for a moment. 'I'll see you later.'

Bridie watched him leave without any feelings at all. She turned to his mother, now seated again in the rocking-chair. Alphonse had said she spoke English. She hoped she spoke it better than her Mademoiselle Charette!

'It's very kind of you, Madame, to bother with me. I'm not feeling meself, as you can see.'

'It's not kind at all,' Madame Duvalier declared. 'I wanted to see for myself what sort of family those two boys come from. I want to ask you about their mother. But we'll have our refreshments first,' she added, as a maid came into the room bearing a tray with a fat teapot and cups and saucers and a small plateful of cookies and cakes.

Madame spoke only of the weather—cold for the time of year—and the health of Mademoiselle Beaupré, of whom she had been the employer for many years. By the time Bridie had finished her second cup of tea and her third cake—so small they just melted in her mouth —Madame had managed to make her smile with a story about her sister and the black hat the Irish girl was wearing. 'She bought it when her second husband was ill, expected to go to his just rewards, and was upset when he recovered, said she never wanted to see it again. I shouldn't wonder if it wasn't Albert she didn't want to see again! But he lived, and she gave the hat to me. I gave it to Mademoiselle Beaupré. It looks charming on you, my dear. Was your sister as pretty as you?'

Bridie discovered that she could speak of Pegeen with pleasure. 'Prettier by far.' She moved a little way nearer her hostess. 'She had my Da's hair—coppery brown —and his brown eyes. She had the looks of the family.'

'Nonsense! You have your share.'

Bridie coloured with such praise. She knew it wasn't true, of course. Black hair and blue eyes couldn't hold a candle to Pegeen's brilliance.

'She'd winning ways, too,' Bridie went on. 'She'd make you laugh when there was nothing to laugh at —nothing at all.'

'You'll miss her, *ma chère*.' Madame leaned forward. 'Tell me, was she healthy? Before the famine, that is.'

'Never a sick day in her life, and even when the potatoes rotted in the ground on our place, Pegeen was lucky in where she was working. They grew wheat, and their crop was untouched. It was Maling wanted to come to the Americas and start again, for when his Da died, he left him no land. It all went to the eldest—to Hugh—and none to himself. Hugh was cruel hard to him. He told him he must shift for himself. Where was Maling to go? But sure you don't want to be hearing all this old talk . . .'

'Yes, *bien sûr*, I like to hear you tell it. Families have interesting histories. Go on, *ma fille*, tell me more. This Maling and your sister married, did they, in spite of the difficulties?'

'Yes, but not at first—not when they planned to. For the blight came to the potatoes, and Maling's Da died. They had to wait, and Pegeen kept on with her work. Maling went to work on the Penny Road. He worked hard and got thinner and thinner. He didn't look like

himself—just a shadow with no spark in him, like my Da
and the others.'

'What's this Penny Road, child?'

'They called it that, for the men were paid a penny a
day. The road didn't go anywhere much. It just kept
them working—and living—a little longer. Their families would have gone very hungry but for the soup
kitchens. Where I worked, the master of the big house
was good. He said the hungry should be fed. I made the
soup. Thick soup it was at first, it got thinner after—but
the women and chil'der were glad to have it—till his
money ran out and he couldn't even keep me on.'

'So you crossed the ocean with your sister and her
husband. How did you pay for your passage if you were
thrown out of work?'

Bridie rocked back and forth in the wooden chair,
conscious of its smoothness, cradled by its comfort,
warmed by the food and drink and the luxury of having a
listener who encouraged her to talk, for the past few
days had been a sore trial to her tongue. 'That was an
odd thing. It was Maling's mother paid for me and for
himself and Pegeen. Mind, she didn't exactly know she
was paying for me.'

'How could that be, *ma fille*?' Madame interrupted,
sitting forward in her chair.

'I'll tell you the way of it. There wasn't any harm in it,
certain sure there wasn't. Maling and Pegeen were to go
to New York. The fare for that was fifteen pounds, a
terrible large sum. But Pegeen was that set on me going
that Maling asked around and found that the three of us
could get to Montreal for six pounds, and we'd have nine
pounds left over for a start. Wasn't that a fine way out of
a fix?'

Madame Duvalier advanced no opinion on this in-
genious solution of a problem. She merely nodded and
asked, 'Did Maling's mother want her son to leave,
then?'

'She did and she didn't: I think that must be the right
of it. She favoured Hugh, but maybe she felt it hard that

Maling didn't inherit any of the land. Where she found the money, I've never puzzled out. Maling couldn't comprehend it either, but it was an answer to prayer. That's what we all thought then, for we had nothing between us, and Maling said we must go, and so did his mother. Except that she didn't know about me.'

'*Oui, je comprends tout ça.*' Madame slipped into French as she followed Bridie's example and rocked back and forth. 'It's a sad little history with only you left—you and the babies. My son will give them a good home, and his wife, Marie-Rose, thinks of them already as her own. In fact, François daren't tell her the truth of the matter—that her own little one died. Perhaps it's better that way, that she should think Jean and Jacques are her own. You understand why Alphonse acted so swiftly to send you away. He didn't want curious neighbours asking questions about them—and the story being known by everyone.'

'Yes.' It was Bridie's turn to sit forward, the comfortable motion of the chair stopped. 'In a way, it's like Maling and his Mam. What a body doesn't know, can't be hurting.'

'*Exactement,*' Madame agreed. 'You have put it in a nutshell. When you first came into the room, I knew you for a girl who would understand. Of course, it's difficult for you. You must forget that the twins ever came into this world. Pegeen's baby died—if anyone asks you.'

'But Father Mulcahey knows,' Bridie protested.

'Priests keep many secrets.' Madame waved that idea away in a gesture which was very much like her son's. 'Remember, you put the babies in Marie-Rose's arms.'

Bridie bowed her head. Yes, she'd started it in her desperation. She had wanted Marie-Rose to think them her own babies. She had often enough seen a ewe adopt a lamb as her own if it was given to her soon enough. Yes, it had all sprung back on her. She would have to be silent, to watch her tongue. No wonder Monsieur Alphonse had been waiting at the church, and stayed while the neighbours talked to her.

'What do you want me to do?' She guessed at the answer before it was given.

'Never mention to a single person here in Montreal about your sister's babies. They aren't hers any more. You signed them away.'

'I promise,' Bridie gulped. 'But—but does this mean that I'll never see them again—never be able to tell them about Pegeen and Maling and how they came to this place?'

'I'm afraid it must,' Madame Duvalier's voice was soft. 'You've given them to Marie-Rose and my son. You can't take them away. They are their parents now as truly as if they had been born to them.'

Bridie felt as though she had been cut in two. She must live with the consequences. 'I understand.' She slid to the front of her chair. Oh yes, she understood very well! This Duvalier family kept adding conditions. Now they wanted her absolute silence. That was all this woman had talked to her for—that, and being assured that the twins came from a healthy family. That's why Alphonse had been keeping the money from her. He must have known exactly what his mother was going to say, even though he had pretended he knew nothing about it. They expected her to beg for the money. She wouldn't. She would demand it!

'If anyone asks,' she agreed quietly, 'I'll say the twins died. They were too small and too weakly to live without their Mam.'

'That will do quite well.' Madame smiled at her. 'You're a good girl—and a quick one. I'm pleased we had this little chat.'

'So am I.' Bridie found she could smile just as sweetly. 'Now I'll be speaking to Monsieur Alphonse again —with your permission, of course, Madame.' She sat back again.

'Now?' Madame Duvalier seemed surprised.

'Now's as good a time as any,' Bridie assured her. 'He said he'd be here.'

'He did mention something like that.' Madame's

hands made a circle in the air. 'I rather thought he meant he would talk to me.'

'So that you could tell him what you thought of me! You can stay if you like. Tell him what you think, then we can finish the business between us. Shall I ring the bell-pull so that you can ask him to come?'

Madame hesitated and gave Bridie a considering look, then she indicated that she should ring. 'I don't believe I'll stay.' She rose to her feet and went towards the door.

Bridie bade her *Bonjour* and watched her walk from the room. She'll be telling him all that went on between us, she told herself. That'll be just as well. She settled down to wait for Alphonse.

It was a longer wait than she had expected. She spent it prowling about the room, fingering the curtains of heavy plush velvet, admiring their sheen when the sun caught their redness. You would think a woman with curtains as fine as that would guard them from fading. She picked up ornaments and examined them. One day she, too, would have fine things. She tried out some of the chairs, and was ensconced in a pale green and gold love-seat when Alphonse entered the room. She stayed there, not rising to her feet, and he came towards her and sat down in the other half so that they faced each other at an angle. His face was very close to hers. It was not quite what she had planned, but she wasn't going to move now. She must be careful not to lose herself in his eyes. She needed all her cunning. She spoke first.

'Your mother's told me I'm to say nothing to anyone here, and I've agreed, for there's enough sorrow in the world without me adding to it. Monsieur François' wife is free to think the babies are hers, for I'll not be speaking anything to the contrary—no, not to a soul.' Bridie sat back satisfied with her little speech. He'd be certain to know what she was driving at. 'Now, if you'll be handing over the money, I'll be on my way,' she added for good measure.

She had the pleasure of seeing comprehension on Alphonse's face before his eyes darkened and he shook his head. 'I don't like threats,' he said softly.

There was something about the tone of his voice that sent a flutter of fear through the girl. 'Wait now,' she said. 'If we're to talk of what we like and don't like, I don't like folk who make half promises and don't even keep them.'

'What promises have I made?' His face was within inches of hers, and his eyes were sparking with anger.

'You promised to help me—to speak with your brother.' She was as angry as he.

'I have spoken to my brother.'

'Has he given you the money I asked?'

'No, he hasn't. He's paid for the funeral, he's given something to Father Mulcahey for his charities, and he's advanced Mademoiselle Beaupré something for her trouble. He thinks that's enough.'

'Oh, he does, does he? And him so pious and holy at Pegeen's Mass!' Bridie seized hold of Alphonse's shoulder. 'I see it now. It's just what Pegeen said. His baby was buried with her—that's why he was there, and why you were there.'

'Pegeen?' he echoed. 'What's Pegeen got to do with this? How could she tell you anything?'

'She came to me in a dream—in a dream only last night.' Bridie put her hand to her cheek, taking it from his shoulder, and conscious still of its warmth. She had felt the effect of her words on him through that hand. They had struck home. 'You needn't deny it, for I see it's the truth. What would he be doing that for—to save on the cost?'

'No,' said Alphonse, and he got to his feet above her. 'Think what you like of him, but he wanted the child buried in consecrated ground—and a stillborn baby can't be, unless he's buried with his mother.'

Bridie's heart softened a little—but only a little. 'Sure, Pegeen couldn't have understood that, or she'd not have made such a fuss.' She half put out her hand to him and then drew it back as he sat down again. 'Well, then, I suppose that makes us almost related. What will the gravestone say? For gravestone there must be, you promised me one. Pegeen Prendergast and baby François? Sure it must—he's part of the Irish family.'

His lips twitched, almost smiled, then straightened. 'I fancy he'll leave it as "baby", with no name.'

'Sure, he wouldn't be wanting a separate grave anyway—not with his wife thinking that Pegeen's boys are hers.' She wasn't too sure about his talk of consecrated ground, for weren't all babies baptised whether they breathed or not? He needn't be thinking she was just a green girl from the other side of the world!

Alphonse put his head in his hands. Bridie could see that he was thinking. She didn't disturb him, just looked at the way his dark brown hair curled over his collar. He had changed out of his funeral black into the grey suit he had worn when she first saw him. The back of his neck looked quite vulnerable, and he sat just like Danny used to sit when he'd been scolded for some piece of devilry.

Suddenly Alphonse sat erect and looked straight in her eyes. 'I'd give you the money myself—if I had it, and if I thought you wouldn't lose it in a matter of weeks. This business you want to start—I don't believe you can do it. You don't speak French, you can hardly write . . .'

'I can sign my name,' Bridie interrupted, and was quelled by his glance.

'You can scarcely write—I don't suppose you can keep any sort of accounts. What am I to do with you, Bridget Langton, when you look at me with those eyes and tell me you're part of the family?'

There was more warmth on his face than she had ever seen there. His voice was soft, too. She realised that somehow, maybe something she'd said, had touched him. Ah, it was the hat—it must be the hat! With that on her head, she looked a different person, a person he'd talk to, not order about. She held his gaze, willing him to go on.

'We owe you something, but I'm hanged if I know what—and how to go about giving it to you. Money's not the answer, I know that.'

Bridie's dander rose again. All these Frenchmen were the same—no wonder they lived well, they wouldn't part with a cent! She bit her lip. The trouble with this one was that she almost liked him. He was so disarming with it. '*Charmant*'—that's what Anita had said about him, and she was right. He could charm the heart from a girl if she'd let him—but she wouldn't! No, never.

'Why isn't money the answer?' she demanded.

'Because you'd never keep it. No, take my word for it.' He put his hand on her shoulder. 'I don't believe François is right either. There's no use trying to bury you in some French household in another town. You'd rise to haunt us—I'd see your eyes looking at me, and know your tongue would be running off with you . . .'

Bridie tried to take her hand away. She was appalled both by his brother's plan for her and by his refusal to give her the money as much as by that reference to her tongue. 'I'll not be insulted!' she snapped.

'I'm not insulting you! I'm telling you the truth.' His clasp was firm, alarming her.

'I'm going to send you back to Mademoiselle Beaupré, and think what to do.' He got up, and pulled her up with him.

Bridie was so close to him as he forced her to walk round her side of the love-seat that she could feel the power of him, the muscle in his back and arms, the sheer masculinity of his body. She yearned to be closer, and swayed on her feet. When his hand steadied her, her legs turned to water and she was held prisoner in his arms. Prisoner! That's just what she was! She straightened and took a step away. He thought he could do with her just as he wished.

'I won't go,' she exclaimed.

'Yes, you will. *Bien sûr*, you will, *ma fille*. You've nowhere else to go. I'm the only one who's willing to help you. You'll go back to Mademoiselle Beaupré, and learn French and enjoy her good meals and the good country air, and next week I'll come and see you.'

'And what then?' She was still held by him, but she thought she saw what he meant to do with her. 'Sure, if you think to have my body, I'll not let you! Not next week—not ever!' She drew herself to her full five feet.

He laughed at her, laughed uproariously. 'You can put that idea out of your head! I don't want your body—nor, if the truth were told, any part of you—but I'm stuck with your problems. I'll call for the carriage.' He released her with a push, and she stumbled against a chair as he reached for the bell-pull.

He escorted her down the stairs, out to the carriage, and helped her into it. There was no escape.

The Duvaliers had the twins, she told herself savagely as the carriage drove off. She had the opportunity to learn French. It didn't seem a very even sharing. But it was all she had.

CHAPTER FIVE

'COME ON, BRIDIE, we shall go to the barn.' Anita tugged at her hand.

Bridie followed her out of the hot kitchen—away from Mademoiselle Beaupré and those other chattering Frenchwomen who were admiring the mountains of food already prepared. She and Anita had done their share of fetching and carrying, of beating eggs and dough, of stirring icings and sauces—let the others finish now. Anita's sister's wedding was tomorrow, and they had been baking all week.

Mademoiselle Beaupré had made the marriage cake in her own house with the girls helping, and today it had been carefully carried to the Beaupré farm half a mile down the road, and duly admired and praised. Then all three of them had turned to for a day's further cooking with the bride and her mother and her aunts and her old grand-mère. Bridie's head reeled with trying to understand it all. The speed with which they spoke and the unfamiliar words had left her thoroughly confused. She'd never master the jabber. Only old Granny Beaupré tried to include her in the conversation, and she spoke to her as if she was a complete idjit, one word at a time. She was more than glad to escape.

The barn was cool and spacious, and it had been cleared and decorated with ribbons and bunches of flowers. the two girls sank on to baled hay in one corner.

'They'll dance here tomorrow—after the feast,' Anita told her. 'Can you dance, Bridie?'

'Yes! If I wasn't so hot and so tired, I'd be showing you.' Bridie fanned herself with the edge of her apron and lay back.

Anita laughed and went to the door of the barn.

'Pierre's coming—and so is Jean-Paul. Now we'll have some fun!'

Bridie didn't move. 'Who are they?' It was surprising how well she and Anita chattered, part in French, part in English, part in signs.

'Pierre's a cousin. He's old—almost twenty. Jean-Paul's one of my brothers—he's only ten.'

'What are they coming here for?' Bridie felt she wanted nothing more to do with French people.

'Pierre has his fiddle with him. He's going to play for the dancing.'

Anita sounded so excited that Bridie sat up. The youngster was already greeting her cousin. Pierre was a small, unprepossessing specimen, dark and very young-looking. In fact he was so short that the ten-year-old Jean-Paul came to his shoulder. He was dressed in a baggy sort of black overall with a bright checked shirt. He looked in Bridie's direction, but didn't even smile at her. Anita was holding on to his free hand and whispering something. Jean-Paul was chasing a large fly round the barn.

'Pierre is going to play for us,' Anita announced, and ran to Bridie, her face alight. 'I'll show you the steps, just follow me.' She pulled her to her feet. 'You'll need to know them.'

'Wait, now,' said Bridie. 'I'll not be coming to the shindig tomorrow. It's a family affair.'

'Of course you'll be coming! I asked my sister Madeleine—she expects you to come. There'll be cousins to dance with, and friends of *son mari*—what's the word?—*son homme*—Georges.'

'Her husband—the bridegroom,' Bridie supplied absently, nearly putting her hands over her ears as Pierre tuned up his fiddle.

'Jean-Paul shall call for us,' Anita decreed, and gave her young brother his orders. He didn't seem to mind, but stood beside his cousin waiting for the tune. He began calling almost at once, tapping in time to it.

Anita began the steps of the country dance. It was one

Bridie didn't know at all, and she had to put her mind to learning it. When she mastered it, even Pierre nodded approval and permitted himself a little smile in her direction. He immediately began on another piece. Bridie succeeded almost at once with this one because it was half familiar.

Pierre's playing was spirited, and by the fourth number, which presented Bridie with a good deal of difficulty, Anita was giving her instructions and Jean-Paul was doing his best to lead her in the right direction. He had no English at all, so his method was more than a little painful. He stepped on Bridie's toe to show her that her foot was in the wrong place, and shouted to her in his own language as though he thought the louder he spoke the more easily she would understand.

'No, no,' a male voice interrupted, 'that's not the way to go about it! She'll have no feet left, Jean-Paul.'

Bridie whirled round. Alphonse Duvalier was in the barn doorway. He came forward and took her hand. Pierre had stopped playing. He stood with his bow lifted, not sure whether to continue. Alphonse motioned to him to do so, and began to show Bridie himself. With Anita and Jean-Paul dancing in front of them, the Irish girl began to enjoy herself. Alphonse was a grand dancer, light on his feet, easy to follow, quick to tell her where she was wrong—and in English. Grand-mère and one of the women from the kitchen joined them, and grand-mère was the best dancer of all. She had them bowing and curtsying, honouring their partners and tripping the length of the barn. They were soon all laughing and breathless and following grand-mère.

Bridie had not enjoyed herself so much in ages—not since the old days in Ireland. Once upon a time, she told herself as she executed a tricky piece of footwork with grand-mère as partner, she had danced like this to different music, in a different place. So had Pegeen. She banished the thought before it got hold of her. There was a time for sorrow and a time for joy. Sure there'd been sorrow enough. She was swirled back to Alphonse, and he held her hand firmly as they promenaded off to the right. Of course her enjoyment had nothing to do with him, nothing at all, save that he was a grand man to dance with. She wished she were wearing something prettier than a blue and white checked gingham dress that was so short it showed her ankles. Still, it wasn't as loose as it had been to start with. She had filled out a little in the bust, and had taken in the dress at the waist, and knew it looked better.

The dancing went on, and Alphonse at grand-mère's urging took off his jacket and loosened his collar and tie. Bridie, the next time she partnered him, could see the dark hair high on his chest. For some reason she couldn't understand, she averted her eyes. It was odd—the sight of her brothers' hairy chests had never given her any occasion to stare, or to look away.

Grand-mère called something to him, and he laughed aloud, throwing back his head like a boy.

'What did she say?' Bridie asked. 'You can be telling me what she said.'

'No, not I!' He shook his head. 'She's a wicked old woman.'

'Wicked? Why? That's a terrible thing to say about an old lady. Have you no reverence for her age?'

'Just as well you didn't catch what she said!' Alphonse laughed again and spun her round to Jean-Paul's care.

Grand-mère called a halt after that, and Jean-Paul and Anita were despatched for refreshments. They came back with a chair for Alphonse. He insisted that the old woman sit there, and she rewarded him with a toothless grin and sat down close to the baled hay. The rest of the company were dispersed outdoors by her, but she signalled that Bridie and Monsieur should stay. Grand-mère took only a glass of lemonade from the tray the two youngsters had brought, but Alphonse and Bridie both had a large slice of crusty bread with boiled egg and tomato for garnish.

'I want to talk to you.' Alphonse, balancing bread and

lemonade in one hand, pointed to the hay with the other. 'Sit down, Bridie. There's no need to be formal.'

The girl did as he bade, and made room for him beside her. She sat as far as she could from the old woman. 'Is she staying for the listening, or for the looks of the thing?'

'For the looks of the thing.' Alphonse tried to imitate the way she spoke.

Bridie, though she was filled with some misgivings about the talking, was forced to smile at the awkward way the phrase fitted in his mouth. She had lost some of her awe of him. With beads of moisture sticking to his face from the exertions of the dance, he was altogether more human, somehow less foreign, too. She bit into her bread.

He leaned back against the wall of the barn and took a long drink, and a small bite of the savoury. 'It's Madeleine's wedding tomorrow. I'd forgotten, but when Mademoiselle's house was empty I guessed you must all be here.'

'Do you know Madeleine?' Bridie spoke with her mouth full. Not for her the dainty nibbling of Monsieur Alphonse. That was all right at the table—but not in the barn.

'I know most of the Beaupré family. As a boy, I used to come to the farm and stay for a holiday. I've baled some of this in my time.' He patted the stack he sat on. 'François wasn't a country-lover, but I always begged to stay longer.'

Fancy that, Bridie thought to herself. Her jaws stopped their steady munching as she regarded him with new eyes. With his white shirt and his loosened collar, the breadth of his shoulders was more pronounced. She could almost imagine the muscle of his arms. Yes, he had the strength for the work. 'Did they let you stay on when you asked them?'

'Sometimes. The height of my ambition was to be a pig-farmer!' He smiled at the memory.

'A pig-farmer,' Bridie echoed the words. He was an

odd man. 'That must be an ambition you left behind you.' She finished her lemonade. 'What trade do you follow now?'

'I sell property—buy and sell it.'

Bridie frowned. 'Is it a good trade? For a grown man? Your brother has a factory where furniture's made —that I know. Is it the same here as in Ireland, where elder brother inherits all? I'm not being nosy; I just like to know.'

'My father left me a share, but I didn't want to work for my brother, so I set up on my own.'

Grand-mère surveyed them with one beady eye; the other was closed.

'Just like me—just like I'd be doing!' Bridie was quite excited to find they had something in common. He wasn't so different after all. People wanted to get on, the world over.

'Yes,' he said slowly. 'Much like you. Bridget, are you really serious about starting this potato business? It's not easy. I can tell you that.'

'You made a go of a business, so why shouldn't I?' She sat back and found the wall as grand-mère closed both eyes and began to snore gently. 'I've a name for it, all planned out in my head. "Hot Potato"—that's what I'll call it, and for those who can't read, there'll be a grand fat potato dancing in its skin, right up by the name, and the scent of the place will run out in the street to entice customers in. There's nothing like a hot potato for that. That's how I came by the name.'

'Yes,' he repeated. '*Bien sûr*, you must know what you're talking of. For myself, I can't recall a potato ever making such an impression on my sense of smell.'

Bridie looked at him in astonishment. Was there a man in the world who didn't relish a potato? His taste-buds must be spoiled with too much meat and rich sauces. Before she had a chance to point out to him what he had been missing, he went on.

'Mademoiselle Beaupré seems to think you could be a first-class cook. Wouldn't you be satisfied with a head cook's position in a big house—with only a family to please, and servants to work under you?'

'Wait, now,' said Bridie. 'You're just trying to get round me with your soft talk and your smiles! I see through that plan. It would be easy for you—for you could wash your hands of me entirely. I'd never be anything but a servant all my life. I've a grander picture of how my life should turn out.'

'Have you, Bridget? Tell me about it. What is it you want?' He set his empty glass down on the floor.

Bridie shrugged. She wasn't certain that he really wanted to hear, but they had all the time in the world, and grand-mère wouldn't interrupt, by the looks of her.

'Every girl's supposed to want a home and a husband. I'll be telling you the truth of it—if I'd stayed in Ireland, I'd not be any different. I'd have been delighted with that. But I've come half across the world and seen some terrible hard things. Why should a girl wait on some man all her life when she could reach out her hand and better herself? There's none to tell me here what's fit for a girl to do. They expect her to work. I'm willing to work —I'm a grand worker in spite of what you say about the Irish! I'll work for myself and keep what I earn, and in a year or two I'll have enough to go home and live in my own place, comfortable and warm. Then I might look for a husband.'

The corners of Alphonse's mouth twitched, but he didn't smile, or if he did, he hid it by smoothing his moustache. 'I could almost believe you—if I didn't know what women were like.'

'What women are like? What are they like?'

'You know perfectly well what they're like! When things go wrong they break down and cry. There's no room for tears and tantrums in business.'

'Why is life full of them, then?' Bridie was no longer leaning back at her leisure. She was sitting up straight, even leaning forward. 'Sure, I've seen men—strong men—break down and cry! And who do they cry to? Some woman, of course. They think she's born to it—born to calm and to comfort, to kiss and make better.'

'Is that what you'd do, Bridget—kiss and make better? *Une crise de nerfs* might be almost worth while!'

Bridie didn't understand the phrase, but she understood full well what he was driving at, for he had hold of her hand and she could see the expression of his eyes, half soft, half amused. Well, she wouldn't let him fluster her! That's what he wanted to do. She snatched her hand away. However comfortable it had been there, he had only been willing to weaken her, to make her change her mind. 'I wouldn't kiss you—or comfort you either. You'd be laughing at me!'

'Why should I do that?' He captured her hand again. 'Anyway, it isn't a man's part to be so weak and soft. He'd be more likely to be comforting the woman. Men are supposed to be strong. That's what women like, *n'est-ce pas?* They like to be pampered and petted.'

Bridie smiled. 'They're sounding more like kittens or babies, these women of yours! Is that really what Frenchwomen are like?'

He countered with a question. 'Are the Irish so different? Why, if you had this shop of yours, you'd be looking to some man for help every time anything went wrong. It would be almost worth giving you the money just to see how you'd go on.' His voice was taunting, but he kissed her hand.

Just as he would if she'd been a fine lady, Bridie told herself in some astonishment, as shivers of pleasure invaded her whole body. With the pleasure came a sense of her own power. If he could tease her so, she'd tease him in return. She made her voice gentle. 'Why don't you try, then? What a grand thing if you proved to be right!'

She could see she had startled him, for he let go of her hand, and his eyes fastened on hers as he drew his face closer so that only inches separated them.

'Take care, Bridget, before you issue any challenges like that! I might be tempted.'

Tempted to what, she wanted to ask, but with him in his shirt-sleeves and his lips so close and the warmth of his body reaching out to her, she didn't quite dare. 'It'd be nothing to you to give what I ask. I'm not like your French girls.'

'No, you're not!' He leaned back against the wall. 'But you can't even imagine the difficulties.'

'What difficulties? You keep putting things in the way. All I'd be doing is cooking potatoes and selling them. What could be easier? I'd soon be counting the dollars.' Bridie had swivelled round on the hay to face him. Absently, she picked a stalk and began to chew it.

'There's accounts to keep straight, money to count, bills to pay and suppliers to deal with . . . No, the whole thing's impossible. You're barely literate.' He took the piece of hay from her and broke it in two. 'Look at that—snapped, broken. That's the way you'd be in no time.'

'That's how you see it, but I've a different picture.' Her voice shook. She hadn't liked the way the stalk had split in his hands. She wasn't going to be cast aside so. 'What does it mean . . . that bit about literate?'

'You can't read or write more than your name.'

'Yes, I can.'

'Why did Father Mulcahey have to read you the paper about the twins?'

'It was in the wrong language.'

'It was in English.'

'English is not my language. In the Gaelic, I'm a grand reader and writer. My Da saw to that. I went to the hedgerow school—all of us did.'

'Is this the truth? Show me, then.' He reached over to his jacket pocket and fished out a small notebook and a stub of a pencil. 'Write something for me.'

'What shall I write?'

'Whatever you want. It's just to prove that you can.'

'Right!' Bridie vowed she would take that look of scorn from his face. She licked the end of the pencil and began to write. When she had filled a page, she handed it to him.

He turned it one way and the other, examining it. 'What does it say?'

'What's in my mind, of course. What should it say?' She found she didn't want to tell what she had written.

'I'll take it to Father Mulcahey if you won't tell me. If he can't read it, he'll know someone who can. You might as well tell me yourself.'

She lunged for the notebook, falling against him, but he held it just out of her reach. His free hand reached out and held her pinioned. She struggled, but she was off balance and couldn't get free for the wall being in the way. 'Let me go,' she whispered, as grand-mère stirred in her sleep.

'Tell me what it says, or pay a forfeit.'

'What sort of a forfeit?' Her heart was hammering so fast she wondered if he heard it. His eyes were smiling at her.

'What sort of a forfeit does a girl usually pay to a man?'

Bridie blushed to the roots of her hair. He meant a kiss. She was sure he meant a kiss. 'You needn't be thinking I'm just a kitchen-maid to be tumbled in the hay! I'll scream, and wake grand-mère.'

'You could have done that two minutes ago! I wonder why you didn't.'

She could not read the expression of his eyes, but they were very close, so close she felt she was losing herself in their brown depths. What was she thinking of, remaining here when all she had to do was tell him what she had written. Why should he think she was enjoying it—even if she was? She liked the feel of him, the strength—and the fluttering he set up in her. 'Let me go! I'll be telling. It wasn't anything much.'

He released her immediately, and she sat up well away from him, scuttling across the bale.

'I'm waiting.' He smiled.

'I wrote just what I felt—like you said I should,' she defended herself in advance.

'Yes, so you said. But what did you write?' He handed her the page. 'Read it out to me, in English, if you please.'

She took a deep breath. 'Handsome men are the worst of the lot. They look at a girl as if they could eat her.' She took a quick peek at him from under her lashes. He was scowling. Her voice hurried on. 'They pretend to offer help when they've no intention of making good that promise.' The paper shook in her hands. He'd be angry. She daren't look up. Her hand dropped the paper and tugged at a piece of hay.

'Is that the way it seems to you, Bridget?' he asked in a much gentler voice than she would have imagined.

This time she ventured a full glance—and couldn't look away. His expression was hurt. She nodded, not daring to speak; if she spoke, she'd tell him she was sorry.

He sighed. It was the first time she had seen him at a loss for words.

'You made me read it.' She bit at the stalk, and was surprised when it broke in her mouth.

'It leaves a bitter taste.'

She wasn't sure whether he meant the broken hay on her note. She rushed into speech. 'I was angry! You made me angry by telling me I couldn't write.'

He shook his head. 'Yes, I'm as bad as my brother. At least he stated what he'd do. He didn't keep you dangling, waiting for more. I see that once having interfered, I'm obliged to go on. I'll help you—and this time I mean it. It's a promise.'

Bridie opened her mouth to thank him, but he held up his hand.

'Keep your thanks till you hear me out. I'm going to put up the money to get your little shop started; but let's have it clear why I'm doing it. It's for Marie-Rose, not for you.'

'Your brother's wife? Why is it for her?'

'Because she thinks the twins are hers. I want her to go on thinking that.'

'Sure, I wouldn't tell her. I've signed the paper.'

'Yes, but if you were penniless and hungry you might well forget that.' She made a motion of dissent, but he brushed it aside. 'That's what you mean now, but an empty belly might dictate a different course of action. No, it's safest to help you to stand on your own, and the best thing of all would be to wave you goodbye as you left for your cottage in Ireland.'

'Yes, so it would!' Bridie put an eagerness into her words that strangely she wasn't feeling. He needn't be in such a hurry to get rid of her! For a while there she had thought he liked her, but she had spoiled it all with that silly writing. Why hadn't she made something up when she'd read it out? He wouldn't have known the difference; he couldn't have known. Why should her wits have deserted her when she most needed them? Of course she wanted to go back to her own country, she chided herself, and spoke up again. 'You must be very fond of Marie-Rose—of Madame Duvalier.'

'I am indeed,' was his emphatic reply. 'She's a very lovable woman. There was a time . . . But that's no concern of yours. Let's stick to the subject of *pommes de terre chaudes*—hot potatoes. That's what you may become for me!'

Bridie ignored the comment; she didn't understand it. He was going to help her, and that was what mattered. He had promised her her shop. 'When can I start?' She knew a moment's dread. It was a big step, a terrible big step all on her own.

'When you're ready. That won't be for a while.'

'Why not?' She was immediately upset.

'Because I'm going to see to it that my money's safe. You're going to learn to speak French, to write in English and French, and to keep proper books on the money which comes in and out.'

Her mouth opened in astonishment. 'Where am I to learn that? Am I to go back to school like a tiny child?'

He was tormenting her again with half promises.

'Not quite. I shall find someone to teach you, just on your own. It'll be quicker that way. You must promise to do your best to learn.'

There was nothing soft about his voice. His face was stern. He had changed back to a business man before her very eyes.

'Who's to say if I don't learn enough? Who's to tell when I've learned what I need?' Bridie didn't like the programme he outlined.

'I'll say,' was the repressive reply—one that brought her no comfort at all.

'Where am I to do all this work?' she asked. 'Will you be taking me back to Montreal?'

'No, of course not. You'll stay here. I'll send you a teacher, and Mademoiselle Beaupré will see that you have time for your studies.'

'Yes,' said the dismayed Bridie, 'but wait! How long will it take?'

'That's up to you. It depends how you work. Perhaps a few months, if you work very hard.'

'Am I never to go back to Pegeen's room? Am I to be held here all that long time?'

'Was there some reason you wanted to go back to your sister's room?'

'To fetch her things—not that there's much.' She swallowed. 'Just a keepsake or two.'

'There's no need for that,' he told her. 'One of her neighbours gathered what was left. I've brought it for you. I think there's only her ring and a brooch and some articles of clothing. I left them inside Mademoiselle Beaupré's porch. They'll be safe enough there, and my mother has sent you some material for a dress.'

'Has she? That's kind of her then, and good of you to bring all the things. Are the twins—are Jean and Jacques—in good health?'

'They're fine. My mother dotes on them already. I think she's been longing for grandchildren.'

Bridie couldn't stop the tears coming to her eyes.

However hard she blinked them back, one managed to overflow and hover on her eyelashes. It ran slowly down one cheek.

'What's this?' His finger reached out and traced its path. 'There's no need to cry. The boys do enough of that. Marie-Rose says they're hungry all the time, and little Jacques is worse than the bigger one for demanding more and more.'

She brightened up considerably, and managed a smile. It had nothing to do with his sympathy; it was the news that the babies were well.

'I'm pleased you're calling them by their French names,' Alphonse went on. 'It tells me you're a sensible girl.'

'I think of them still as Sean and Sennen. I just had a notion to please you.'

He smiled at her. 'I hope you'll go on having notions like that. We'll get along better that way.'

He was so matter of fact that Bridie realised he meant exactly what he said. He wanted her to make as little trouble for him as possible, and fall in with any plans he made for her. She sighed. She would do all he asked. She might as well say so.

'I'll study and learn,' she promised him. 'Then you'll not have to bother any more.' She jumped down from the hay. 'I'll be getting back to the kitchen.'

'And I'll be getting back to town.' He stood beside her and shook her hand. 'I'll hold you to your promise.' With a wave he was gone, striding out of the barn.

Bridie watched him go. She was glad it was settled —or if not settled, at least on its way.

She jumped when grand-mère spoke in English. 'He'll make a fine husband. He has a soft heart—and a hard head!'

The girl looked at her in astonishment. 'I didn't know you could speak English! Have you been listening all the time?'

'Not all the time, but long enough to hear he's setting you up in a shop.' Her smile, toothless as it was, was more of a leer than an expression of amusement.

'It's not what you think!' Bridie protested. She didn't want any false ideas circulating among the Beaupré family.

'What is it, then?'

'I can't tell you—it's a promise I made.'

'Child, I don't ask you to break a promise. Besides, you wouldn't know how to pleasure a man. You could have kissed him! Why didn't you? I would have done —so would any French girl.'

Bridie was considerably ruffled by this slur. She was as warm-blooded as any French girl. 'You're a wicked old woman, just like they said.'

Grand-mère's laugh was a crowing cackle. 'Better to be wicked than to be slow. Here, take this chair and get back to the others. I'll come on my own.'

Bridie picked up the chair. She was angry enough to let grand-mère go on her own, but she was a very old woman and needed help. 'I'll bring the chair later.' She took hold of her arm.

The old woman laughed again and muttered to herself all the way back, 'This cold girl wants a shop when she could have a man! What's the world coming to?'

Bridie made no reply. There was no method of making her understand. She was only relieved that the English changed to French as they approached the house. But she liked the sound of it no better in that tongue. She didn't want Alphonse, or any man. She wanted her little shop and her freedom, and she would have the both of them soon.

It was strange that she didn't feel the kind of excitement that she should. Ah well, that was the way of it. She still grieved for Pegeen. That must explain it.

'Don't say anything to the others,' she begged the old woman. She wanted to shake her, to make her stop talking, but she was old and a grandmother.

'What's there to tell?' Grand-mère leered at her again. 'Monsieur Alphonse won't be back—not for such a cold piece.'

Seething, Bridie left her and went back for the chair. She didn't want to kiss Alphonse, never had wanted to kiss him. It was a business arrangement. She wanted to shout that out—to tell them all. Was that not the truth of it?

CHAPTER SIX

BRIDIE HAD NO need to remind herself in the next few weeks that it was a business arrangement between her and Alphonse Duvalier: it was borne in upon her with all the work she was set. He had been as good as his word and had found her a teacher. Monsieur Dupuis was a retired schoolmaster with a good command of both French and English, and of arithmetic. His cottage was about half a mile away and nearer to the shops. It was smaller than Mademoiselle Beaupré's, and the tiny garden was filled with flowers. The only edible things he grew were onions and herbs.

Every other morning she went for her lessons. They worked in a room with books everywhere—on the chairs, on the table, on shelves in the wall, on the floor. On the first day, she knocked on the door but there was no answer. She had had to track him down by calling and searching, and eventually ran him to earth sitting on the floor behind a pile of books. All she could see of him were his white hair and beard and two dark button eyes looking through a pair of spectacles whose frames were sadly out of shape.

Like a child he looked up at her happily. 'Ah, the Irish girl—Bridget, isn't it? Take a look at this, *mon enfant*, it's something I'd forgotten I had—a history of the early days of the colony when there were only French people here. It's a child's book, really, but it'll do to start. Come, we'll sit at the table and see what you can do.' He moved some books so that she could sit down, and cleared a space for himself.

He shot some questions at her in French, and Bridie did her best to answer him.

'The accent's good,' he assured her, 'but you've no idea of grammar or gender. How are you at sums?'

Before she could make any answer, he took some coins out of his pocket and said he was buying some apples and some pears. 'The apples are half a cent each and the pears are four for three cents. I want six of each. Count out the money.'

Bridie puzzled over the pears for a moment, then counted out seven cents. 'We'll forget the other half cent, since there aren't any coins quite so little and you're a grand customer anyway!'

'*Bon!* I'm likely to remain a customer if you treat me so well.'

His brown eyes twinkled. 'Now say it in French.'

She translated as best as she could. Of course she made mistakes, but she couldn't help being a little pleased with herself. It was surprising what she had picked up already. Monsieur Dupuis said he liked a pupil who tried.

When it came to her writing, he exclaimed over that. 'I've never seen Gaelic written, nor heard it. Read it out to me in the original.'

He was delighted with the sound of it. 'Old Breton has the same sort of sound. That's where I grew up, and the peasants there spoke a very similar tongue.' He rubbed his hands. 'Take hope, Bridget. If you can write in one language, you can write in another. If you're willing to learn and to work, I'm willing to take you as a pupil. We'll begin. It'll be a pleasure to set you on the road to books.' He picked up the little history book. 'By the end of the week you'll be reading from this and understanding it.'

Bridie was not quite as optimistic as her tutor, but he was quite right—if not in the exact timing, at least in her ability. After ten days, she did read from the little history to Anita, who was so enthusiastic that she began to teach her to read English.

'*Très bien,*' was Monsieur Dupuis' verdict when she told him how quickly Anita was learning. 'I felicitate you. If everyone taught one other person, the whole world could soon read and write.'

'Would there be enough books to go round?' Bridie asked. 'Mind, it'd be a grand thing if it happened. My brother Patrick can read the English, but he never taught me. He said I'd never be needing it. Do you think I could write him a letter, when I'm cleverer with the pen and the ink, and tell him all that's happened to me and Pegeen? He'll be wanting to know.'

'Why not?' Monsieur Dupuis smiled at her. 'Maybe next week, when you're a bit stronger on spelling.'

It wasn't the next week nor yet the week after, but there did come a day when Monsieur Dupuis declared she was ready to write to her brother.

'Here's paper and pen,' he told her. 'You can say what you like. You're quite able to write on your own, and I won't look at what you've written. Letters are private, but I'll tell you what I'll do. I'll pay for the postage and see that it's sent off safely.'

'That's terrible kind of you,' said Bridie, 'but what shall I say? I've never concocted a letter. Where would have been the use with Patrick not able to read the Gaelic and Michael not able to read at all.'

'Don't look so worried, *ma fille*. It's easy enough. Just put the date, your address, then "Dear Patrick and Michael" and add whatever you want to tell them. Just write it as though you're saying it. You're a girl who's seldom at a loss for words.' He smiled at her.

Bridie wrote as he said. Date and address: August 28, 1847, were easy enough. 'Dear Patrick & Michael' tripped off her pen. She sucked the end of it for a minute or two. How to tell them their sister was dead? Perhaps not in the first sentence of all. She'd ask were they well. She began to write, and it got easier as she went on. When she had finished, she held it up to see what she had said. She read it to herself:

Dear Patrick & Michael,
Is the old place just the same? Are you both in good health? I've sad news to tell you. Pegeen's gone with the angels. So has Maling. He died of

the fever on the long cruel way over. He's buried
with the others on the first landing here. You'll
need to be telling his mother. Tell her too she's a
granny, for didn't Pegeen give birth to twins on
the last night of her life—two boys—Sean and
Sennen she called them, and fine fellows they are.
She had a proper burial with a gravestone to
come and Father Mulcahey said a Mass for her
soul. There weren't many there, but her neighbours turned out and they all said kind words,
kind and true. I've put the boys with a French
family and they're coming on grand. I've learned
English writing as well you can see, and French
too—for that's the main tongue here. I've
enough to eat and I'm to have a little shop, so
don't you be worrying on my account. All my
love to you both.

She signed her name with a flourish. That should put
their minds to rest, for she knew they'd be fretting to
hear. She had said she'd put the boys with a French
family—well, that wasn't exactly the truth of it, but
there was no sense in their being further upset. The loss
of Pegeen was enough to be telling them—that and
Maling's death was a terrible catalogue of distress,
wasn't it so? And it was all right to tell them of the twins,
for her promise was only not to let it be known here. She
addressed the envelope and sealed it up.

'How long will it take?' she asked her teacher.

'A few weeks, if you're lucky. At this time of year the
ships only take a week or ten days. It's longer in the
winter, for the river's frozen all the way to Montreal. I'll
send it off this very day. Are you pleased with yourself,
Bridget? You've written a letter all by yourself. I think
you're ready for the next stage in your learning.'

'The next stage in my learning?' she repeated. 'Does
that mean you're finishing with me?'

'Not entirely, but there's no need for you to come
quite so often. Two mornings a week will do. You've

done very well—the first girl I've ever taught! You've worked hard, and you deserve your success. Promise me you'll keep reading and learning. I've a little present for you—a book to enjoy.' He produced a volume from the side of his desk.

Bridie took it. It was in English; a romance, it was called. She handled it gingerly, turning the pages. The words looked long and some of them hard. But it was her own, her very own book. She stammered her thanks.

'Nonsense!' said Monsieur Dupuis. 'My best thanks will come when I know that you've read it, because you'll find it a struggle. You don't know everything yet. I think you'll like it. It's the story of a man and a maid. A story of love.'

'Do they write books of that?' Bridie marvelled. 'Sure, I didn't know that! I'll read it for certain.'

'See that you do. Now, this next stage that you're starting involves book-keeping and accounts. I'm not competent for that sort of thing. You're being passed to another.'

'Another? What other?' Bridie's heart sank. Why could she not stay with Monsieur Dupuis? She liked him, and he made learning easy. She told him so.

He waved aside her protests. 'I don't know who your tutor will be; someone in the business world, I fancy. I'll let Monsieur Duvalier know, and you'll soon hear.'

Bridie had to be content with that. Wasn't it just like Monsieur Alphonse to keep her in the dark? He hadn't been to see her. Why, she might have been dead and gone for all he knew—or cared. The very thought of being dead and gone made her laugh. How could she be dead and gone with so much good food to eat? Why, she was no longer just skin and bone. Her figure had plumped out, her face was no longer gaunt. There was colour in her cheeks, a sparkle in her eye.

Mademoiselle Beaupré had told her so only last week. She had announced, too, that it was time the dress material Alphonse's mother had sent her was made up, and they had taken it out and looked at it again. It was a

deep rose cotton with a little sprig of a white flower, and
Bridie had at first put off the very notion of it, of making
it up. 'It's too light and too cheerful,' she'd said, 'with
Pegeen scarcely cold in her grave.' But that had been the
first time after the day at the farm. That parcel from
Pegeen's had contained an old black dress of her sister's
as well as the ring and the brooch. She had looked hard
at the brooch. It looked like silver, but where had it
come from, and how had it not been pawned with the
rest of their things? It was a mystery, a real puzzle, but
one she didn't have time to ponder over. She had put the
ring and the brooch away, and worn the dress. It fitted
her better than the blue and white gingham.

The week before, Bridie had agreed with Mademoiselle Beaupré that it was time to make up the new dress,
but she hadn't allowed her to cut it out. She'd talked
about style and about fit, and promised to speak to yet
another of her nieces. This one was a dressmaker who
would be pleased to do her auntie a favour for a few jars
of plums or a bottle of chutney.

Bridie had gone with Mademoiselle to call on the
niece, and the material had been cut after she'd been
measured for size. Both sides were well satisfied with
their bargain. Anita and Mademoiselle and Bridie had
been stitching and hemming ever since. The dress was
going to be lovely. In her unexpected free time, she
decided to finish it. It was the afternoon when she tried it
on for its final fitting and the size of the hem, that
Monsieur Alphonse chose to call.

A giggling Anita brought him into the kitchen, where
Bridie was standing on the table so that Mademoiselle
could cut round the bottom to the right length. She
wanted to hop off the table; she didn't want his eyes
upon her. But Mademoiselle insisted that there was only
a little more to do. She snipped away, and stood back in
satisfaction.

'*Comme c'est belle, cette robe! N'est-ce pas?*' She
addressed Monsieur Alphonse.

'*Elle est vraiment élégante, charmante,*' he agreed.

Bridie was fairly at home in French now and knew what the words meant, but whether he had used them to describe herself or the dress she wasn't so sure. Elegant, charming—she said them over to herself, but aloud she exclaimed, 'You'll be turning my head.' She said it in English and quickly translated it into French.

Alphonse smiled at her and offered his hand to help her down. She could easily have stood on the chair that had made a step up, but instead she let him swing her down and catch her to steady her. She had meant it to be graceful, but she managed to trip over her hem, and it was only his close embrace which saved her from falling. She blushed to the roots of her hair, as Anita giggled and even Mademoiselle smiled.

It was mortification at her clumsiness which made her breath short, not the fact that he held her. As she disentangled herself, she had the satisfaction of knowing that at least the dress suited her. It was very fitted in the bodice, and emphasised her small waist before the skirt flared out round the hips.

Alphonse sat her down in the chair. 'Shall we speak here?' He looked to Mademoiselle Beaupré for permission.

She nodded, and he continued as Anita found him another chair. 'I shall be teaching you book-keeping myself. I've brought some paper and accounts.' He spread some large ruled sheets on the table without even bothering to clear the few pieces of material that had fallen there.

He might have said she had done well, that he was pleased with her progress, that she had worked harder than he had expected, Bridie told herself mutinously. But no, didn't he just go ahead with the explaining and the columns of figures, till her head began to swim with the addition and the subtraction and the red ink and black. It was a hot day, too, and she would have preferred to get out of her new frock into her old comfortable blue, for she didn't want to mark this one with all colours of ink.

Anita made herb tea for them all, and Bridie's cup was untasted as she wrestled with the dullness of entering the right place with the right sum. She'd never master this lot! She gritted her teeth and went on as Alphonse sat back, all at his ease sipping his tea and chatting to Mademoiselle about Madeleine's wedding. Poor Bridie wished they would talk somewhere else. She wished it even harder when Anita began to tell him about the dancing, and how Bridie had found herself a beau.

'It was cousin Albert, and you know what a gawp he is! So tall and so thin. He hasn't a word of English, but he couldn't take his eyes off Bridget. At last he made up his mind to dance with her, and he just came up and swept her away. He wouldn't give her up to anyone else, and kept jabbering the whole time in French. At last it was cousin Pierre who saved her. He stopped playing his fiddle and came over to them. You know Pierre has never gone with any special girl: he's always said he was waiting for the right one to come along. Most of us thought it was because he was so small and the girls wouldn't bother with him.' Anita winked at Monsieur Alphonse. 'He seems to think he's found the right one in Bridget! He keeps calling on her. Wouldn't it be nice if they made a match of it? He'll have the shop when his father goes.'

Bridie had slowly become conscious that Anita was speaking in English. The little minx! If she had used French, her aunt would long since have stopped her. She looked up and found Alphonse's eyes on her.

'*Ma foi*,' exclaimed Alphonse. 'I wouldn't have believed it possible.'

'What wouldn't you have believed possible?' Bridie sat erect and pushed her pen behind one ear. She was ready to do battle. 'There's no reason why someone shouldn't find me attractive, is there?'

'None at all,' he assured her. 'But you misunderstand me. I'm marvelling at the way this child rattles on in English! She's even caught some of your expressions and odd words.'

'What odd words are you meaning?'

'Things like 'jabber' and 'gawp'. I don't know how you've done it in the time!' He beamed at her.

'She's a bright little thing. She's learning to read as well.'

'Well done, Mademoiselle Anita!' Alphonse was quick to compliment the girl. 'You'll never regret learning.'

Anita giggled and poured Alphonse more tea. She was clearly delighted with his praise.

Bridie jabbed her pen at the account sheet, making a blot which spoiled the whole page. Why was Anita congratulated for speaking a bit of English when there was no value put on her efforts with French and writing and sums?

Alphonse saw the blot spreading over the page, and took the pen from Bridie's hand. 'You'll need to be more careful than that. I can't see what's under the stain. Start the page over.'

She bit her lip and did as she was told. If every lesson was going to be like this, she'd be old before she finished—and likely blind as well—the columns were so small.

Monsieur Alphonse came once a week, and succeeding lessons were less harrowing. In fact, by the middle of October, Bridie felt she had mastered ledger-keeping as well as she needed. He seemed to be in agreement with that, for one afternoon when he came earlier than usual, he announced that they were to go into Montreal and look at shops. He had two shops to show her, and in a way it would be a test of her ability to judge location and suitability. Anita should come with them.

'You mean where it should be to do the best trade?' Bridie was excited at the prospect and pleased that she had put on the new rose-coloured dress. Her old one was discarded, except to do cooking and cleaning.

It was a lovely mild day, with the leaves changing colour on all the trees and the harvest mostly gathered from the fields. Mademoiselle Beaupré had insisted that the girls take their shawls, but once away from her gaze, they had slipped them from their shoulders. This time, Alphonse's carriage was a low open one pulled by a small rough-looking horse. It moved in a kind of amble faster than a trot.

'That's a strange-looking animal,' Bridie told her host. 'Is it healthy? Its chest is so narrow. What's happened? Have you come on hard times?'

He laughed and slapped the reins against the board at the front. 'That's a French Canadian horse, not showy, but serviceable. When you go looking at property, Bridget, you don't want to look as if your pockets are bulging with money.'

That made sense. So there was to be bargaining, then. Bridie was thrilled at the prospect. It would be grand to hear a bit of haggling. She was sure Alphonse would know how to go on. That's why he wasn't wearing his smart grey outfit but was in sober dark blue, a little frayed at the cuffs. She smiled to herself and breathed in the fresh air. It was a darling of a day, even if the nights were getting quite a nip to them. By the hard days of winter she would be in her own place, snug and warm —not like the voyage over, when she had nearly perished with the cold.

As they came within the city limits, Anita exclaimed over everything. She had never seen such big buildings or so many people. And the shops! If she lived here, she'd go in them all. Her eyes were everywhere, praising the silks and satins displayed along Notre-Dame Street.

This was a part of Montreal that Bridie had never explored. She was almost as excited as Anita, but couldn't resist saying, 'If you'd no money to spend, they would not want you tramping through and touching the finery.'

'Anyone can look!' Alphonse brought the horse to a stop. He jumped out and hitched the reins to a post, throwing a coin to a small boy to stand guard. He helped them both out. 'The first shop's just up this side street.'

He led them to it. There was a hotel on the far corner, and a livery stable to one side of the hotel. A few steps brought them to the shop, tucked in behind a much larger store. Alphonse had the key, and opened the door. It was empty, but quite a good size. A counter of sorts ran along one wall.

Bridie stood in the centre. She stamped the bare floorboards with one foot. They were firm, but some dust rose from them. The condition of the room was reasonable. She noticed it had gas lighting when Alphonse pointed it out. Slowly she went to the back room. Good, there was a sink there, and an oven with an open fireplace.

'Could the wall be taken down between?' she asked, greatly elated. 'For I'd want to see the customers from where I was working.'

'Perhaps part of it could be removed.' He tapped at the wall with his knuckles.

'I like it,' she said. 'There's building going on at this end of town.' She had noticed that as they came up the street. 'It'll be busy enough soon.'

'I wish I could have a little shop!' Anita sighed. 'Did you see the barber's and the locksmith's? And there's a horse-market near by.'

'The new university is just up the road,' said Alphonse. 'The English one. McGill they call it.'

Bridie let them talk on while she examined every single item in the kitchen. The oven looked old, so did the sink. She came back to the others.

'How much rent do they want for this place?' She was determined to show she could be business-like.

'A few dollars a month.' Alphonse examined the front window. 'We might get the owner down a little. Let's talk about that when we've seen the other one. You might like it better.'

Anita wanted to know where the other one was.

'In a very busy street, the main street of the town. Let's go upstairs now. You want to see everything while you're here. The owner says there are three rooms up there. I didn't see them when I came before, so shall we look?' He gave Bridie his arm.

She took it, but had to relinquish it as they approached the narrow stairs. They went up to the living quarters. There was one larger room with a Quebec heater in the centre and several doors leading off. The first two opened on to bedrooms. There was a water-closet behind another, and finally a scullery with a large sink and very little else.

It was certainly more than enough space for her, Bridie told herself as she went to the window of the first bedroom. It framed a view of Mont Royal, the mountain at the summit of the city. She drew in her breath at the imposing sight. True, she had to ignore some of the chimneypots of adjoining habitations, but there it was just the same, something to lift up her eyes to every day.

'Would you live here all on your own?' Anita's eyes were full of wonder.

'Unless I rented a room, or took on help in the shop.' Bridie couldn't get over the spaciousness. It certainly was nothing like the crowded family place she had grown up in. She almost had to pinch herself to believe all this was within her grasp. She stole a look at Alphonse, and found that he was frowning.

'I think we must discuss your living arrangements,' he said. 'But we'll leave it for now.' He ushered them down the stairs and out to the waiting carriage.

Bridie asked herself what there was to discuss about her living arrangements, as he so grandly described them. What could he mean? She was still puzzling about it when they bowled along St James Street and then Notre-Dame. It was all very busy here, with more shops than she had ever seen before, and houses as well. The streets had names which were a little familiar to her, for it was in this area that she and Pegeen had worked and lived for those few months.

The carriage turned up St Lawrence Main and came to a halt before a small shop. This, too, was vacant and rather down-at-heel-looking on the outside. Inside, a man was waiting for them. He was sitting on an old chair, his feet on the window-ledge as they approached. He got to his feet and let them in with a bow.

'Just what you're looking for,' he assured Alphonse, directing all his attention to him. He spoke in French. 'Good position, nice and roomy, a real little gold-mine of a place.'

Bridie looked around as he led them through. It was very small—and very dirty—and it smelled. She couldn't decide what the smell was, but she knew she didn't like it. She didn't like the man either. Both he and his shop needed a good scrub. The rooms upstairs were not as bad as she had feared, and to her surprise the windows were big and let in a good deal of light.

Yes, the shop itself, cleaned throughout, might be just what she was looking for. It was in a very busy street and something could certainly be made of it. It was exactly the kind of place she had intended all along. Why was she hesitating? She knew the area was right. There were plenty of workpeople around, the very sort of men and women who would want her hot potatoes because they would be cheap and tasty. It was just the kind of place she'd meant to have, and yet . . . She couldn't get that view of Mont Royal out of her mind. Scenery was for the rich, she told herself. A business woman should be practical, her mind on dollars and cents and getting ahead.

'We'll think about it,' Monsieur Alphonse was telling the man. 'I'll let you know.'

'Don't spend too much time thinking,' was his admonition. 'There are others after it.'

'Of course, that's true,' Alphonse exclaimed as they went back to the carriage. 'But it never does to look too eager. We'll go and talk about the possibilities over a cup of chocolate, shall we?' He helped them in. 'We'll try somewhere a little quieter than this, where we can talk without being disturbed.'

The place they drove to was not far away, but it was in a small street, one lined with trees, and was really the front room of a house which had been turned into a welcoming coffee-room. The chairs were large and comfortable, the room was cool. Hot chocolate with whipped cream floating on the top was brought for all three of them in a secluded alcove. It was followed almost immediately by a plate of cakes—cakes which had Anita and Bridie Oh-ing and Ah-ing in anticipation.

Alphonse let them make their choice, smiling as an indulgent uncle might have done. He let Bridie finish her drink before he began. 'This last place we've been to has great possibilities, *n'est-ce pas*?'

'Ye-es,' she agreed, without the enthusiasm which she felt she should show—if only for his trouble and effort.

'You hesitate because it's not in good condition. I assure you that it could be made very presentable. The location's good—ideal for what you have in mind.' He smiled at her.

It was such an open smile, such a pleased smile, that it set Bridie's pulses racing. He was delighted for her. She liked him better than she ever had. He was like a small boy. She wanted to agree with him, to say it was indeed the very thing, but the words stuck in her mouth. They just wouldn't be said.

Anita eyed the plate of cakes longingly, and he passed them to her. 'Help yourself, *mon enfant*; this is a time of celebration. You have one as well, Bridget.'

Anita's hand hovered over the cakes. Eventually she chose a *mille-feuille*. Bridie was tempted, diverted from her thoughts, but she shook her head.

'What's the matter?' asked Alphonse.

'You said I might choose—about the shops, I mean. That we'd talk about it, that . . .' She faltered to a stop as his smile faded.

'What is there to discuss?' he asked. 'The first shop was well enough in its way, but the location leaves something to be desired. The second has everything, has it not? A good clean through, and a coat of paint, and you won't know it.'

'Everything you say is true,' she admitted as much to herself as to him, 'but . . .' Again she couldn't go on. This time because he interrupted her.

'But you want the first one. Is that it?'

'Yes.'

'Why, when you know I'm right?'

How could she explain it to him when she didn't know why herself? 'The first place is where I want to be. Just something about it said it was my place.'

'Well, if that isn't just like a woman!' He set his cup down with a bang on its saucer. 'We are talking about business, about success in business—not about feelings. Have some sense, girl.'

Bridie could see that Anita had stopped eating her vanilla slice and was looking from one to the other of them anxiously. She didn't care. The more he pointed out the advantages of the second shop, the more she wanted the first. 'It's myself that'll be living there and working there,' she pointed out. 'Not you. Isn't that the truth of it?'

'Oui, vraiment.' His dark eyes were angrier than she had ever seen them. 'We might as well have that out, too, now that we've started. You can't live in either of them without a companion.'

'A companion?' Bridie echoed. 'What can you mean? I see it all, now we come to the heart of it! There's strings on it! It's you we're talking of. I won't have it. I'm not up for sale!' Her breathing was uneven, her cheeks fiery red.

'Don't be ridiculous,' he snapped, drumming his fingers on the table. 'That's not the way I do things! I've told you before you're not quite my style.'

His tone was drawling, his words insulting. They stung Bridie into retorting, "I'm delighted we're in accord on something! What would you be meaning about a companion? You'll have to explain it, for it's not clear to me.' She tried to get some dignity into her voice. He needn't tell her that she didn't have style. What was this 'style' of his, anyway?

'You can't live on your own. Girls don't. Besides, you'll need someone to help in the shop.'

'I can't afford to pay anyone while I'm starting up.'

'Yes, you can, and you must. I'll see to it.'

'Then I'll have Anita. We'll get on together. She's a good girl and a worker . . .' She let her eyes go to the girl.

'No, you'll not! No criticism of Anita—I know she's a good little thing.' He patted Anita's hand. 'But she's too young. You need someone older and steadier—like Anita's cousin Adèle. I've spoken to her, and she's quite willing . . .'

'What right had you to do that?' Bridie was stuttering, enraged.

'Cousin Adèle,' echoed Anita. 'You met her at the wedding, Bridie.'

'The one with the face like a board,' Bridie exclaimed. 'I could see she thought I was flighty, and she hates all the Irish! I heard her say so to Mademoiselle Beaupré. She was after telling her they shouldn't be allowed into this city, that the ships should be turned back, that they only bring fever and death to all who live here.' If there was one thing Bridie knew, it was that she didn't want anything to do with Adèle. How had he got her to agree?

'She only said what a great many other people are saying,' Alphonse pointed out. 'You must know there's typhus in the landing-sheds at Goose Village. Hundreds of Irish immigrants are dying of it. Weren't there deaths on your ship? You were lucky you and your sister didn't catch it. And not only the Irish are dying, but the nuns and the priests—all the people who are ministering to them are suffering and dying. I've heard a rumour that Father Mulcahey has caught it.'

'I hope it's not true,' said Bridie. She was pulled up short. 'But, couldn't you, wouldn't you, consider some-one else? Someone I could like? Perhaps an Irish girl like myself—an orphan or a widow with no one to turn to? Sure, Father Mulcahey would put us in the way of someone . . .' She looked at his set face and knew the answer before he spoke.

'Adèle is entirely suitable, and in any case I've spoken to her. I can't go back on my word.'

Bridie bit hard on her tongue. She was very conscious of the fact that it was his money that was going to be used for Adèle, his money for the shop. Could she be bargaining with him? 'I quite see that,' she managed to smile at him. 'It looks like I'll have to give way just a little. Can we not settle this thing like the good friends that we are? I'll have to pretend I never heard those hard things Adèle was saying behind my back! I'll be just like a saint, wear a smile like a plaster statue, and the pair of us will move into the first shop, at peace with the world.'

'Into the first shop?' Alphonse looked at her hard. 'That's your saintly smile, is it? Take it off your face. It doesn't fool me! You'd be wise to remember that the man who pays the piper calls the tune.'

Bridie glared at him. Wasn't that just the luck of it to tangle with a cruel hard man set in his ways. What did he want of her? Abject obedience to his wishes? Well, he'd not have it! She wanted that first shop with all her heart, even if it was a bit on the edge of things and not in the centre.

'Will you not meet me half-way?'

'How can I, when I'm sure you're wrong? I want you to succeed, whatever you may think.'

That softened Bridie, but it didn't stop her. 'That's what I want, as well. Can't you see I have to feel that it's mine, and I feel it in the first shop. What if I make you a promise?' She leaned forward and spoke more softly. 'If I fail, I'll not be bothering you again. I'll find a job as your brother wanted me to do, and pay back all I owe—if it takes all my days.'

She heard Anita draw in her breath, but Alphonse was silent. He took the spoon from the saucer in front of him and idly tapped it against the cup.

'Do you know what you're saying, Bridget?'

She nodded, frightened and yet exhilarated. 'Certain

sure! It's further I'll go: I'll leave Montreal and seek my future in Toronto, where all they speak is the English, and you will not hear from me—not ever again!' She didn't explain how she would pay back the money if he was never to hear from her again, but she saw he was considering her words very carefully.

'It means that much to you?'

She nodded.

He was silent for a long time.

She waited.

Anita's hand reached out for hers, and she held it. They waited together.

CHAPTER SEVEN

The Hot Potato opened in the beginning of November on McGill Street, off St James. It was Bridie's chosen location; Alphonse had given way on that.

He had done more than let Bridie have her heart's desire. The place was now comfortable and convenient. He had brought in a carpenter to make counters, to break down part of the wall between kitchen and shop. A painter had transformed the dingy interior, and now it was sparkling white. Alphonse found an enormous wood-burning stove for the shop itself, and provided from his brother's factory some chairs, stools and tables. A cord of wood, was now stacked neatly at the rear of the premises, under a shelter. He supervised the laying of black and white linoleum throughout the shop and kitchen.

He brushed Bridie's thanks aside brusquely. 'It's part of my investment in you. If it doesn't work out, at least I'll get some of my money back on furnishings!'

Mademoiselle Beaupré helped Bridie to hem curtains, and lent Anita to help her scrub and polish. She also gave her a rag rug and blankets for the two bedrooms, and located two beds going very cheaply and got one of the nephews to transport them.

The place was a picture. Bridie moved in after a tearful farewell with Anita and Mademoiselle Beaupré. She was glad she had gone to the pawn-ship with Pegeen's wedding-ring and brooch. The brooch had fetched the most, which only added to the mystery of how her sister had come by it. With the proceeds, she had bought a present for each. François Duvalier had never sent the wages he owed her, and she hesitated to ask Alphonse when he had done so much.

The wooden-faced Adèle arrived, escorted by a

cousin with a load of potatoes. She said very little, except to announce that no fault would be found with the tubers, they were first class. She put her things in the room assigned to her and ate a meal of baked potatoes and sausage (provided by Mademoiselle in a basket with other provisions as a parting gift on setting up house).

Afterwards the two girls sat together. Adèle, with her feet on the fender of the glowing Quebec heater, took out her knitting without a word, and the garment, whatever it was, grew steadily longer to the swift click-click of the needles. It set Bridie's teeth on edge and made her long for the easy chatter of little Anita.

'It's a grand little heater, this fat little stove. We've nothing like it where I come from—just open fires.'

Adèle's shrug seemed to imply that nothing better could be expected in Ireland.

Bridie tried again. 'Monsieur Alphonse said that you're a good cook and a good manager.'

'Yes.'

'I'll be needing your help. You must say if there's any part of the work you're not happy about.'

'Yes.' The steady click-click went on.

'In a week or two, we'll be used to each other's ways.' Bridie spoke in French to make her feel at home. 'Do you speak English at all?'

'Yes. I've worked in a hotel this past two years. You need both languages for that.' Adèle answered in her own, making no attempt to prove her ability.

'Did Mademoiselle Beaupré train you, as she's doing with Anita?'

'Yes.'

'Sure, she's a grand woman. She's been very kind to me.'

'Why wouldn't she be?' Adèle examined her work and began to count stitches.

Bridie could see that was what she was doing, for her mouth framed the numbers. What was the matter with the girl? Were words gold or silver—so precious they mustn't be used? Puzzled, she examined the averted face. Adèle wasn't as old as she'd first thought—she couldn't be more than twenty-five. It was the expression-less face that made her appear older—that, and the cruel way she had drawn her black hair tight and skewered it into a bun at the back. Her features were good, only her nose a little too sharp, maybe. The eyes were lovely —deep grey and large—if only they held some warmth! She longed to shake her to life.

She sighed, but did not give up. 'Is everything all right in your room? The bed should be comfortable. Anita tried it the other day, and said you'd like it.'

'Yes. Yes, I do.'

'I hope there's blankets enough. They're old and a bit thin. When we start earning, we'll buy new for the winter.'

'Yes, I'll manage till then.'

There was another long pause. 'I'm an early riser, myself. Are you hard to get up?'

'No. I'm used to being early.'

That was all Adèle was willing to do; just answer questions, but not contribute anything at all. Had she no opinions, no feelings? What was working with her going to be like?

Bridie sat brooding over the problem while the needles clicked on. She yawned and she stretched, built up the fire for the night and decided the best thing she could do was go to her bed. Her companion finished her row and rose to her feet.

'Good night,' said Bridie. 'Sleep well, and wish us good luck. Say a prayer for us both.'

Even that didn't elicit much of a response. There was no answering smile, no good wishes, just the folding of her knitting into a cloth bag and a murmured, '*Certaine-ment*, I shall offer a prayer. *Bonsoir*, Mademoiselle Bridget.'

Bridie woke the next morning to the sun on her face. She had left the curtains open because she wanted her first sight in her new kingdom to be of Mont Royal. And there it was! She lay in her bed and looked at it. She vowed to herself she was going to succeed. She had to. She would.

To her surprise she heard Adèle go downstairs, and then the sound of fires being shaken into fresh life. In a matter of minutes, a cup of herb tea was handed to her, and Adèle whisked out of the room before she even had time to thank her.

Bridie drank the hot brew, her excitement mounting. This was the day, the day she opened the shop. She rose from her bed and began to sing an old Irish tune that had more to do with going to war than going to work. By eight o'clock she was dressed and breakfasted, and the first of the potatoes were washed, ready for baking. She was in a fever of impatience.

'What time shall we open the door and let the grand smells of cooking float out to the street?'

Adèle only shrugged. 'Perhaps it would be as well to let the potatoes part cook.'

It was the first sentence the French girl had uttered which made Bridie feel that she had any interest in the whole business. 'There won't be any shoppers about for a while, but there might be people on their way to work. At least they'll know that we're here. Yes, put five or six of them in, and I'll unlock the door.'

The door was unlocked for a long while before the first customer came, and then it was a young boy, one of those who hung round the livery stable at the corner to look after the horses. He was followed by another smaller lad, who stood just inside the door.

'We'll have one baked potato,' said the big one firmly.

Adèle reached into the oven and extracted one. 'That'll be one cent, please. Are you going to eat it now?'

The boy nodded and paid.

Adèle cut the potato in two and put butter in each half. She gave him salt to help himself.

That attended to, he gave half to the little lad by the door.

Bridie had been watching the whole transaction, smiling. 'Wait, now!' she exclaimed. 'There should be something to mark this. It's an occasion—our very first customers! You shall have one each for the same price.' She took another potato from the oven, and cut and treated it as Adèle had the first. She handed it over the counter with a curtsy. 'I'll make a wish that this is the start of success for the Hot Potato.'

Both the boys beamed at her and sat down on the bench that ran round the room. The two potatoes were quickly demolished.

'That was good,' said the older one.

The little one smiled, and kicked at the floor. 'It was hot. The wind's like a knife today. It's nice and warm in here.'

Bridie's heart went out to him. He couldn't be more than six or seven, and wasn't warmly dressed. In fact, neither boy had gloves or scarves, though they seemed to have two layers of ragged sweaters, and both wore red woollen caps. The older one's hands were chapped and red, and his boots were stuffed with rags, which peeped over the sides.

'What are you called?' she asked.

'Why do ya want to know?' He was on guard.

'Just to be friendly. I'll tell you mine. I'm Bridget. She's Adèle.' She pointed to her unsmiling companion.

'Jim,' said the bigger one. 'He's Davey. He's my brother.'

'It's a pleasure to have two working men as our very first callers!' Bridie gave them a little salute.

'I'm only starting, same as you,' Davey piped up. 'Jim's putting me wise to the job, then he's going to try to get taken on at that building-site round the corner. Jim's pretty strong.'

That wasn't the way Bridie would have described the lanky thirteen-year-old, but she didn't say so. 'That'll be grand,' was her comment.

'Some of the men might be in here at lunch-time—if just to get warm. Are you two girls all there is?'

'Yes. Why do you ask?'

'They're big and they're rough—some of them. You could tell them there's a man in the back.'

'There's no man in the back,' Adèle broke in.

'You could say it just the same,' Jim got to his feet. 'But suit yourself, it's nothing to me.'

'It's terrible kind of you to set us straight.' Bridie could have shaken Adèle; the boy was only trying to help. 'We'll say me brother's back there—he's six foot two and watching out for us both.'

'That sounds about right!' Jim grinned at her. 'What'd ya say his name was?'

'Paddy,' Bridie was quick to reply, in spite of Adèle's outraged expression. 'What else should he be called, and him as Irish as me?'

Jim winked at her. 'I'll spread it about to the other boys. You've done us a favour.' He put his hand on the door.

'Is it only the first customer gets two for the one price?' Davey asked as he paused before following his brother.

'Only the first.' Bridie softened the words with her smile. 'Come again, won't you? You'll be welcome each time.'

He gave her a wave, and sidled out.

Bridie looked at Adèle and clapped her hands. 'That's the hard one, the very first one. Weren't they grand little lads?'

Adèle only frowned. 'They'll be in for a warm every time you move round.' She sniffed.

Bridie was indignant. 'Would you have us turn away custom?'

'There's a difference between turning them away and encouraging them to stay.'

'It never hurts to be welcoming.' Bridie took out a large bowl and banged it down. She started to measure out ingredients. 'Paddy's that fond of potato pancakes, I'll just be mixing some up for his lunch.'

'Paddy? What Paddy?' Adèle's face was surprised into genuine expression.

'Him in the back.' Bridie jerked her thumb in that direction.

Adèle's face was once more wooden as she realised what the Irish girl meant. 'Imaginary brothers,' she muttered under her breath. 'Whatever next?'

Bridie beat the mixture, a little pleased to discover it was possible to jerk Adèle into some sort of reaction. The pancakes were ready in no time, and as if by magic, customers began to trickle in and were tempted by them. Adèle had a busy time serving, while Bridie began on potato scones.

All in all, the first day passed pleasantly enough, and there were spurts of real activity at lunch-time and then again later in the afternoon. They had done just about the right number of baked potatoes and sold out of pancakes and scones, and when the men from the building-site had come in at noon, Bridie had remembered to call out, 'Paddy, we'll be needing more logs, and could you just bring in that other sack of potatoes like the darling man you are.'

Adèle had glanced at her darkly, but kept her tongue still.

The second day was even busier than the first, and Bridie added potato cakes to the menu. They went well, too. The horse-boys loved them.

'What do you think about potato soup?' she asked Adèle as they sat by the glowing Quebec heater that evening. 'We would need bowls or cups—something to serve it in. I'll buy a dozen or so. The money is coming in well. Then I'll make a pot tomorrow, just for the try.' Happily she planned how they would manage the extra item.

There was one good thing about Adèle, she mused, as she outlined the plans. She was willing to work, even though she had come up with no ideas and never pretended she knew anything about 'Paddy in the back'. Bridie had grown so accustomed to carrying on a conversation with him for the benefit of customers that she almost believed he was there.

The third morning she was in high good spirits as she looked out at Mont Royal. It was all working out just like a dream. Even the weather was good today. The sun was shining, and it was a lot milder. It would be even better with more customers in.

For a while it looked as if she might be right. The morning was busy enough, but there was no lunch-time crowd, only a straggler or two—and a pot of soup made and all sorts of baked potatoes without buyers. The afternoon was dismal as far as business was concerned. One woman came in for six pancakes.

Bridie saw ruination staring her in the face. Just as hard as that thought was the idea of throwing out good food. The soup they could use for their supper, and most of the potato cakes. It was the bakers which vexed her—two dozen of them going to waste. It was because they took so long to cook, and they had to be started early. People wouldn't want to wait more than a minute or two. It was a puzzle what to do, how much to prepare. There was nothing for it now. If they couldn't be sold, she'd give them away. She didn't tell Adèle, as she knew what she would say. She slipped out and went round the corner to the hitching-rails and found Jim.

A crowd of ruffianly boys followed him in at her heels, and she dispensed the hot potatoes to them all without any payment. They were delighted, and she was congratulating herself on a solution that gave pleasure to some, when Monsieur Alphonse chose to arrive.

'Ah, business is good!' he raised his hat to the girls as the boys shuffled out. 'That's excellent news, Bridget.' He looked from her to Adèle's glum face. 'What's wrong? Have I said something to offend?'

Why did he have to come just then, Bridie asked herself. She had been expecting him yesterday. Yesterday, they had been busy. 'We're just closing,' she said to him. 'Would you like something to eat? There's soup and potato cakes . . .' For some reason she couldn't quite explain to herself, it gave her great pleasure to offer him food. It put their relationship on a different footing. She was inordinately disappointed when he refused.

'No, thank you, I've just had a cream cake and coffee.' He sat down on one of the stools. 'Have you food left over after the day?' His eyes roved round the place.

Bridie did not want to admit anything of the kind. In a minute, he would be telling her that the shop was in the wrong place. 'I made a few things too many. It's terrible hard to judge right.'

'A few things too many,' Adèle sniffed. 'You've just given away twenty baked potatoes. It's not for me to say, but you could have saved them against tomorrow.'

'And passed off day-old tatties to my customers? How many would come back for that sort of thing? I'll not be known for stale food and for cheating!' Bridie was angry for her reputation, and even angrier that Adèle had given away the state of affairs to Alphonse.

'Were you giving those potatoes to the boys when I came in?' he asked, looking from one girl to the other.

'What if I was? Isn't it my shop, and can't I do as I see best?' Bridie snapped at him. 'Yesterday I ran short, so I did more today. I couldn't know that folk wouldn't be coming.'

'Better to go short than to give it away. It's no use scowling at me, Bridget Langton! You can't afford costly mistakes. And there's no sense in getting a reputation for handing out food free of charge at the end of the day. If people get to hear about it, they'll wait until late and then offer you less. Where will your profits be?'

Bridie bit her lip. She knew he was right. 'I'll not see food wasted when folk are going hungry,' she protested.

'Then you'll soon be joining them. You'll be one of the hungry. Is that what you want?'

'No, it's not. I've had enough of going hungry.' She stood facing him.

'Sit down there,' he indicated the bench, 'and let's have a sensible talk.'

Bridie didn't want to, but she did as he asked while

Adèle, silent now, leaned on her elbows at the other side of the serving-counter.

'The first thing you must do,' said Alphonse, very seriously, 'is to forget the past. You're not in a famine-stricken land any more. There's more than enough food to go round.'

'You may think there is,' Bridie muttered, 'but I've seen hungry people here. Those boys outside—the ones I've just given tatties to—they're hungry most of the time, and cold as well. I can't be thinking it's right that lads as young as that Davey should have to find work.'

Alphonse shook his head at her. 'You can't change the world, Bridget. You have to take it as it is. You're in business. Act like a business woman.'

'Hard, you mean? Without any heart?'

'I didn't say that. I'm just trying to tell you that you must look out for yourself. If you're going to have food left over, make some sort of arrangement with a pig-farmer. Charge him for swill. In that way you'll at least break even and be able to pay your bills by the end of the month.'

Bridie felt a chill of fear. There would be bills to face—potatoes to pay for, more wood, Adèle's wages. 'You'd put pigs before people,' she accused him.

'Stop turning my words around! You'll do no one any favours if you close up your shop—yourself and Adèle least of all. You're not stupid, just stubborn and blind. Wake up before it's too late!'

Bridie glared at him. It was all very well for him to give advice, good advice maybe. She curbed her temper. Perhaps it would help to talk it over sensibly. 'The thing is,' she began, 'they take so long to bake. People can't be standing waiting. It means they have to be started and then kept warm for a while. What we're needing is a quick-cooking potato and no waste at all.'

'There's no such thing,' said Adèle.

'Come down to earth, Bridget! Don't put your mind to the impossible. Find a solution to what's happening here and now.'

'Wait a bit,' said Bridie. 'What if . . .'

'Never mind the what ifs!' Alphonse got to his feet. 'There's no talking to you, is there? Sit down with Adèle after you've eaten and listen to what she has to say. Between you you might—in fact you must—come up with something clear.'

That inflamed Bridie. 'Talk to Adèle?' she shot back at him. 'Has she a tongue in her head? All that comes out is yes and no—nothing else.'

Adèle gasped. Bridie heard her, but she didn't care. She was standing facing Alphonse.

'Only yes and no,' she repeated, not caring in her anger whom she hurt. 'But she's willing enough to talk to you and tell you about giving away food.'

'Just as well she did,' was his answer, 'otherwise you'd be heading for ruin.' He took hold of her by the shoulder. 'Did you ever think of listening to her? Or is your own tongue so busy that she can't get in a word however she tries?'

Bridie was left for once speechless at the unfairness of his attack. Had she not been doing everything in her power to get the wretched girl to open her mouth? She spluttered and stammered in her rage. 'You know nothing! Nothing at all!'

Alphonse shook her—shook her hard. 'Settle it between you, and settle it now. Go over there and take her hand and ask for her help.' He smiled at Adèle.

That smile did it. With a cry of rage, Bridie kicked him in the shins and managed to secure her release. She ran from him. Through the cubbyhole in the counter she darted, past the simpering Adèle, through to the scullery and up the stairs to her room. She threw herself on her bed and cried her heart out. All the disappointments of the day crowded in upon her.

Neither of them came to her—to help her or to soothe her. She heard the sound of their voices and then the slam of the front door. That was Alphonse leaving. Good! She cried harder than ever. Gradually her sobs lessened, and she heard Adèle moving about below. She would be setting things to rights, washing up, putting away. It wasn't fair to expect her to do everything, however she felt.

Bridie sighed and sat up. Her face felt a sight. Her nose was red and shining. She was bathing it with the water in the bowl when the shriek rang out. Mother of God, what was that! Was Adèle being attacked? Another scream followed the first, shrill and ear-splitting. Was she being killed? What could it be?

Bridie looked wildly around the room, her face dripping wet. A weapon, that's what she needed! She snatched up the jug. It wasn't much, but it would have to do. She flew down the stairs and into the scullery.

Adèle was perched screaming on a stool, holding on to her skirts. The gas-lamp had been lit both there and in the shop. Bridie couldn't believe her eyes. No one else was in the room.

'Where is he?' she demanded. 'Has he touched you? I'll be killing him now.' She clutched the jug to her, and ran to the back door. There was no one there. She ran to the front. Not a body in sight. She ran back to the scullery and the moaning Adèle still high off the floor.

'Tell me what's happened,' she begged, but could get no sense from the girl.

Exasperated, she threw the contents of the water-jug on the quivering figure. 'Stop that wailing and tell me what's wrong!'

The sudden dousing with water startled Adèle into quiet. 'It went over there!' She pointed to the sack of potatoes in the corner, but did not get down from her perch.

Bridie looked where she pointed. 'What went over there?'

Adèle hugged herself and trembled. 'A mouse, Bridget! A great big mouse. I can't stand the filthy creatures! Chase it out—kill it—Bridget! Then I'll come down.'

Bridie couldn't help it. She sat down on a chair and laughed till she cried, wiping her face on her apron. 'You screamed like that for a mouse?' She giggled again. 'For goodness' sake, come down! I thought you were scalped or burned at the stake.'

Adèle stayed where she was. 'I'm not coming down until it's out of this place!'

'Then you'll be a long time up there,' Bridie told the cringing girl. 'How I am supposed to catch a wee mouse who's gone to hide in a sack of tatties or back to his hole, I just don't know.'

Just the same, her feet took her to the other room and she picked up the poker by the stove. She would frighten him out if he was nibbling her food store! Back she went, not relishing the job in hand in the slightest.

'Should we get a cat, do you think?' Adèle suggested as she passed. 'A cat wouldn't take up much room or eat very much. I'd feel safer if we had a cat of our own.'

'So would I,' said Bridie through her teeth. Wasn't it the funny time though for Adèle to be finding her tongue?

She lifted the poker and approached the sack. If it jumped out at her, she didn't know if she'd have the stomach to kill it with the poker. Gingerly, she opened the top. Nothing happened. She pushed the poker in, and potatoes tumbled all over the floor. No mouse followed them out. She sighed. That was only the top layer. 'Paddy!' she shouted out loud. 'Where are you, Paddy? Just when we're needing you!'

Adèle gave her the ghost of a smile. 'You're doing well, Bridget. You don't need any Paddy! Dump out the whole sack and then be quick with the poker. You'll have him before you know it.'

'It's terrible brave you are up there,' said Bridie. 'Sure I wish I had your courage now!'

Another layer of potatoes rolled over the floor. If only she could lift the whole lot at once. The mouse must still be in there. Well, there was nothing for it; she must get them all out. She heaved to the task and was halted before she could manage it by a great knocking at the front door, the shop door.

'Let me in,' shouted a strong male voice. 'Open up! There's two hungry men on the step.'

Bridie's hands flew to her face. What to do? That was money on the doorstep! She went to the door, poker still in her hand. 'I'm coming,' she called out, and undid the bolt.

Facing her were two soldiers—British soldiers! She took one look at them and would have shut the door in their faces, but one of them managed to get his foot in and then the rest of himself.

She cringed back, shaking. What were they doing here? She forgot where she was. In Ireland, British soldiers meant trouble. Why had she opened the door?

'Put your weapon away, Miss,' said the big blond one. 'We've come for food—not for war!' He put out his hand to touch her, to reassure her. 'We've just been to the livery stable. They thought you might feed us.'

Bridie sprang back. 'No, I don't want you here. You must go away.'

The two of them laughed. They were both in the shop now, the door firmly closed.

In her fright, Bridie ran under the counter and out to the back. If she thought to escape them, she was sadly mistaken. They followed right after.

In the scullery, with potatoes all over the place, Bridie made her stand in front of the astonished Adèle. 'You'll not come a step further. We'll fight to the death.' She raised the poker in her hand and reached out for the jug sitting close by on the bench. Adèle must be armed as well, then she waited for whatever was coming. They'd give a good account of themselves! Of that she was sure, certain sure.

'Paddy,' she called out. 'Where are you, Paddy? We're needing your help.'

CHAPTER EIGHT

IT WAS ADÈLE who brought order to the whole scene. She cried out, 'Bridget, put down your poker! These are officers of the regiment, and they mean us no harm. They'll pay for their food.' She said the last in French.

The poker wavered in Bridie's hand. She looked up at Adèle. 'Do you know them? They're British soldiers. Why should they come here?'

The two officers remained motionless. In fact one of them smiled, the tall blond one. 'It looks like a siege in here! What happened?' He leaned against the shelves at the side of the room.

The other—the brown-haired one—had stepped back out of range of the poker. 'She's a madwoman! Let's get out of here, Hartley. We came only because the boy at the hitching-post said we could get something filling here. He's played some sort of trick on us.' He walked as far as the serving-counter in the shop.

'Hold on, Viv!' exclaimed the first. 'I like the look of the girl. She's got lots of spirit, but if her food's as uncertain as her temper, I'll follow you out.'

'Wait, now,' said Bridie and she put down the poker. 'There's no need to be going. If one of the boys sent you, you must be all right. You mustn't pay any heed to the muddle here. Adèle sighted a mouse, or thought she did. I'm not so sure.' She didn't want these officers thinking vermin swarmed in her kitchen.

'And you were throwing potatoes at it from a great height?' The officer gave Adèle his hand and helped her down from her perch. 'Is it good sport?'

Adèle said nothing, just smoothed her skirt, but Bridie wasn't going to let his jest pass.

'We weren't throwing potatoes! I was trying to upend

the whole sack in case the little creature was nestling in the inside.'

'You went the wrong way about it,' the big blond man told her. He walked over to the corner and lifted the sack. 'I'll put it outside.' He opened the back door, and dumped the whole lot on the little cinder path that served as a yard. Potatoes scattered everywhere, but there was no little mouse.

'Imagined it, more than likely!' He gave a great laugh. 'Get your Paddy, the one you were calling for, to pick them up.'

'Yes, when he comes back. That's the way brothers are—never there when they're wanted. What can I do for the two of you now?' Bridie managed a smile.

Adèle was busy picking up the potatoes scattered over the kitchen floor. She had found a bucket, and was filling it quickly.

'We've hot soup and potato cakes, and some ham if you're wanting something substantial.'

'That sounds fine to me. Is it Irish potato soup—like yourself?'

Bridie nodded and favoured him with a smile. 'Ah, you've guessed that I'm Irish. You'll be knowing the country then?' She was bustling about, putting the pan of soup on the stove.

'I was stationed there before my posting here,' was the reply. 'I've never forgotten the soup. Come on, Viv,' he called to his friend, 'you're in luck's way. You're in for a treat.' He took off his hat and laid it on one of the shelves.

Bridie could see how young he was and how pleasant his face. His hair was very fair. In fact, in the light of the lamp as he sat down at the table before her, he looked so young that she lost all her fear and hatred of the British uniform he wore.

His friend joined him, his hat in his hand. The pair of them were scarcely more than boys, though they were full grown and strong-looking.

Adèle turned up the gas-lamp on the wall, for the short November day had darkened into evening. She got out the ham and began to cut it in slices.

'You can eat in the shop,' said Bridie, busy with starting the potato cakes in a frying-pan.

'Can't we sit in here and talk to you both? Come, say we can? I've fond memories of Irish kitchens and the colleens who always had time for chattering to a man.' He gave her such a friendly smile that Bridie began to like him.

'I suppose there's no reason why not.' Bridie set a steaming bowl of soup on the table, and he drew the chair up to it and sat down. His friend lost no time in pulling another forward and dipping his spoon into a second dish of soup.

Bridie found that she, too, was suffering the pangs of hunger. How long was it since she'd eaten? Absently she poured herself a cup of soup and one for Adèle. It would stave off being famished.

'You must tell us your name, and how you come to be here,' said the blond officer between spoonfuls.

'If you'll first tell me who you are.' Bridie was beginning to feel he might be a friend.

'Lieutenant Hartley Brooke, at your service,' he sketched a salute. 'My friend is Lieutenant Vivian Roberts.'

'Bridget Langton, Adèle Beaupré—we run the shop between us.' She smiled at them both, but Adèle merely took a sip of her soup and busied herself with the potato cakes warming in the pan.

'Who's Paddy? The one you called out for—the one who's going to pick up the spuds?'

'My brother,' Bridie replied swiftly. 'A terrible fellow he is for going off and leaving us to it.'

'He's an Irishman.' Lieutenant Vivian Roberts shrugged as if that explained everything.

'Oh come on, Viv,' Hartley intervened before Bridie could explode. 'Not all Irishmen are afraid to work! Look at young Bridie—I'll wager she works from morning till night. Tell me, Bridie, how long have you been here?'

'Just a few months.'

'Come to make your fortunes, have you, you and your brother?'

'Yes.' Bridie didn't want to deny Paddy's presence, but if she were not careful, she would be getting herself in a pickle remembering he was supposed to be there.

'Adèle is a French name. How did you two get together, or is she a friend of your brother?' Hartley smiled at Adèle to take the sting from the words, but she gave him the most haughty of looks.

'Doesn't she understand much English?' he went on. 'Well, I suppose it's sensible to have one who speaks the native language. Still, she can't be much company for you.'

Bridie opened her mouth to agree, but managed to close it in time without uttering a word of disparagement. Her tongue had done enough running away with her an hour or so since. She removed the empty bowls, and Adèle slapped the heaping plates of ham and potato cakes on the table in front of the two soldiers with no ceremony at all.

'That was splendid!' Hartley wiped his mouth with the back of his hand. 'You've no idea what you're doing for two starving men. We've been drilling all day.'

'Drilling? Where do you drill?'

'Of course you wouldn't know, as you've been here such a short time. The regiment marches and drills on the Champ de Mars. I suppose you've never even seen the place. You've missed something, I can tell you. It's the true centre of the city, this Champ de Mars.'

'Just because of you soldiers?' Bridie didn't know whether to believe him or not.

'Not only because of us.' Hartley's knife and fork stopped their dance on his plate. 'The citizens of this fine city promenade there. On a fine afternoon, they come in their hundreds. You'd love it of an afternoon or an evening, when one of the military bands is playing and the people are strolling in the sunshine. You must come one day soon.

'There won't be many more fine days, now that we're into November,' said Vivian. 'The snow will soon come, so they say. My Captain says it's going to be a hard winter, and he's been here for two. He declares the only thing for us is to get a sleigh and a horse.'

'To be getting about, you mean?' Bridie looked from one to the other.

They both laughed together. Even Adèle smiled.

'What did I say that was funny?' Bridie demanded. 'What else would you be using a sleigh for?' She trembled a little. She hadn't seen the snow yet. It had all gone by the time they had landed, but she had heard talk of it often enough.

'For the sport,' Hartley explained. 'For racing and winter picnics. All the officers who've had a tour of duty in Canada speak of the winter with affection and longing. It's almost as if they wish they were back.'

Bemused, Bridie finished the last of her soup. Hartley's words opened a picture of Canadian life that was entirely new to her, and something in her yearned for the sort of excitement he spoke of. She liked the thought of mingling with crowds of people, of winter picnics. It wasn't for the likes of her, she told herself. She had a shop to run, a business to build up, but just the same she wished that sort of life was open to her. Alphonse and his brother would know about it—even join in—for they were well born and no doubt went to garrison parties and outings. The twins would have such a life. She sighed for the opportunity, but could not be sorry that the boys would share in it. She had seen great parties in the house where she had worked back in Ireland, but always from the wrong side of the table. She sighed again. Perhaps it was different here. 'Can anyone promenade on the Champ de Mars?' she asked.

'Why not?' Hartley finished his meal, and poured himself a cup of tea from the pot Adèle put at his elbow. 'It's for everyone.' He added sugar, and stirred it. 'I'll make you a bet! By next summer, you'll be treating it as your village square.'

'Oh, I'll never!' Bridie laughed at the very thought.

'Of course you will. You'll find life here is a lot freer and easier than it was where you come from.'

Adèle produced two baked apples, piping hot from the oven, and set them before the two men.

That was our supper, thought Bridie without any rancour—and a kind of peace-offering intended for me? It would be easier for her and Adèle to come face to face after the breathing-space provided by the officers.

Hartley and Vivian paid for their meal, and Bridie escorted them to the front door—to lock up after them, she told herself. She carried a candle, but somehow the wind blew it out as she opened the door.

Hartley paused in the entrance, and his arm slid round her waist. 'I've always liked Irish girls,' he whispered into her hair. 'You're pretty by gas-light. I intend to come back and see you in the day.' He gave her a squeeze for good measure.

Bridie smiled up into his face. She didn't believe him for a minute! Why would he bother with the likes of her—until the next time he was hungry? All the same, as she shut the door behind him, her smile stayed on her face.

'We've made a profit for the day,' she told Adèle as she went back to the scullery. 'It's a strange kind of life, isn't it, all ups and downs.'

Adèle was washing dishes. 'Shall we have the last of the ham? There's a bit of bread in the bin, and some pickles left from the basket Aunt Beaupré gave us.'

It was the first real thing Adèle had ever said to her. Perhaps there was hope for them yet—and she had been grand about serving and fixing the meal for the officers. 'Yes,' said Bridie. 'I'm so tired of potatoes—and there's all that lot to pick up outside the back door.' She began to laugh. 'What a sight we must have been when they came in—me with my poker and you up on the stool! It's a wonder they stayed.'

Adèle gave her a real smile for the first time since she had known her. 'All the same, they're a pair to watch out for.'

'How do you mean?' Bridie buttered two slices of bread and fitted ham between them.

'The fair one liked you. He'll be back.'

'Never!' said Bridie. 'I know his kind. He'll want a girl of his own station.'

'Only for marriage.' Adèle started drying the plates. 'But officers such as he often want a girl for a bit of fun. They don't want girls from really good families. It never works out—not when they go back to England.'

'Why ever not?' Bridie made more tea. They would have a treat tonight—never mind the expense! Adèle had found something to talk about, and she would keep her going. The two girls sat down at the table and attacked their sandwiches.

'Montreal girls get homesick and long to come back. England doesn't suit them. It's not as free as it is here.' Adèle sipped at her tea. 'That's why the Army frowns on such marriages now. They send an officer back to Britain the minute he gets serious with a girl he might marry.'

'How do you know all this?' Bridie was interested.

'I worked in a hotel before I came here. I've seen some strange things, and kept my ears open and learned all the gossip. You'd be surprised how some people live! These officers are the worst of the lot. They're young. They like girls, and they especially like girls who are willing—girls who fancy themselves in love. Mind, they can be generous, but there comes a day of reckoning for the girl—there always does.'

'Yes,' said Bridie. 'Yes, I see what you mean. The officers go back to England when they're sent.'

'Not only that,' Adèle paused. 'The girls find themselves in trouble—expecting and alone.' She whispered the last three words.

'Babies,' Bridie whispered back. 'Poor little souls.'

'The wages of sin—that's what the priest calls them.' Adèle bit into the second half of her sandwich. 'Why is it the women who always have to pay the wages of sin?'

Bridie shook her head. She had never considered the matter before, and didn't want to now. She took a drink of her tea, and found it scalding hot.

'I wondered about you and Monsieur Alphonse,' Adèle went on. 'My aunt said there was nothing in it . . . It was just a business arrangement.'

'That's all it is,' Bridie defended herself. 'What else could there be?'

Adèle gave her a very serious look. 'Sometimes you're very young—and very unworldly. It could lead you into trouble. I wish I could be like you, so friendly and open. There's no question but that Monsieur Alphonse does as you bid, and yet the way he spoke to you tonight . . . It's not the way of romance.'

'Certain sure it's not! That's because there is no romance.' Bridie wanted to make it crystal clear to Adèle. Of course she wasn't interested in Alphonse. It was a business arrangement. That must be understood. It was unfortunate that she had this strange reaction every time he came into a room.

'Yes,' said Adèle. '*Bon Dieu*, but I'm tired! It's been a long day.' She yawned and she stretched, and put her plate and cup in the washing-up water.

'You go off to bed,' suggested Bridie. 'I'll finish up here.' She poured another cup of tea, and rested her chair against the wall, balancing on two legs.

'*Bien,*' said Adèle. 'Have I talked enough for the once?' Her eyes held Bridie's.

'I'm sorry! I didn't mean all I said.'

'Yes, you did,' corrected Adèle. 'Shall we think about the pig-swill tomorrow?'

'Tomorrow will be soon enough,' Bridie agreed. She held her cup in her hands, the warmth of it comforting. '*Bonsoir*, Adèle. Sleep well. We'll ask Jim about a cat.'

'*Et vous aussi,*' Adèle called as she went up the stairs. 'A cat will be company. *Bon soir*, Bridget.'

Bridie blinked tears from her eyes as she sat sipping the last of her tea. You just could not tell about people.

Adèle wasn't so bad. Fancy her being scared of a mouse!

She rose to her feet and soon had the few dishes finished. She had her foot on the bottom step, when she thought of the potatoes out at the back. They could wait till morning . . . No, they couldn't. Sighing, she fetched a lantern and lit it, and went to the door.

It was very dark outside and cold too, and so quiet. There were stars in the sky, but no moon. She would need more light. Going back in, she found and lit two candles, and set them on two large stones. With the lantern on another, she could manage to see. The kitchen door she shut gently behind her. There was no sense in waking Adèle. The sack was where it had been left, and she bent to her task. There was quite a quantity of tatties spilt all over the place. Humming softly, she gathered them. There was no use in hurrying. Now that she was working, it was warmer. She scarcely needed the shawl she had thrown about her shoulders.

She was into a second chorus of 'Danny Boy' when she felt she wasn't alone. She straightened and looked about her, still singing. Sure, she was imagining things! Her voice faltered. Was that a darker shadow over there by the gate to the lane? Yes, it was, and she wished she had not left the poker inside. 'Who's there?' she called out in more of a squeak than a shout.

Monsieur Alphonse detached himself from the depths of the darkness. She knew it was he, even before he spoke. 'Sh-h-h, Bridget! What are you doing?'

'Picking them up.' She pointed to the ground, but kept her other hand on the mouth of the sack.

He came closer. 'I was passing the front of the shop and saw the light of the lantern through the window. My first thought was fire, so I came to investigate. I never expected to find you here playing *boules* with potatoes!'

Bridie stamped her foot. 'I'm not playing bowls! I'm sick of people asking me silly questions about sport.' She saw Alphonse's look of astonishment and didn't care.

'Haven't you got over your fit of the sulks yet?' he

asked coldly. 'I'll go if you can't talk to me civilly.' He half turned on his heel.

'No, don't go.' She took hold of his sleeve. 'I behaved badly. I'm sorry you left in a huff.'

'It was you who took the huff—not me,' he contradicted, but he smiled.

She saw the flash of his teeth in the starlight and breathed deeply. What was that strange smell about him? Fire—smoke—that's what it was! 'Are you burning?' she asked. 'It's smoke I smell.'

'I've just come from a fire. I suppose you're just too far away here to have seen the flames, and the wind's in the wrong direction. It was a big one.'

'Where was it? Were you in it?' She still had hold of his jacket.

He put his hand on hers. 'I helped to haul buckets of water, trying to put it out. The volunteer fire-fighters were out in some force, but everyone turned to. It was that shop in the Main—the one we quarrelled over. To think I almost insisted you take that one!'

Bridie was too shocked to tell him that he *had* insisted, that there was no 'almost' about it. Instead she asked, 'Was anyone hurt?'

'They say a girl was killed—overcome by the fumes before they could get to her. One of the firemen was burned, too.'

She shuddered. She felt death brush straight past. 'It wasn't my time to go,' she said stoutly.

'No, thank Heaven it wasn't.' His hand closed on hers.

They stood close, so close that they could see into each other's eyes in spite of the paleness of the light. She saw concern in his—concern and something more. 'Would it have mattered to you?' she breathed the words.

'Of course it would.' He drew her closer, his arm round her waist, and she didn't resist.

Before she knew it, his lips closed on hers. Her hands crept up to his neck and fastened behind his head. It was sweet to be kissed and to kiss in return. She forgot the scattered potatoes, the cold of the night, the troubles of the day, and gave herself up to the warmth and the comfort of his embrace.

'I would have missed you,' he whispered against her hair, tickling her ear. 'Funny little Irish shamrock, always fighting, always wanting. I knew you'd be like this to kiss.'

'Like what?' she whispered back, her body tingling with pleasure.

'Welcoming, warm. They say the Irish girls have the softest hearts of all! They're wild and yet tender—is that true of you?'

His lips brushed her cheek, then her neck and the V of her bodice. His hands slid down her back, pulling her to him, closer, so that she could scarcely breathe and she was totally conscious of the strength of his desire.

'No,' she managed to gasp, and she tried to pull away. She said the first thing that came into her head. 'There's all the potatoes to pick up, and Adèle may wake and look out and find us.'

He released her at once. 'You're right, of course. We've all the time in the world.' He held her hand only, and placed a kiss in its centre. 'Bridget, you don't have to work so hard cooking potatoes.'

'What do you mean?' She didn't like the sound of his words.

'You could have a place of your own.'

'What sort of a place?'

'A comfortable little apartment with a servant to wait on you.'

'And what would I have to do to—earn—this comfortable place?' Her eyes were flashing. 'I'll not be your mistress, if that's what you're after! I'm me own mistress, no one else's.' British soldiers, she told herself sternly, weren't the only ones to beware of!

'Then why did you kiss me in that fierce way you did? I know you want me as much as I want you.'

'You don't know anything of the sort!' she denied his words hotly.

He laughed. 'You don't know yourself, Bridget

Langton! You've such an unquenchable spark of life in you that you're bound to settle on someone—why not me? I'm prepared to put up with your temper, and not everyone would.' He pulled her to him once again.

To her shame, she didn't struggle as much as she should. She let him hold her and kiss her, and his lips were gentle and sweet. A fire of longing took possession of her, but she wouldn't give in.

'No,' she repeated with very little conviction in her voice to her own ears. 'You should be ashamed of making such a suggestion to a good Irish girl.' It was hurt and anger that gave her the strength to say it. But why should she be hurt? The likes of him would never suggest marriage to the likes of her. She had known that all along. It was what Adèle had said of the officers. They weren't looking for wedding—only for bedding! Alphonse was just the same. There was no cause for anger. He hadn't forced himself upon her . . . she'd been willing enough. That make her blush and thank her stars for the darkness of the night. It was up to her somehow to put things right between them—without accepting his offer.

'We'll forget that you've said it.' She spoke aloud, without harshness.

'Will you be able to forget, Bridget?' he asked very softly.

'I shall put it out of my mind.' She tried to sound sure and dignified as though such offers came her way every day. Well, there had been the butler in the great house where she'd worked, but he had tried with all the girls, and none of them took it seriously—not at all. 'You needn't be thinking that I don't know how men are, for I'm aware that the devil is in them where girls are concerned!'

'You're adorable when you're serious and trying to act the woman of the world,' he told her. 'But don't worry too much about being a success in the commerce of potatoes. You may turn to me yet!'

'Never!' said Bridie, bending down to retrieve two

potatoes that had rolled almost under her feet. His easy
confidence stiffened her resolve.

'Here's another—and his friend.' He tossed two more
into the sack. 'Why did you throw them out here? Were
you tired of them?'

'It's a grand tale!' Bridie kept her hands busy and her
body some distance from him. He might have put up
more of a fight for her favours. She tried to banish the
thought. Hadn't he said he had only to wait? Well, it
would be a long wait for him. She launched into the story
of Adèle and the mouse, but didn't tell him about the
two officers. Let him think the business was on the verge
of ruination. That way, she'd be one step ahead.

She ended her account with her resolve to ask the boy,
Jim, for a cat. 'Sure, Adèle's human like the rest of us,'
she added. 'She's found the tongue in her head. We had
quite a cosy gossip about men and their ways.' She
pulled her shawl tighter round her. Somehow the
warmth had gone from the night. 'I think that's most of
them now. Any others hiding away can wait till the
morning, and the sunshine will find them.'

'If there is any,' Alphonse amended, taking the sack
from her hands and lifting it through. 'There's a nip in
the air. It won't be long before the snow arrives and the
winter sets in.'

Bridie was forced to hover near the door, since he
blocked it with his bulk. She picked up the candles and
blew out their flames, then wished she hadn't, for the
lantern flickered out with the last of the oil. There were
only the stars and him blocking the way of her escape to
the kitchen.

'Afraid, Bridget?' he called to her as she paused out of
reach.

'No, I'm not.' She came a step closer.

'What if I don't let you pass?'

She looked into his eyes. 'I'll scream, and Adèle will
poke her head out of the window.'

'Ah, yes! Adèle—I was forgetting her.'

'I'll bid you *Bonsoir* and ask you to move.'

'Go ahead! Bid me good night.' There was challenge in his voice.

'Good night, Monsieur Alphonse,' she said very formally, 'I believe you're standing in my way.'

'How could that happen? A gentleman wouldn't allow such a thing. *Bonsoir*, Mademoiselle Bridget. Don't let me keep you.' He stepped away from the entrance and gave her a bow, making no attempt at all to touch her.

That piqued her considerably. Only a few minutes ago he'd been kissing her and holding her. Now he was as cool as cool. See if she cared—no she didn't! Slipping through the door, she shot the bolt tight through its length. She thought she heard his soft laugh as she ran up the stairs, and only hoped Adèle had heard nothing. She didn't want to make any explanations in the morning. Her clothes she threw off and left them lying on the floor. She would sleep well tonight after all the excitements of the long day!

Why wouldn't sleep overcome her, she fretted, as she lay in the narrow bed. Why did Alphonse's face keep appearing before her eyes as though he were there? How was it that she still felt his kisses on her lips, his hands on her back? She'd forgotten his offer. She'd forget him as well. Ah, it was easier said than done. It was because he had not touched her again. He could turn himself off and on at his ease, and she didn't have the knack. It was the devilry of man to blind a poor girl to all else save his wanting. She would put him straight out of her mind. By tomorrow, her senses would have returned . . . Pray Heaven they would! She sighed again, and tried to sleep.

CHAPTER NINE

DIABLE! WHATEVER HAD got into him tonight? Of course he was attracted to the little Irish girl—he had been, from the very start. There was that way she looked at him, half innocent, half inviting. It was those blue eyes; he had never seen anything like them before. They were the colour of the river on a soft summer day, and they changed from light to dark as her mood changed. There was no doubt about it she was a pretty girl, and, now that she had filled out a bit, an inviting one. But he had not meant to let it go any further than looking at her. The sooner she was out of Montreal the better, as far as he and his family were concerned. Marie-Rose would never recover if she were informed that the twins were not, in fact, her very own, and as long as Bridget remained, so would the threat of her finding out.

Alphonse let his horse slow down as his hands slackened their hold on the reins. Thank Heaven Bridget had said No! She had saved him from a very awkward situation, albeit one that might have had its moments of pleasure. What a strange little thing she was—one moment full of fire and the next reverting to childish friendship with him. She had made no fuss about being insulted, nor had she pretended not to know what he had meant, yet there had been a kind of dignity about her that he had been forced to admire. She might have been flattered by his offer, but she hadn't liked it. He had sensed that.

He sighed. It had not been his intention to make her any offer . . . the emotion of the evening had put the thought in his mind. Seeing that other shop going up in flames and hearing the screams of the poor girl inside had had a profound effect upon him. What if it had been Bridget in there? As soon as he could, he had left the scene of the fire, but on his way home had gone more than a little out of his way. Just to make sure everything was all right at the Irish girl's shop—he admitted it to himself. And when he had seen the flickering candles casting such odd shadows through the window, he had to stop the horse and rush round the alley to see what was happening.

The relief he had felt had been out of all proportion to the event. She was alive—and flesh and blood called out to celebrate that! There was no coquetry in her. She was direct in her mind, even if her speech sometimes skirted a subject before going to its heart. He liked that directness. If she was angry, she let it show. When she was pleased, the whole world could witness it and was invited to be pleased as well. He thought of the scene with Adèle and the mouse, as she had described it. Well, Adèle was a bit of a facer. He himself had never taken to her. She was too stiff and too correct, but that was why he had picked her. His hope had been that she would keep Bridget safe and respectable. Now he wasn't so sure —afraid of a mouse!

Ah well, he'd get them a cat. That should be easy enough, and it was the kind of gift she could accept. She had no need to depend on this Jim, whoever he was.

Why was it that this stubborn little girl occupied so much of his thoughts? He'd never mooned like this over any other—not even Marie-Rose. He had let his brother take her away from him without any struggle: it had not mattered enough. Yet, in a way, it had put him against the thought of settling down. His mother talked about his marrying, and often introduced him to suitable girls. 'Good matches', she called them and talked about their father's wealth and the size of their dowries. He supposed that, one day, he would have to decide on one of them, but not yet. If he had won Marie-Rose, he might have been father to that poor little mite buried in Pegeen's arms; he might have been raising the twins. Fate had played an odd hand to François, and to himself!

He flicked the reins over the horse's back. It was late;

time to be home. Maybe one of these days he would do what was expected of him and make a good marriage with some suitable girl. What was the name of the latest one his mother meant to parade before him? Gabrielle Truteau, that was it. She was reputed to be quite a beauty, only eighteen, and high spirited. Perhaps she was the very one to erase Bridget Langton from his mind.

Alphonse called out to the horse. 'Move along, old friend. *Dépêche-toi*, hurry up home!' He made a snapping sound with the reins, and the horse obeyed him.

'Devil take that creature!' Bridie was fast losing her temper. 'It's done nothing but fight with the other. I never wanted two cats.' She picked a small potato from the ones she was cleaning and aimed it at the big black cat, the gift of Alphonse. 'I don't know what Monsieur Alphonse was thinking of, and him so pleased with himself when he carried it in I didn't have the heart to tell him of the other Jim had brought the day before.'

'We could give back the first,' Adèle suggested, as she put some logs in the stove. 'It wouldn't do to offend Monsieur Alphonse. I wonder how he thought of a cat.'

'I'm wondering, too,' Bridie assured her. She had kept her lips sealed about the night visit he had paid. She had never asked him for the black devil! She was positive she had told him she meant to ask Jim. Well, she wasn't going to return Jim's cat—she liked it better, anyway. It wasn't fat and pampered like this one. She fixed it with a baleful stare. Jim's cat was more of a kitten; half grown, scrawny, not sure even of the colour of its coat. Its underside was creamy white, its back tabby, and the two strains met on its face, giving it a clownish look that made Bridie laugh. She liked its spunk, too. It stood up to the big black one and gave as good as it got. But what was the use of two warring animals underfoot in the kitchen? Adèle had named them 'Noir' and 'Blanche', and that didn't make sense, because they were both males, or so it was said. Blanche had retreated behind the stove, and Noir licked its paws near Adèle.

'About the pig-swill . . .' began Adèle.

'What about it?' Bridie interrupted. 'We don't need to do anything about it.' She washed another potato, and cut out its eyes. 'I've a better notion. We'll scoop out the day-old potatoes and mix the flesh of them with cheese and butter and whatever else we may think of, and sell that as a sort of savoury. We'll charge two or three cents a scoop.'

'We can try, I suppose.' Adèle wasn't too eager.

'And another thing,' Bridie went on. 'I've remembered how my mother used to fry potatoes in deep fat. I'm going to make some. That's why I'm cutting these tatties up in sticks.'

'*Bien.*' Adèle disappeared into the shop to serve the first customer. Some ten minutes later when she tasted the result, she was much more enthusiastic, and wanted to know how they were made.

'Ah, that'll be my secret,' said Bridie, 'but I'll tell you this much. It's the heat of the oil and knowing when to plunge them—that, and the salt you put on after. I shall call them *patates frites*. We'll put up a sign.'

'*Pommes de terre frites,*' corrected Adèle.

Bridie turned obstinate. 'When the men from the building-site come in, they call potatoes, *patates*. That's what I'll call these: *patates frites.*' She made out the sign herself. And, in the days that followed, *patates frites* they were known as, and very popular they were. Bridie had found herself a winner. It was a turning-point for the shop. Business began to pick up and the money to come in very nicely. Bridie was able to buy more supplies, even to redeem Pegeen's jewellery and to wear the brooch herself under her apron.

Anita had found a position in a large house quite near, and planned to spend her time off with Bridie. On her first free Sunday afternoon, she came to call. Adèle had already gone out with a friend, so the two girls were on their own. They attacked bread and jam and tea with appetite, and were in the middle of talking and eating when there was a heavy knocking at the front door.

Anita could not resist peeking, even though Bridie advised being quiet and letting whoever it was go away.

'It's two soldiers out there. They look splendid in their red tunics! They're calling your name. Do you know them? Oh, let them in. They're so handsome.'

Bridie went to the door. The two British officers, Hartley and Vivian, stood there, smiling.

'As good as my word,' exclaimed Hartley. 'We've come to take you to promenade on the Champ de Mars. It's a lovely afternoon. The sun's shining, even if it's a bit nippy. It's probably the last of the good weather. The Highland band will be playing, and we're off duty for once. Get your bonnet and shawl. Viv's hired a buggy.'

'Grand!' exclaimed Bridie, face all alight. 'But I'm not on my own. I've a friend with me. Anita's her name.'

Vivian saluted the girl who was hovering behind Bridie. 'So much the better! She's younger than that Adèle who was here the last time.'

'And prettier!' Hartley bowed over her hand and Anita dimpled and blushed. 'Are you both ready now?'

Bridie was glad she had worn her rose frock. Both of them fetched bonnets and shawls and, the door locked behind them, they were helped up into the open carriage by their escorts and were soon bowling through the streets.

Bridie told herself that Adèle would be sorry she had missed the outing, but she soon put her out of her mind. Anita was so excited and pleased, and so was she. It was grand to be out and to have friends—friends who knew how to treat a girl!

It was indeed a lovely afternoon, with warm sun. 'Unseasonable for late November,' Vivian told them, making Anita giggle because he sounded so pompous.

Hartley devoted himself to Bridie, and Vivian seemed to enjoy Anita's company. Between them, they pointed out all the landmarks and waved to other officers who, like themselves, were driving about with girls beside them.

'None of the other girls is as striking as ours!' Hartley spared a moment from guiding the horses. They were travelling at a spanking pace for city streets. 'Look, there's old Fortesque-Brown! He's been here six months, and that's the first time he's ever squired a woman.'

'How long have you been here?' asked Anita.

'Only a month.'

'Oh, Bridie,' she sighed, taking hold of her hand and whispering. 'Isn't it good to be out on our own with no one to tell us what we must do?'

Bridie agreed. It had all happened so quickly that she hadn't even thought of whether it was the right way to go on. Still, there were two of them, and it was broad daylight. She dismissed from her mind the idea that it would not have been possible to go on like this in Ireland. It wasn't Ireland, and she was managing her own life: no brothers to nag her, no mother to advise.

When they reached the Champ de Mars and hitched the horses to wait for them, Bridie was amazed at its size. Why, it was like a large park, and the promenade place surrounded the huge square where Hartley said the exercises and the drilling took place.

There was no drilling that afternoon, but a military band was playing some very stirring music. They were all in kilts with red jackets, and there were two of them with bagpipes. Not Irish bagpipes such as Bridie was familiar with, but bigger versions of the same. Anita put her hands over her ears and complained of the piercing skirl, but Bridie stood stock-still—transported to home.

Hartley pulled at her wrist. 'We must walk, and smile Hallo to our friends.'

'I've no friends here,' Bridie protested, but she walked on just the same.

'We'll make you known to some,' Hartley assured her, tucking her hand into his arm. 'The others in the regiment are a friendly lot, and they're all out with their girls.'

He was as good as his word, and did introduce them to several. Some of the girls were French, some English. All were well dressed and spoke nicely to them. It was good, Bridie reflected, to have two languages at her tongue's end. She even found herself translating for Hartley's benefit, for his French was not as fluent as hers.

The promenading seemed to take place in two directions, so that people actually did meet and sometimes stop to talk in little groups. It was very pleasant indeed, and Bridie was quick to tell Hartley how much she was enjoying it.

He smiled down at her and held her hand tight. 'Wait till the winter, and the picnics and dances. We'll have a fine time! It's great to have a friend like you who understands that soldiers love to play and need company —female company . . .' He broke off as he forgot to look where he was going and collided with a smart couple conversing in French.

Bridie looked up with a start. It was Monsieur Alphonse—with a girl.

'*Bonjour,*' she stammered. '*Bonjour*, Monsieur Alphonse.' She could not take her eyes off the girl. Black haired, brown eyed, wrapped in furs, she was smiling up at him as if she might eat him, her tongue licking the tip of her top lip.

'I didn't expect to see you here, Mademoiselle Langton,' Alphonse said.

'No,' said Bridie. 'Nor I you.' She recovered enough of her composure to introduce her companion.

Alphonse hesitated, and she wondered if he meant to make the girl he was with known to them. 'This is Gabrielle Truteau. Bridget Langton, Lieutenant Brooke.' He was formal, if not welcoming.

Gabrielle acknowledged Hartley's bow with a gracious smile. She nodded briefly to Bridie. 'Nice to meet you.' She spoke in English, but there was no smile for the Irish girl.

'Are you two old acquaintances?' Alphonse asked Hartley.

'No,' he replied, 'but we are friends just the same. I've been in Montreal only a month, but I'm enjoying the experience. There are so many pretty girls—as you, too, seem to have found.' He smiled at Gabrielle. 'I suppose it's because there are so many French beauties. And they all speak such good English!'

'My English is not so very good,' Gabrielle protested, her dimples very much in evidence, 'But it is kind of you to say it is.'

Indeed, to Bridie's ears, Gabrielle's English was very careful and very stilted. She didn't say so, of course. She was too busy wondering what Alphonse was thinking about her presence here with the Lieutenant. Why had she not told him about the officers the other night?

'I see young Anita Beaupré is here with a British officer, too,' Alphonse remarked to Bridie.

'Yes, so she is,' she managed to reply without offering any explanations. Let him think what he would!

'That's your doing, is it?'

'What makes you think that?'

'It hardly seems likely that a child of Anita's age and inexperience would have met such a one on her own.'

'Anita's fifteen. She's small for her age.'

'And a young fifteen—not schooled in the ways of the world.'

'And I am, I suppose! Is that what you're meaning?' Bridie was glaring at Alphonse, who was looking down at her with a disdainful expression.

She felt Hartley's hand on her arm, and knew that he and Gabrielle were regarding her in some astonishment. Hot words trembled on Bridie's lips. The only experience she had had as a woman of the world was Alphonse's own suggestion of ten days ago. She wanted to throw that information at him, but bit her tongue just in time; she wouldn't let him spoil her afternoon. 'So nice to have met you,' she said stiffly to Alphonse, and tucking her hand into Hartley's arm, she added, 'isn't

that Adèle over there with her friend? We must go and
speak to her.'

Hartley looked for a moment as though he might not
be ready to leave. His eyes lingered on Gabrielle, but as
Bridie exerted considerable force, almost pushing him
forward, he was obliged to go with her unless he wanted
to release her hold.

'Dash it all, Bridie,' he protested, managing after a
few yards to disengage himself. 'What's the hurry? A
chap likes to stand and talk—that's what the promenading is for. Besides, she was a right corker of a girl! Did
you ever see anything like her dimples?'

'No,' said Bridie. 'Never. And I've never seen anything like the furs she was wearing. What kind of fur
might that be, so soft round her face?'

'Fox. I'm sure it was fox, but that was only the collar
and the bonnet. The coat might have been beaver. I've
seen coats like that in the Hudson Bay Company's shop.'

'It looked expensive,' said Bridie.

Hartley laughed. 'It is expensive! I expect her father is
a wealthy man. Is the man she was with wealthy too?'

'Why? How should I know?'

'He'd need to be, to provide such furs. Don't you
know him well? You seemed to be well acquainted with
him. Who is this Monsieur Alphonse?'

'Just someone I know.'

Hartley stopped where he was in the middle of the
path and forced Bridie to face him by holding both her
hands. 'How do you know him?'

Bridie didn't know how to answer. She couldn't tell
him the truth, not when she was sworn to secrecy. Nor
did she want to tell him that Alphonse had supplied the
money for her to set up shop. What was she to say? She
had to make up a story he would accept—as close to the
truth as she could. She only hoped the tell-tale colour
wasn't rising in her cheeks as she looked at the fair
officer.

'Monsieur Alphonse is a business man. My brother
was after doing him a grand favour, and didn't he help

him start off the shop in return?' Her tongue nearly tripped over itself.

'Your brother Paddy, you mean? The one you called out for that night in the shop—the one who picked up the potatoes later on?'

'The very one! Fancy you remembering his name all this long time.'

'Not such a long time. I'm good about names. I'll have to meet this Paddy. What's he like?'

'He's a grand fellow, is Paddy. Big and tall, with black hair and blue eyes; but he leaves most of the work to me and Adèle.'

'Just like an Irishman! I'll have to meet him, just the same.'

'Of course you will,' agreed Bridie, wondering how her inventive tongue had trapped her in this tangle. She crossed her fingers, telling herself it wasn't such a lie after all she almost believed in him. Ah, if only Patrick were here! If he had been, instead of safely in Ireland, he would have seen the sense of handing over Pegeen's twins. As it was, he had replied to her letter about them, telling of his concern and wanting to know who they favoured—had they red hair or black? Bridie had searched her mind what to tell him. They'd both been bald at birth.

Again she tucked her hand into Hartley's arm. 'Let's walk on,' she suggested. 'The music of the band is telling my feet they must move to it.'

'The Highlanders are always like that.' Hartley began to march in time with the tune.

Thankfully she matched her steps to his, laughing because she had to lengthen her stride. But if she thought Hartley was going to leave the subject of Alphonse, she was mistaken.

'Does this Monsieur Alphonse have a lot to do with the Hot Potato?' he asked, as they marched.

'He does have an interest in it.'

'Does he come round often to check up?'

'He doesn't come every day—if that's what you're

meaning—but he looks at the books. Paddy's not too grand at the figures.'

'Does he have much to do with you?'

'Not very much.' Bridie crossed her fingers again, amending her words to herself: 'Not as much as he'd like.' She didn't say it aloud. Besides, it wasn't true, else he would not have had that Gabrielle Truteau with him, would he? Would he have promenaded her around the Champ de Mars if she had been willing to his wishes? She rubbed her mouth. She still felt the mark of his lips there, turning her weak.

'You spoke to him as if you didn't like him very much. He didn't seem to like you much, either!'

'I'm not sure that he does.'

'Does it matter?'

'It makes it difficult with Paddy. He won't be hearing a word against him.'

'Is there a word you could say against him?'

Bridie bit her tongue; she'd have to be careful. 'He's always giving advice.'

'Advice to you?'

'To Paddy or me—it's all the one thing.' She managed to smile. 'There's no need for you to be bothering with my troubles. They'll come right in the end.' She doubted it herself, with all the half-truths she had been telling.

'But they are troubles. He upsets you.'

'Sometimes he does.' She was getting breathless from the pace the music set—breathless and bothered. She didn't want to go on talking about Alphonse, and they were going to meet him soon again if they kept on the path. She did not want to see the way Gabrielle looked at him—the way he might look at her. She was delighted when they caught up with Anita and Lieutenant Roberts, who were chatting with Adèle and her friend.

More introductions followed, and Bridie pretended to be looking the other way when Alphonse and his companion passed all of them. But she could not resist giving Gabrielle's bonnet a quick glance from the back. With such a confection, any girl would look great. Ah, if she had some money to spend on clothes . . . But she did—or at any rate she would soon, the way things were going.

Clothes—that's all she can talk about, Adèle thought sourly as she sat by the fire with Bridie that evening in the little upstairs parlour. She doesn't want to tell me how she arranged things so that Anita would go with the officers this afternoon—and not I. I'll not talk of it either. Just the same, the idea rankled, however hard she tried not to let it.

'The fair one wants to meet your brother, doesn't he?' she asked softly. She saw with a sigh of satisfaction that Bridie's attention was brought away from the new frock she was planning.

'Hartley is the fair one. I don't know what I can do. Just keep them apart.'

Adèle finished another row of her knitting. 'You could tell him the truth.'

'I can't—not now.'

'Why not?'

Bridie looked away from her. Adèle knew she was making her uncomfortable, and was glad. It had something to do with Monsieur Alphonse. If only she knew what that was! She thought of bringing the conversation round to him, and decided not to. The Irish girl could be very stubborn when he was mentioned. But there was something between them; Adèle was sure of that. She had only to wait to find out. She'd be patient—and quiet. Bridie would give herself away, one of these days. She'd trip over her tongue the way she had over Paddy. Fancy anyone fool enough to invent a brother, and then to believe he was there and keep talking about him! Maybe something could be done about that. There were a lot of poor Irishmen around Montreal. One of them might be prevailed upon to turn fantasy into seeming fact. Adèle toyed with the idea, turning it over in her mind. She didn't know any Irishmen, but if there were a man of her own race near at hand, Bridie might get interested in him. She might rely more and more on herself. It would be surprising if she didn't marry. She was a pretty girl, and marriage would surely mean the end of her shopkeeping. Adèle began to see herself as the natural heir to managing the Hot Potato.

She pulled herself up short. It was Bridie's shop, but, just the same . . . No, it was wrong to covet! And it was wrong, too, for them to have excluded her from the outing this afternoon. She hadn't been taken in by the fuss they had made over her and her friend Hortense. Hortense had been foolish enough to think they were being friendly and pleasant, but she herself knew better. They had been trying to butter her up, to stop her asking awkward questions. She had seen through them. That Vivian—the dark one she had thought had liked her —she had seen the way he looked at Anita. She was only a child.

Adèle went on with her knitting, her mouth a straight line. Let Bridie watch out!

Alphonse called on the next Friday. It was his habit to come in at least once a week and inspect the book of expenses and profits. Adèle fetched it for him, and he and Bridie retired to the table in the back kitchen to study it.

'What have you told Adèle about why I take such an interest in you?' he asked.

Bridie toyed with a pencil. 'I haven't told her anything.' Her reply was equally low. Even if Adèle was straining her ears, she couldn't possibly hear. 'What should I tell her?'

'Has she asked you anything?'

'Not really, but she hints around the subject. I just change it.'

'Good.' He opened the book without looking at it. 'It might be best to let her know you pay the rent.'

'Is that for the sake of your reputation, or mine?' Bridie wondered why the subject was important suddenly.

'Yours,' he told her impatiently. 'How can it matter to me?'

To Bridie's eyes he looked angry. 'They might talk about it in your family.' She might have added that Gabrielle Truteau might, as well!

'They don't know anything about it. In any case, why should they care?'

Bridie didn't answer that. If any of the Duvaliers heard about it, they would just think he was doing it for her favours. 'What should I tell Adèle?' She went back to the original subject.

'Why, just that I'm helping you because you're new to the country—because you're so young. I'm sure you'll be able to think up some story. Anyone who can invent a brother shouldn't have much trouble.'

She coloured hotly. Why did everyone tease her about the non-existent Paddy? She took the ledger from him and opened it at the current page. 'Just take a look and see how well we're doing. It's the *patates frites* and the doughnuts that are bringing in the money.'

Alphonse studied the entries. 'It's going very well,' he conceded.

'I've a mind to try apple turnovers and apple pie,' Bridie confided. 'And perhaps sausages at lunch-time.'

'Go slowly,' he cautioned. 'Don't overstep yourself. Something that didn't sell immediately could turn profit into loss.'

'Yes.' She couldn't understand why he was always so careful in his advice. If she listened to him, she would never try anything! 'I'm doing well. You've said so yourself.'

'I'm only speaking for your own good.'

'Are you?' She felt mutinous. 'You could admit that I've surprised you.'

'It's early days yet.' He closed the book with a snap. 'While I'm here, there's something else we must talk about.'

'Something else for my own good?'

'Yes. I don't know why you should sound angry. You don't even know what it is yet.'

'Say it, then!' Bridie was defiant. 'There's nothing so full of righteousness as a body who thinks he knows best.' She knew she was provoking him, but she didn't care.

Alphonse looked as if he might hit her. He raised his hand, then put it carefully down so that it lay clenched in a fist on the table. 'I won't let you provoke me—it must be said. I don't know where you found those two officers you introduced to me on Sunday. I don't suppose for a minute you had a proper introduction to them or know anything at all about them?'

'I know that I like them,' Bridie interposed, as he drew breath to go on. 'They treat me like a lady.'

His laugh was scornful. 'That's hardly the reputation officers have! You'd be wise to have done with them before your reputation's tarnished.'

'You mean one or both of them might make me an offer.' She was incensed at his high-handedness. 'Like you did,' she added softly. 'Take care, it might be a better one!'

Alphonse's fist unclenched and reclenched. 'I suppose I deserved that.'

'Yes, you did.' There! That showed him she didn't care about Gabrielle Truteau. She wasn't sure how it showed him.

'Don't do it, Bridget. Don't go on seeing them. Think of your family. They brought you up to be a respectable girl.'

'I have no family,' she pointed out. 'You saw to that. You don't even bother to tell me how the twins are.'

'Does it matter to you?'

'Yes, it does. I haven't forgotten them—perhaps I never shall.'

'What do you want to know about them?' His voice softened only fractionally. 'They're well, and they're thriving.'

'Have they red hair or black?'

The question seemed to take him by surprise.

'Neither. They're fair—like Marie-Rose.' He unclenched his fist and would have taken one of her hands
which rested on the table, except that she removed it
when she saw his intention. She didn't want to know that
they were light-haired, like Marie-Rose. She wanted to
cry out that Marie-Rose wasn't their mother, but that
wasn't fair. It had been her own choice.

As if sensing the chaos of her feelings, he rose to his
feet. 'Bridget, promise me at least to think over what
I've said. I've no power to make you do what I will. Your
own good sense must prevail.'

Because he didn't press her any further, Bridie felt her
defiance slipping away. She looked up at him. 'I'll be
thinking it over,' she murmured, finding kindness in his
eyes, and concern too.

'See that you do! And another thing you might remember. Anita Beaupré is too young to go out with
soldiers. At least think of her. Don't include her in your
outings.' He put his hands on her shoulders.

Bridie wanted to go on arguing, but the touch of his
hand made her want to please him. Did he touch
Gabrielle Truteau in this fashion, give her unasked-for
advice? She bit her lip, and shrugged his fingers away as
she, too, stood up. He didn't think of her. He thought of
Anita—and of Gabrielle Truteau. Now she knew
exactly what her position was. She was her own woman.
She must remember that. She was free to do as she
chose—and she chose to go on seeing the two British
officers. Let Alphonse just wait and see! She didn't
bother to follow him into the shop, but fetched some
apples and flour. Apple turnovers would sell—she knew
they would. Whatever else, Gabrielle Truteau couldn't
make apple turnovers like she did! She took pleasure in
telling herself that as she pounded the dough with her
rolling-pin.

CHAPTER TEN

BRIDIE OFTEN WISHED she could share the news from Ireland with someone. She re-read her brother's letter, sitting at the kitchen table in that short unbusy time of the afternoon she looked forward to, drinking hot soup. Ah, but it was cosy here, with Adèle minding the shop.

Patrick had written that things were a little better with him and Michael. Hugh Prendergast had given them some wheat-seed back in the spring for a few days' work they had done for him. They had planted it, and when it had been harvested it had brought them in enough to manage on for the winter. The potato crop had failed again with their neighbours, and more of them were leaving the land. Big tracts of it were lying useless. Hugh was buying up great pieces of it, but wasn't that just like him and his luck? They still talked of Maling and Pegeen, and Hugh and his Mam always asked for word of the babies.

Why did Bridie mention only French people in her letters? There must be some nice Irish families she could make friends with. They couldn't all have died of the terrible ship-fever.

They wondered how Bridie had started a shop of her own and how she was managing. Did she go to church regularly, and wasn't it good fortune she had learned French so quickly?

Bridie smiled at that bit. It hadn't seemed all that quick to her. She would have to make Patrick see that things were different here. She knew only French people. She sighed as she thought of the Irish. So many of them had died in the fever-sheds in Goose Village —some said as many as five thousand. Why, only last week she had heard that Father Mulcahey had died of the fever he had caught from nursing the victims. She

had cried at that news. He had been one of the last to
suffer, for the port of Montreal was closed for the winter
and there wouldn't be any more ships arriving till the
spring.

She would tell her brothers about the snow when she
wrote next. It had snowed for two days and two nights,
and everywhere was blanketed with it. The boys from
the livery stable had helped her and Adèle to shovel it
from the path in front so that people could find their way
to the shop.

'What you need is a man about the place,' the lad, Jim,
had told her. 'I'd come myself, but I've a job with a
builder for inside work. I start next week.'

'Do you know of anyone?' Bridie had asked him.
'Mind, it'd need to be someone honest—and agreeable.
Maybe someone Irish like myself. There must be lots of
them willing to work.' Jim had promised to ask around.
She might tell her brother of that.

She was roused from her reverie by the sound of
voices. Adèle called to her, and she put her feet down
from the chair where they rested, and walked into the
shop.

Adèle was behind the counter, and a man in thread-
bare clothes stood warming his hands by the stove. He
wore faded overalls, and a checked woollen shirt that
had once been red and now was faded nearly to pink. His
black jacket was thin and several sizes too large for him.
It matched the colour of his hair. His eyes were very
blue, his face parchment white and pinched-looking.
With something of a shock, she realised he was a young
man, probably in his middle twenties. When he'd had
flesh on his bones, he must have been a handsome
fellow.

'He says he's looking for work,' said Adèle. 'Jim
didn't send him. He liked the sign on the door.'

Bridie didn't take her eyes from the stranger. 'Where
are you from?'

'Killarney,' was the reply. 'I'm Irish, too.'

Bridie hesitated. She could see for herself that he

needed work, but he didn't look strong enough to hold a shovel or bring in loads of wood or potatoes.'

'What's your name?'

'Paddy—Patrick O'Leary.'

She drew in her breath, and heard Adèle exclaim, 'Is it a sign?'

'A sign of what?' He swung round to the French girl.

'A sign that you're meant for us.' Adèle crossed herself.

Bridie looked at her in some surprise. Was Adèle seriously thinking that this scarecrow might take the place of the imaginary Paddy? The Paddy she called to had become almost real; he was big and strong. This one was neither, and she knew nothing about him. 'Is there anyone to say you've a decent character—honest and that?' It might be better to give him a plate of *patates frites* and a bowl of onion soup, and then let him go.

'Who could be saying?' he countered with another question. 'I've not been here long—and most of that time I've been in the fever-sheds. They say I'm one of the lucky ones: I've lived through it. But where's the luck in it? I've nothing and nobody, only the clothes I stand up in. My two brothers came with me but they died, and if I don't get work soon, I'll be joining them. The cold is fierce, and I've never seen the like of the snow.'

Bridie nodded her head. Of course she felt sorry for him, but she wanted an able-bodied man.

He must have sensed her doubts, for he turned to Adèle again. 'I'll soon get back my strength with some food inside me. You look like you've a heart under that apron.' He smiled at her. 'Where's the chap you work for? Put in a good word for me, and you'll not be sorry. Let me see the gaffer.'

Adèle might have been a simpering milkmaid for the smile she gave him in return, Bridie thought to herself, as she said, 'I'm the gaffer! It's my shop.'

He swung back to face her. 'Give me work? For the love of the saints you pray to. I'll not last without work.'

Still Bridie hesitated. She couldn't deny being moved by his plea, but she could well imagine what Alphonse might say.

'We could try him for a week or two,' Adèle suggested. 'If you're willing. At least he would have a few meals inside him.'

Bridie wavered. It wasn't like Adèle to be soft-hearted. 'There's snow to be shovelled, sacks to be hefted, wood for the stoves—could you do it?'

'I could.' This time the smile was directed at her. It lit up the whole of his face, made her notice again the blue of his eyes. When he was well, his black hair might shine again, his face fill out.

'I don't know what you'd expect to be paid.' She knew she had given in.

'Two dollars a week,' suggested Adèle, 'and his food.'

'I suppose that would be fair,' Bridie agreed. 'In the first week you'll eat double that figure! When can you start?'

'Right away.' Paddy twisted a disreputable cap in his hands. 'Would I lodge here?'

Bridie shook her head. She didn't want a complete stranger here to live. Besides, there was no room for him. She told Adèle so in French, asking her why she was so determined to help him.

Adèle replied that she didn't know, but she thought he was right for them. His name was Paddy, after all!

Paddy spoke up, and addressed Bridie. 'How long did it take you to speak French like that?'

'A few months.' She recalled that they had been a very intensive few months.

'I can do the same, if you help me.'

That decided Bridie. At least he was willing, and he spoke confidently and politely. 'Take him to the kitchen, Adèle, and give him something to eat. Then he can bring in some wood.' Maybe it would work out, she told herself as she patted the pocket with her brother's letter. 'He can start tomorrow.'

'After that,' offered Adèle, 'I could take him to the Widow Mulvaney's. She rents rooms quite cheaply.'

'Yes,' agreed Bridie. 'He might as well be near. You haven't any place, have you?'

That being established, Adèle took him to the kitchen and ladled out soup, gave him bread and a baked potato. When she had fed him, she took him out the back way to arrange about a room.

First thing the next morning, he was waiting at the back door, offering to clean the fires or peel the potatoes. His appearance improved dramatically in just a few days. His cheeks lost their grey look, and he began to put on weight. Bridie told herself it was no wonder, for he ate enough for three! She couldn't begrudge him the food, but she couldn't get over her feeling of wariness, try as she might. He slipped very easily into the role of 'Paddy in the back', and the customers never questioned his presence.

The two British lieutenants, Hartley Brooke and Vivian Roberts were delighted to see him. In fact, Hartley shook him by the hand. 'I'm pleased to meet you at last, Paddy. I'd have known you anywhere! Bridget's the image of you—same blue eyes, same black hair.'

'Pleased to meet you, I'm sure.' Paddy didn't appear surprised, but his eyes danced as he looked to Bridie. From his side of the counter he measured out two orders of *patates frites*. 'You'll be wanting to try these, if you haven't before. They're our speciality.'

While the two officers were tasting the free sample, he sidled over to Bridie. 'Who am I supposed to be?' he whispered.

'My brother,' she murmured back. 'I'll be explaining later.'

He put his arm round her waist. 'I couldn't ask for a lovelier sister!'

She slid away from him. She was grateful, just the same, that he'd been so quick-witted.

The two officers were full of plans. 'We've bought a sleigh and a horse between us. Will you come out with us on Sunday afternoon, you and Anita? I say, these *patates frites* are really great, just the thing for the cold weather.'

When the officers had left, she explained matters to Paddy. 'The way of it was, we had no man about the place, so I invented a brother, and when rough-looking customers came in I called out to him in the back, "Paddy, fetch more wood" or "Paddy, we're needing the tatties"—you can see how it was. Then when you came along and looked so much like my brother Michael, it seemed as if someone was looking out for me and solving my problems—or some of them, for the British officers wanted to meet my brother . . .'

She stopped for breath, and Paddy supplied, 'Else they'd wonder how you came about owning a shop—and what sort of a creature you were.' He winked at her. It wasn't quite the way she would have put it, but he went on, 'I'm not minding having a sister. You can take the place of the family I've lost, for if you hadn't taken me in, I'd have been with the others under the snow.'

'Wait a bit, Paddy! I only gave you a job.'

'You gave me more than that. You gave me a life.' He put out his hand.

Bridie put hers in it. 'I'm glad you're here. Now I have two brothers called Paddy—one in Ireland, one here.' She put her doubts away very firmly. Perhaps she could trust this man.

Paddy kissed her cheek. 'A brother can kiss his own sister.'

It was a quick, light kiss—a brotherly kiss, Bridie told herself, but just the same she moved away. It wasn't the same as Patrick kissing her. He always grabbed her about the waist and lifted her up in the air. She wasn't going to tell Paddy that. She had better let him know that brothers and sisters in her family only kissed at partings and Christmas and the like. She told him so, and he laughed and hugged her instead.

'Things are different in the New World!'

Adèle came to the kitchen door. Her face was like

thunder. 'If you've finished the family reunion, there are customers waiting.'

Bridie hurried to serve them, and Paddy went for wood to build up the fire. She wondered if she hadn't gone from one trouble to another. She didn't want a brother who felt he was free any time to hug her or kiss her—not that she hadn't enjoyed it. It was grand, was it not, to have a friendly relative? Especially now, with Christmas just a week or so away. But still, she didn't like the way Adèle had looked.

Snow fell again all day on Saturday, but Sunday dawned bright and clear and cold. Paddy called for the two girls in the morning, and they both exclaimed at what he was wearing. He sported a navy-blue suit and a black over-coat.

'I'm buying them second-hand from my landlady, the Widow Mulvaney. She said they were her husband's, and him not long since gone and just my size, and what was the use of them hanging there lonesome? She pressed the suit, and I sponged down the coat a little. Do you like it?'

The girls circled round him. 'Don't you look dif-ferent?' Bridie was delighted. 'You're so grand and so rich.'

'What kind of payment did she want?' asked Adèle. 'The Widow Mulvaney isn't so old, and she's handsome in a hard sort of way,' she added in a sour voice.

Paddy only laughed. 'You mustn't believe all you hear about widows trapping men! She's a decent sort of body and makes me very comfortable there.'

'Yes,' said Adèle. '*Bien sûr.*'

'Oh, Adèle,' said Bridie. 'It's Sunday, and we're on our way to church. Let the two of you not be snapping at each other.'

'I was only teasing.' Adèle's voice was stiff. 'I'm sure Paddy looks very nice. Whatever he paid for his finery was well spent.'

It wasn't a very handsome apology, but Paddy made

no fuss about accepting it. He took his place confidently enough between the two girls, and offered each of them an arm to hold on to. 'It's slippery today,' he told them.

Bridie looked down at her feet in new boots, and at Paddy's. He had replaced the old tattered ones with quite a respectable pair, not entirely new, she guessed. Part of the Widow Mulvaney's bounty? The thought sprang into her mind—a result of Adèle's words, no doubt—but she didn't voice it. They walked on, and went quietly into church. When they came back, it seemed too nice to go in. They stood outside the shop, talking about the service and the people they had seen.

Adèle started it by throwing a snowball at Paddy, and then the three of them were into it, scooping up the snow, laughing and throwing it at each other like a pack of children. Adèle was quicker than either of the other two.

'Not fair!' shouted Paddy. 'You've had more practice than us.' He ran towards her again, loose snow in his hand. She evaded him, sneaking down the small alley at the side of the shop. He shot after her, laughing.

Bridie seized the opportunity to go inside. She had had enough of the snow, and lunch was cooking in the oven. She had best have a look at it, and leave Paddy to Adèle. It was nice to see her having a bit of fun.

Adèle found herself cornered by Paddy in the angle of a wall. 'No, no!' she cried out in mock alarm, as he raised his hand with the snow in it. There was no way of escaping.

He smiled at her, his blue eyes ablaze with merriment. 'Pay a forfeit and I'll spare you, otherwise it goes straight down your neck!'

Adèle shuddered. She was not really frightened, but the snow would be cold. 'What forfeit?' Paddy was very near her.

'A kiss for the snowman.' He held the loose snow over her head and let a little of it trickle out of his fingers on to her face.

She said nothing, not even when Paddy threw the ball

of snow on the ground. His arms went about her. His lips
fastened on hers. With a sigh, she returned his kiss. She
didn't ask herself why she did it. Her lips opened to him
of their own accord. There was something about this
man that called out to her. She could not deny him.
When he released her, she didn't move—couldn't move.

He stood looking down at her, his hands still at her
waist. 'Who'd have thought it?' His voice was very soft.
His fingers found a curl near her face which had freed
itself from its usual tight bun. 'You're a pretty girl,
Adèle, with your bonnet off and your hair looser.'

'Nonsense!' She couldn't meet the challenge in his
eyes. She tried to put, pat, her hair into place, but he
wouldn't let her.

'Leave it be!' He untied the ribbons of her bonnet and
took it wholly from her. Then he kissed her again. This
time it was a lighter kiss, softly lingering.

Adèle's pulses leaped; her sense almost deserted her.
She dared not touch him. 'A forfeit is only one kiss,' she
managed to whisper.

'The second is for helping me to find work in the shop.
I'll never forget it was you changed Bridget's mind. Can
I be asking you why?'

Adèle looked into his eyes. 'I liked the look of
you.'

'Never! I was a poor, starved wretch, so desperate
when I first entered the shop that I might have pushed
you aside and taken the money just under the counter.'

Adèle shivered. She wasn't sure she liked such
honesty. 'But you didn't.'

'You cried out for Bridget, and she came straight
away. The moment passed.'

'You saw Bridie—that's what it was.' She tried to
stifle her jealousy. 'She's beautiful.'

'She's like every other Irish girl, but you've more to
you than she has. You're fire. She's water.' He didn't
touch her, but his voice was a caress.

Adèle began to be a little afraid—afraid of herself. On
first sight, she had not been attracted to Paddy. She had

supported his plea for work because she saw the possibilities for herself in having an Irishman for Bridie, but it didn't seem to be working out that way. She found she had no wish to think of Bridie and Paddy together. She was roused and excited. She had never felt like this about any man.

He spoiled the moment for her by asking a question. 'Someone must have put up the money for Bridie's wee shop. Would you tell me who would have done such a thing?'

'How would I know?' she snapped at him, and slipped from her position in the corner. She began to walk down the way she had come.

He followed her, tugging at her sleeve. 'Don't be angry, Adèle! I asked only because I've a hankering for setting up on my own, and I'll need backing.'

She stopped. That made sense. 'We'll talk about it another time, perhaps. She'll be wondering where we are. She's going out this afternoon with the officers.'

'And you're meeting your friend. I heard you say so.' He took her arm and began to walk with her, very close to her, because the alley was narrow. 'I expect you'll be back before Bridie is.'

'Maybe.'

'If you should be, we could share a cup of tea and an apple turnover,' he suggested. 'No one would be any wiser. There'd be just the two of us by the fire in the kitchen.'

They came out into the street, and Adèle hesitated. Things were moving too fast.

'You know she won't be home till late, and Anita's going too.'

Yes, Anita had been invited as well, and she felt that was unfair. 'All right,' she conceded. 'I'll see if I can get rid of my friend early. I'm not promising—but I'll see.'

Paddy patted her hand. 'Till this afternoon.' They both went into the shop.

*   *   *

Just before the two lieutenants were due to call, Bridie received a note from Anita saying that she was sorry, but she would not be able to come. Her father had arrived unexpectedly, and was taking her home for a visit. She couldn't put him off. Bridie was disappointed. So was Vivian, when the pair of them arrived.

'Never mind,' said Hartley, his blond good looks heightened by the glow in his cheeks, 'we'll both squire Bridie! She shall have the first ride in our new sleigh with just us two.'

They were so pleased with the prospect that Bridie felt she had to go. What did it matter how it looked to anyone else? Who else was to know? She was her own mistress. She allowed them to help her up into the high-runnered red sleigh drawn up to the very door.

'Not for us those little carioles like the Montrealers use,' said Hartley.

'Nor those unkempt Canadian horses either.' Vivian pointed to the two sleek animals who pulled the vehicle, one behind the other, not in tandem as Bridie would have expected.

'It's for the narrowness of the road,' Hartley explained as he cracked the whip over their backs, and the sleigh sprang forward. Bridie commented upon the luxurious robes over her knees.

'Bear and buffalo skins,' Vivian informed her. 'You'll be surprised how warm you'll feel.' And indeed it was very cosy, as they sped over the snow.

To her eyes, moving out as they now were among the snow-covered fields was a little like putting out to sea from Ireland had been. Perhaps it was because of the vastness of the sky and the beauty of the landscape. Only white cottages and the solitary gigantic tree marked its surface. The horses pranced along in their handsome harness-trappings from which bells jangled, and there were other sleighs about that now and then came close enough for waves and greetings. The whole garrison seemed to have taken to the roads.

Bridie sat happily between Hartley and Vivian, her

hands under the fur robes for warmth, for she had only woollen mitts. It was grand to be alive, and to be with such good companions. The afternoon passed so quickly that she was astonished when darkness began to fall and it got much colder.

'Paddy'll be expecting me home,' she told them. 'He is careful, and doesn't like me being too late back.' She took pleasure in saying it.

'Very proper,' Vivian agreed. 'But he looked a reasonable chap. He'll understand that you'll be all right with us.'

'I'm glad we met him at last,' Hartley added. 'You're very alike in your looks. It's good for a girl to have some family around her. He's lucky that the shop belongs to him. It seems to be doing very well.'

Bridie bit her tongue to prevent herself from contradicting him about the ownership of the shop: she had said it was Paddy's. Wasn't it hard, though, to be always remembering about how people felt about women in business? 'Yes, it's doing well,' she agreed. 'Paddy wants to put more tables and chairs in it and let folk eat there in peace.'

'Quite a good idea,' agreed Vivian. 'People like a bit of comfort. Are you quite warm enough in the rugs?'

Bridie assured him that she was, and they turned for home. At first they travelled at an easy pace, but it was a corner taken too fast that was their undoing. Before Bridie was really aware of disaster, she found herself sliding, slithering, knocked hard against Hartley as the sleigh overturned. Then she was thrown out into a snowbank, so heavy and clinging that she sank into it face first and fought for her breath.

Mother of God, could she be suffocating in snow? She knew her arms were flailing wildly and her legs were immovable. She was going—she was drowning! Silently she screamed for help.

She could see nothing. She could hear nothing. She was going to die! She could not prevent the approach of

CHAPTER ELEVEN

PADDY HAD THE tea brewing when Adèle returned to the Hot Potato, letting herself in by the back door. She took off her boots and her bonnet. It was good to be in the warmth of the kitchen, for she was cold and tired from battling the new fall of snow. Her friend had hurried home. There had been no need to suggest anything else.

Paddy waited on her, pouring tea, insisting she sit close to the heat. He was so normal, so friendly, that she began to relax, and to bite into her pastry. Her hair was wet from the snow, and once again it had escaped from its moorings. She didn't mind that it curled round her face.

In the soft light of the gas-lamp, he helped himself to another turnover. 'You're grand cooks—both you girls!'

Adèle toasted her feet. Feeling was coming back to them, and she curled her toes as it did, holding them up to the heat.

'What elegant feet you have, and neat ankles.' Paddy surveyed them from the other side of the table. 'I like a girl with good limbs.'

Adèle let her skirt fall over her toes.

'Don't cover them up.' Paddy knelt at her feet, and started to massage them.

His touch was soothing and surprisingly gentle. It was very pleasant. Really there was nothing to fear about being here with no one but him; they had been alone in the shop many a time. 'Bridie'll be late, with all this snow falling.' She didn't envy her, out in a sleigh, trying to find the way home. 'If Monsieur Alphonse hears of it, he'll be cross with her again,' she went on without thinking about what she was saying.

'Who's Monsieur Alphonse?' Paddy looked up from kneading her feet.

'Just a friend of hers.' She bit her lip. She hadn't intended to let Paddy know right away like that, but where was the harm? He would know soon enough, with Alphonse visiting the place.

'What sort of a friend?' Paddy pulled up a chair, and sat down with Adèle's feet on his lap.

'I'm not sure, exactly. He comes and does the accounts with her. He hired me—but she pays me.'

'Ah-ha!' Paddy tickled the sole of her foot, sending delicious sensations up her leg. She half thought of taking her foot away, but it was so comfortable.

'Did he put up the money?'

'He must have. Where would she get it? But I don't understand why. He doesn't take her out. She doesn't meet him anywhere. They aren't lovers, I'm sure of that.'

'Then why would he help her?' Paddy tickled the other foot.

'I don't know. It's a mystery.'

Paddy shrugged, and his hand stole to her ankle, and then to her calf. 'Let's not be bothering with mysteries that don't concern us.' His hand had swung the length of her dress away from her legs. He leaned forward and kissed her knee. 'Ah, Adèle, you drive a man wild!'

She knew she should protest, should put her feet to the floor and tell him to leave. She wavered, and his hand circled her waist as he dropped to the floor before her, his head on her lap. Her hand touched the blackness of his hair, and stroked it. All the pent-up longing of her heart and her body seemed to explode, and she wanted him to take her, did not repel him when he pulled her towards him. He was life, and she was ready for living and for loving. There was no one to disturb them.

He sat astride a chair and entered her quickly, his hand on her breast, his lips on her mouth.

She shuddered in rapture and freed her breast from the buttoned bodice of her dress to the caress of his

tongue, and then the soft bite of his teeth. She was
drowning in passion and in pleasure, and crying out his
name. He wasn't Bridie's Irishman. He was hers!

It was Alphonse who pulled Bridie clear. His was the
face bending over her as she opened her eyes, gasping
for breath. She didn't ask how he came to be there; it was
enough that he was. She couldn't see the expression on
his face, for it was dark and he was blocking whatever
light there was from the lamp on his sleigh. He was
holding her to him and shaking her as if to force life into
her.

'Just breathe deep, *ma chère*. You're safe now.' She
heard his voice from a great distance, and tried to do as
he said. What had he called her? *Ma chère*—my dear.
No, she couldn't have heard aright. But he was holding
her, stroking her hair, and she closed her eyes. If this was
a dream, she wanted it to go on. She became conscious
of screaming, and stirred, and looked up.

'It's the horses,' Alphonse told her. He took a flask
from his pocket and made her drink from it.

She let the fiery liquid trickle down her throat. She
started to cough and to beat at the air with her hands.
Her legs moved, too.

'Good!' He made her swallow again. Then he lifted
her and carried her to his sleigh. 'Here, Gabrielle, cover
her up. She's had a bad shock.'

Gabrielle tucked furs round her, and propped her
against the hard wood.

Bridie was like a rag doll, with no strength in her
limbs. She heard the girl exclaiming over her, but she
was only aware that Alphonse had disappeared. She
struggled to see him. 'Where's he gone?' They were the
first words she managed to whisper.

'To help the other two to free the horses. The dark
officer seems to be hurt. I can see blood on the snow.
Young fools, that's what Alphonse called them. He
seemed to know what was going to happen. We've been
following you for a while, and could have passed you,

but Alphonse held back. It's a good thing for you that he did.'

'Yes,' Bridie croaked. 'A very good thing!'

She watched the struggle to get the horses on their feet. They were tangled in the reins and the harness. Alphonse slashed them free with a knife, and they scrambled clear after all three men had pushed at them. They appeared to be unhurt, but stood trembling until the two lieutenants began to walk them up and down.

Alphonse was inspecting the sleigh. 'We'll never right it. You'll have to leave it. Is one of you able to ride bareback? We're not very far from the town.'

In a very short time the whole thing was organised. Hartley agreed to deal with the horses, and Vivian was bundled into Alphonse's sleigh and the cut on his head bandaged with Gabrielle's scarf.

'It's not very deep,' Alphonse assured him. 'But we'll drop you off at the doctor, just the same. You've lost a fair amount of blood, and he'll probably want to stitch it.'

Vivian slumped into the far corner of the open four-seater sleigh. Gabrielle offered him the brandy flask. He took a deep draught, and then fell immediately asleep.

'Leave him,' Alphonse instructed, and took hold of the reins. He had only one horse to pull all four of them, and it looked too small for the task. Their pace was slow, and Hartley followed behind, riding one horse and leading the other.

If Vivian was allowed to sleep, Bridie wasn't. Gabrielle, under Alphonse's instructions, rubbed her hands, removed her boots to make sure her feet hadn't frozen, gave her more brandy, and finally was ordered to talk to her.

'What shall I talk about?' Gabrielle wailed. 'I don't even know her.'

'What difference does that make? Tell her where you've been, what you do. Ask her where she's been —whatever girls talk about. Most of the time, *she* doesn't stop talking!'

'You sound as if you know her very well.'

Bridie was beginning to be interested in this exchange. More than a little influenced by the generosity of the helping from Alphonse's flask, she entered the conversation. 'Of course he knows me,' she asserted. 'And I know him. We're nearly relatives.'

'Nearly relatives?' Gabrielle's careful English questioned this statement. 'What does that mean?'

'You'll have to be asking him, for it's a secret between us.' She raised her finger to her lips. 'Perhaps he'll tell you.'

'How much of that liquor did you give her, Gaby?' Alphonse did not take his eyes from the horse.

'As much as she'd take.' Her voice was sulky. 'What's this secret you have with her?'

'I'll tell you about it some other time. Look, Bridie's closed her eyes. Shake her, keep her awake.'

'Why does she have to be kept awake while the soldier sleeps?' Gabrielle sounded sulky.

'Because he has a head wound—he mustn't be touched. She was buried in the snow. She'll keep warmer if she's awake.'

Gabrielle shook Bridie with considerable force. 'Keep your eyes open, or I'll slap you as well! I'll tell you where I've been,' she said in rapid French. 'I've been to visit Alphonse's family—his brother and his wife. They're staying with her father, who has a big farm at the end of this road. They're going to be there until after Christmas. They've brought the twins, for the old man dotes on them. He's always trying to persuade Marie-Rose to bring them out into the healthy air of the country.'

Bridie closed her eyes in involuntary pain. This girl was allowed to see the twins. She was brought by Alphonse to visit them. A hard slap on either cheek jerked her eyes open. She looked into Gabrielle's eyes, eyes with more than a trace of malice in them. 'Keep awake—that's what he said. I warned you I'd slap you!'

Bridie raised her mittened hands to her cheeks; she had been stung into soberness. 'I wasn't asleep!'

Her hands were taken from her face, and forced under the fur robes.

'There was no need to be so fierce,' Alphonse protested.

'You said to keep her awake! I did what you told me.'

'*Chérie*, be a little gentler. The girl's had a shock, and doesn't know whether she's on her head or her heels.'

'*Bien,*' said Gabrielle. 'Perhaps I was a little too fierce. She's not very big, is she?' She smiled at Alphonse, then looked down at Bridie. 'What shall we talk about? Marie-Rose's babies? Every girl exclaims over babies. Are you different from the rest of us?'

'No different,' Bridie agreed. If this girl wanted to talk about babies, she was more than willing to hear about the twins. 'What are they like, these—these twins?'

'Very fair, and getting very fat. They're nearly sitting up, and Jean smiles at everybody. He adores his grand-father. Jacques hangs on to his mother, and cries when she puts him down. But why do you want to hear about them? They're nothing to you.'

Bridie felt Alphonse's eyes on her. 'No, they're nothing to me. Is it a big farm that you visited?'

'The biggest in the area, and the old man has no one to leave it to except Marie-Rose and the twins. Still, I don't suppose this can interest you very much. Or maybe it does—you said you were almost relatives.'

'That was the drink going to my head,' Bridie was quick to tell her. 'My tongue isn't used to it. How could Monsieur Alphonse and myself be relatives when I'm from Ireland and he's lived here all his life?' She felt she had better make what amends she could. She hadn't meant to give anything away. The twins' future was secure, and that was the way she meant it to continue. It seemed to be taking an interminable time to get back to Montreal. She looked around, and saw that Hartley on his horse was just visible through the snow. He must be finding it cold.

'I'm very grateful to you, Monsieur Alphonse,' she

ventured. 'I don't know what would have happened without you.'

'You'd have died in the snow! You were buried,' Gabrielle told her.

Bridie shivered, as she continued, 'Are they the same officers you were with the other Sunday on the Champ de Mars? The fair one is very handsome. How did you meet them?'

Her tone was friendly, but Bridie wasn't sure she didn't prefer it hostile. 'They came into the shop.'

'What shop?'

'My shop, the Hot Potato.'

'Oh, that shop!' Gabrielle's voice was interested. 'It's the shop where they make *patates frites*. Everyone is talking about them, but I haven't tasted them myself. Anyway'—she dismissed the subject of the Hot Potato —'these army officers came and talked to you, one supposes. Did you know them in Ireland?'

Presented with such an opening, Bridie couldn't resist taking it. 'They knew one of my brothers.' It was nearly the truth, and she consoled herself with the thought. Why should this girl be allowed to think she didn't know how to behave? Gabrielle was lucky that she didn't have to make her own way. Any man she met would be properly introduced to her by her family or friends.

'That was very fortunate for you,' said Gabrielle. 'To be taken up by an English officer must be great fun. Everyone says they have lovely parties. One of them invited me once, but my mother wouldn't let me go. She said I was too young to mingle with older men and men who had seen the world.'

'Quite right!' said Alphonse. 'Thank goodness we're nearly there. I can just about see the lights of Montreal. I think, if you're willing, Gabrielle, we'll deliver this chap to the doctor first, leave him there, and escort Bridget home next. Then we can go on to your home.'

'*Bien sûr*. I suppose the other officer will see to his friend. That seems quite agreeable.'

'Your mother won't worry?' he questioned.

'Why should she? She knows I'm with you and she has
every confidence in you, and your driving.' Gabrielle's
voice was soft.

Bridie wished suddenly she had a mother—a mother
who was waiting for her to come home—untroubled
because she was with Alphonse.

The horse, as if recognising it was on home ground,
began to go faster and it was only a few minutes before
they turned up McGill Street. They had left Hartley and
Vivian as arranged. Gas-lights were glowing in the shop
window, and as the sleigh stopped, the door opened and
Paddy stepped out with a lantern in his hand, Adèle
close behind him. Bridie did not wonder why they were
both there.

'Thank Heaven you're back!' Adèle fussed over her as
Alphonse carried her into the shop. 'What's happened?
Where are the Englishmen?'

Paddy walked behind with Gabrielle. 'Of course you
must come in for a hot drink and a taste of our thanks!
Sure, Bridie'd never forgive her old brother if he didn't
offer you hospitality on a night such as this.'

Alphonse deposited Bridie on a chair in the warm
kitchen. 'Your brother? Since when did you have a
brother here?' He swung round to face Paddy.

Bridie was vexed. What was Paddy doing here, anyway? She was tired and cross, and she didn't want Paddy
here. She didn't want Gabrielle either. Alphonse was
waiting for an explanation. 'This is Paddy O'Leary. He
works for me now. He was just joking about being my
brother.'

Alphonse looked from one to the other of them.
'Now's not the time to talk about it. What you need is a
hot drink and your bed.'

'Yes, of course.' Adèle came to the rescue. 'I've some
soup on the boil, and there's enough for all. Just sit
down.' She waved Alphonse and Gabrielle to seats.
'Paddy was worried—as I was—when you weren't back.
We were sure something had happened.'

'Something did happen. The sleigh overturned.'

Alphonse gave his listeners a quick account of the accident as Adèle ladled out potato soup. There were exclamations of concern, and Bridie had to assure them that she was unhurt. She was wide awake now, and kept looking from Adèle to Paddy. They seemed different, more alive. No, perhaps it was her fancy because *she* felt more alive. A brush with death seemed to have that effect.

'Aren't there any *patates frites*?' Gabrielle, at least, was enjoying herself. She smiled up at Paddy.

'Not tonight, I'm afraid.' He patted her hand. 'You must come back another time. I don't even know your name.'

Introductions were quickly made, and Paddy repeated, 'Alphonse Duvalier, delighted to meet you. You're the man Bridie's to thank for the shop.'

Bridie drew in her breath sharply, and was conscious that Gabrielle did the same. They both looked to Alphonse.

He was equal to the occasion. 'There's nothing very surprising about that—nothing to thank me for. You must know that the whole French community is worried about the influx of Irish immigrants, and not enough jobs for them. A few of us got together with some of the Irish clergy, and decided to give money and advice to a small number of the newcomers who wanted to start off in business for themselves. Father Mulcahey recommended Bridget as one who might be helped.'

Bridie crossed herself. 'God rest his soul,' she muttered under her breath. Lucky that Alphonse had picked on a dead man—there'd be no asking him if it was true.

Alphonse was warming to his story. 'I wasn't too pleased to be helping a girl—and a young and pretty one at that, but Father Mulcahey seemed to think she was worth helping and he must have been right. She seems to be doing remarkably well.'

'I never heard of any such scheme,' said Gabrielle, her big dark eyes shining in the candle-light.

'Never let the right hand know what the left hand is doing,' said Paddy piously. 'Charity is best done in secret.'

'Something like that,' Alphonse agreed. 'And now, Miss Bridget, it's time for bed. Off you go. I must escort Gabrielle home, but thank you for the soup. It was delicious.'

Gabrielle pulled a face, but Bridie was glad to go upstairs with Adèle, carrying a hot brick for her comfort.

'You needn't worry about anything,' Adèle told her. 'Paddy's letting the visitors out, and we'll lock up together. You look exhausted. Sleep in in the morning, and we'll see to things.' She settled Bridie in bed, and the girl heard her run downstairs before she drifted off to sleep.

Back in the kitchen, Adèle was enfolded in Paddy's arms.

'Did you ever hear such a story?' he asked. 'There was no committee handing out money to immigrants—that's one thing I'm sure of!'

'There might have been,' she temporised. 'He had his explanation ready.' At this moment she didn't care.

'He would have, wouldn't he?' Paddy laughed, and put his mouth to her ear. He kissed it lightly. 'No, there's something between the two of them: I can feel it in the air. It's all about them, in the way he looks at her. He doesn't look at the little Gaby in the way he does at Bridie, and she's a handsome piece—that little French girl!'

Adèle stiffened in his arms.

'There's no need to be jealous,' he laughed softly. 'Her family would never consider the likes of me. But I'll tell you something—I mean to get to the bottom of it. I'm a grand one for unravelling secrets, and for turning them to my own ends.' He kissed her on either cheek lingeringly. 'And you shall help me, Adèle.'

Adèle shivered as his lips found hers. This was what she wanted, wasn't it? To be held in his embrace—to work with him. Yes, of course it was, she chided herself.

But somehow he had taken command of the situation, and that wasn't the way she had planned it. She dismissed the thought as his demanding body pressed against hers.

Christmas Eve was beautiful. The sun shone from a cloudless sky; the sun sparkled; the air was clear and pure.

Bridie had been invited to spend Christmas with Mademoiselle Beaupré and accepted with delight. Adèle was to be with her family, and Paddy had announced that he had found an old friend and was spending the holiday time with him and his wife. That had been a surprise, because Bridie had not known he had any friends in Montreal. She was beginning to think there were many surprising things about Paddy, not the least of which was his interest in her affairs.

He had said nothing the morning after the sleigh accident, but had watched when she had received a gift from Alphonse. He had exclaimed almost as much as Adèle had about the fine wool shawl she unwrapped. It was blue—the same blue as her eyes, his note said. The others were not shown it, but she treasured it as well as his expressed hope that she was quite recovered. She pushed it into her pocket, and swung the shawl over her shoulders with gentle hands. It suited her. It made her feel that he cared what happened to her. For no reason at all she couldn't stop smiling, and the feeling warmed the whole day through. She kept remembering the way he had called her *ma chère* when he had rescued her.

Paddy brought her back to earth later on by commenting that it was a sad thing for Father Mulcahey to have died so suddenly. 'Not long since, God rest the poor gentleman's soul. I suppose he was the leading spirit in the French–Irish shenanigans.'

There was no question in his voice. Just the lift of his eyebrow made her feel a shiver of uneasiness. It managed to convey the faintest trace of doubt—that, and his use of the word 'shenanigans'.

*   *   *

There was that same lift of Paddy's eyebrow when Hartley and Vivian appeared at the shop two days after the accident of their sleigh. They had brought the most enormous box of chocolates as an apology to Bridie, and an invitation to a party between Christmas and the New Year.

'The sleigh will be in tip-top form again by that time,' Hartley assured her.

'It had better be,' Viv added. 'We're paying over the odds to make sure it is! These tradesmen don't know what it is to be in a hurry. They always tell you they have more work than they can possibly get through, but it's odd how the work melts away when added cash is mentioned. Anyway, you needn't bother about it—it'll be ready. This is one of the best outings of the winter, at a hotel. I'm going to ask Anita, your little friend, if she'll do me the honour.'

'There'll be two bands,' Hartley broke in. 'I say, Bridget, that shawl is uncommonly attractive. You've a fine pair of eyes, and it's the exact same shade. You will come, won't you?'

What could Bridie do but accept such a kind invitation? She pointed out that Anita might not be able to get the time off.

Paddy, who had been standing close by, brushed that aside. 'If they won't give her the time, surely she can invent an excuse—a sick mother, or some such ploy—and can stay here the night.'

Bridie demurred. She knew Alphonse had not liked the young girl being in the company of the officers. He would be even less favourable if lying was included in the relationship. She insisted that Anita must ask permission.

'I hadn't expected you to be so strait-laced about a little deception,' Paddy told her, after Hartley and Vivian had made their farewells. 'You must know that the rich enjoy saying "No" to their servants. It's one of their ways. And isn't she too young to be going about with a harum-scarum pair like your soldiers?'

'They're hardly more than boys!' Bridie hadn't expected censure from Paddy. It stung her into saying, 'You're as bad as Monsieur Alphonse! He sees danger in every one of the regiment.'

'Does he now?' Paddy laughed softly. 'Maybe he's right. I've noticed your two cavaliers still think of me as "brother Paddy". I'm wondering why I'm still your brother to them; or do you want me to tell them otherwise, sister dear?' He put his hands on her waist and gave her a squeeze.

Maybe it was no more than a brotherly gesture, but he wasn't her brother. It made her feel uncomfortable. She didn't like the look Adèle gave her, either. Really, the pair of them were hard to live with, these days! She was always finding their eyes on her, and they said such strange things, too. As Paddy had, that time when she had slipped away from his reach.

'Don't answer,' he had told her. 'We'll leave it as it is, where the Englishmen are concerned. I rather like the feeling of them thinking I own the whole caboodle,' he raised his hand to encircle the shop, 'even if you and I know it's not the way of it.'

Before Bridie could say a word to deflate him, he had gone on to ask, 'Is Monsieur Alphonse, as well as myself, a brother to you?'

'No, he's not. He isn't anything to me.'

'Just the man who put up the money—who set you up in the Hot Potato. Well named, was it not?'

'I know what you're thinking, but it's not so.'

'What am I thinking? What is it that's not so?'

'It's a business arrangement. That's all it is, and it's all it's ever been. You can see why he didn't want his good deed known.' Bridie had been angry. 'If you can't accept what I've told you, you can be looking for another job. Today, if you like.'

'Whoa!' said Paddy. 'Have I ever said I wasn't believing you? I like working here. I like having a sister I can squabble with and tease a little. The feathers do fly when Monsieur Alphonse comes into the conversation!'

*   *   *

Nothing more had been said, and all three had busied themselves with hanging a few decorations around the shop for Christmas. It was a hectic last week at the shop, with more customers than ever, and presents to buy. Bridie had had a new dress made, of jade green, off the shoulder, and very tight in the waist. The bodice was decorated with black lace, and she had a fan to match and little black mittens. When she had tried it on, her pleasure was less than complete. If only Alphonse could see her in it! She made him a cake for his Christmas present and gave it to him when he came to do the accounts. She was glad she hadn't had to do that under Paddy's and Adèle's eyes, though they both knew what she planned.

There was a letter from her brothers in Ireland only this morning. It made the day less sad for her, for she had found herself missing Pegeen . . . yet it was odd, for the news in the letter was bad—not about her brothers, but about Hugh Prendergast, Maling's brother.

> Some say it's a judgment on him for turning off his brother, and him dead this six months or more, but hasn't Hugh had a loaded farm-cart roll over on him and he pulled from it senseless and mangled as well. They thought at first he'd lose his right leg, but they've managed to save it. His old mother says he'll never be the same man again, but his wife—did you know he'd taken a wife? Maureen O'Shaughnessy as was and her with a bit of property and cash of her own—says it's too soon to tell. All goes well with us, and hasn't Michael found himself a little widow with a stretch of ground of her own? They'll be marrying in the spring, and I could be doing with you home on the place. Do you not sometimes get homesick for Ireland and your own brother?

He had signed himself 'Patrick', and Michael had added a row of XXXXs and a scrawled 'Merry Christmas'.

It meant, Bridie told herself, that she could go home

any time she had a mind to. Why was the thought of going home suddenly less attractive? It was what she had intended all along. Yes, when she had had enough money for a place of her own. She had never meant to go back to her brother and keep house for him. One of these days, he would be bound to find himself a wife. Still, she should be pleased that he had thought of her. Wasn't that so?

She dragged her thoughts back to the present.

Mademoiselle Beaupré had been pleased to welcome Bridie and had made her very comfortable. They had a long gossip about the shop after they'd eaten, and the old woman nodded approvingly to hear about the British officers and the sleigh parties. 'I'm glad you're not wasting your youth cooking potatoes. Montreal is a sociable sort of place, and you'll want people about you who speak your own language.'

Bridie was sure that was a way of telling her that Monsieur Alphonse wasn't for her. Well, she knew that. She began to tell her hostess about the sleigh overturning and the girl who had accompanied Alphonse. Mademoiselle wanted to know all about her—what she looked like, how old she was, how she was dressed, and if she had seemed serious. Bridie found, strangely enough, that she did not want to guess whether Gabrielle was serious about Alphonse or he about her. She offered to show Mademoiselle her new dress, for Adèle had insisted that she would want to see it.

'Perfect!' said Mademoiselle when she brought it down from her bag. 'You can wear it tomorrow night.'

'Tomorrow night?'

'Didn't Adèle tell you that the whole family gather on Christmas night and they all dress up in their finest things? You'll be greatly admired. I shouldn't wonder if Monsieur Alphonse didn't come—he usually does.'

Bridie felt her cheeks flushing. She hoped Mademoiselle didn't notice, but she must have, for she looked at her sharply. 'That pleases you, does it?' Her tongue clicked against the roof of her mouth. 'Off to bed with you now, for I see you can scarcely keep awake.' She patted her hand and murmured in French, 'A moth to the flame. Good heads were never on young shoulders. Child, child, be careful.'

Bridie fled from the room. Of course she would be careful; Mademoiselle didn't need to worry about that. But, all the same, she did feel delighted that Alphonse would see her new dress. Of course that was why she felt happy. What else could it be?

CHAPTER TWELVE

ON CHRISTMAS MORNING, Bridie and Mademoiselle Beaupré went to Mass in the village church. Later, nephews kept dropping in with presents for Mademoiselle, and usually there was a little something for Bridie as well. She was quite overcome with the family's generosity. 'How can I possibly give them anything in return?' she wailed to Mademoiselle.

'There's no need,' she was told. 'They are only *des petits cadeaux* to acknowledge you as my guest.'

Just the same, Bridie felt very touched. It was true they were only small things—a ribbon for her hair, a hanky, a needle-holder, a tea-cosy for a tiny pot—but she was pleased to be remembered. It was kind of the Beaupré family.

In the evening the two of them dressed for the soirée. Mademoiselle was magnificent in deep purple velvet with a lace collar. Bridie wore her jade green and carried her dancing slippers, for Christmas Day or not, Mademoiselle declared, there would be dancing. 'We French love to dance.' Her eyes twinkled, just to talk about it.

At the farm, there were greetings and hugs and kisses for all the ladies. Bridie was kissed by every member of the family from the smallest child to the old grand-mère, whose first question to her was, 'Well, fixed yourself up with a young man yet?'

Bridie only laughed, but the next moment she was swept into Alphonse Duvalier's arms and given a re-sounding kiss to a sharp cackle from the old lady. '*Bien sûr*, if you wear a dress like that, you will attract the men.'

'I didn't know you were going to be here.' Bridie ignored grand-mère, and spoke to Alphonse.

'I always come to spend Christmas evening at the farm,' he told her. 'They always ask me, and I enjoy it tremendously. I know all the sons and daughters and the cousins and the aunties, even the tiny babies—and every year there are more of those. You must meet the latest one. Anita's sister's baby is just two weeks old. His name is Hercule, after the old man—now gone from us. Grand-mère is delighted with the choice of name.'

Bridie met Hercule, a bundle of sleepy content in his mother's arms. She and Anita drooled over him.

'Do you have any nephews or nieces?' Anita asked her.

Bridie, standing beside Alphonse, shook her head, unable to acknowledge Sean and Senan's existence. She was surprised when Alphonse slipped his arm in hers as if he understood her sadness. 'One day, you'll have sons and daughters of your own. *Maintenant*, the dancing starts. Will you partner me, Mademoiselle Bridget, in the first dance? May I say how beautiful you look tonight? Green suits you, and so does a little plumpness.'

'I'm not plump!' Bridie denied the very idea, but she was pleased to be complimented on her looks just the same, and somehow the evening had assumed a feeling of excitement with Alphonse's presence. She fancied she could still feel the pressure of his lips against hers, taste the masculine scent of his mouth. She matched her steps to his, recalling the first time she had danced with him to the music of the same fiddle in the barn that summer afternoon. It was odd, was it not, that he was so much more at ease here on the farm than he ever was when he came to the shop to inspect the books or give her unasked-for advice.

'Tonight you are *jeune fille*—the young girl you must have been back in Ireland before all the troubles,' he told her. 'If I had been an Irish boy from the same village, I would have been courting you.'

Bridie dipped and curtsied in the patterns of the dance. 'Would you so?'

'How could I help myself?'

'But you're not an Irish boy,' she whispered, as the next sequence brought them together and he was holding her.

'Tonight, I might be!' His hold tightened, and she was conscious of his body fitting neatly against hers. 'Have you never imagined how things might be—might have been?' He swung her in a circle, as all the other men were doing with their partners. 'Just suppose it so—for a single evening.'

Bridie was swept back into his arms. 'Shall I call you Danny or Micky or Paddy?' The last name slipped out without her even thinking.

'Not Paddy. There's one of those already. Does he mean anything to you?'

She was swept away in the order of the set before she could answer, and by the time she was returned to him, had decided to ignore it. What did it matter how she felt about anyone else? She was here, dancing with Alphonse. She smiled up at him, and his arms closed about her, more tightly than the custom of the dance permitted. In the soft candle-light it didn't matter. Who was there to notice?

It was several dances later before Alphonse claimed her again. He danced with grand-mère, who flirted wickedly with him before Bridie's very eyes. He danced with Mademoiselle Beaupré, too, and with all the plump matrons of the family, and Bridie danced with their husbands and with some of the younger sons.

It was a great party, with food and drink for all. The fiddler, cousin Pierre, had a girl-friend hanging on his arm at the refreshment table. Bridie was glad to see that, for she had felt rather guilty when she had discouraged Pierre's attentions after her move into Montreal.

The big front room had been cleared for the dancing, and the fire in the enormous fireplace was burning merrily all evening. The room got hotter and hotter, and cold drinks were very welcome. The men drank beer, and the ladies a light punch with very little wine added to it. It was while Bride and Alphonse were fetching more punch for Mademoiselle and grand-mère that he drew her into the darkened recess of a room in the long corridor which led to the kitchen, and pulled her to him and kissed her again.

This time there were no onlookers. His lips fastened on hers in a long searing kiss that seemed to draw the soul from her body. Bridie was shaken to her very core. She might have pushed him away; she might have freed herself, for his hold on her was light. She was not a prisoner. But, instead, she clung to him, returning kiss for kiss in a long embrace of pleasure.

It was he who stopped. 'I don't know what it is about you,' he whispered. 'What madness claims me when you're near. Your lips are so kissable, your body so inviting.' His hands touched her shoulders and slid to her waist. 'I want you, Bridget. You want me, too.'

She neither admitted nor denied it. 'Wait a bit,' she exclaimed softly, 'it's only the magic of the night. It's half because I'm just one of the farm girls here and half because I've said No to you once before. It's a bit of foolishness on both our parts. I'll not be telling you I don't like you—for I do—but it's time to be getting back to the others, else they'll be wondering where we are.'

'Let them wonder!'

'That's all very well for you, but I've no intention of being gossiped about. Not for a few kisses—a few stolen kisses in the dark.'

'Is that what they are, Bridget, stolen kisses?'

'Not stolen, exactly, more exchanged; but I've no intention of its going any further, any more than you have.' Bridie had a struggle to say it so baldly, but he had started it, with his talk about wanting her and her wanting him. He would have to go on wanting her, for she had other plans for her life—and they did not include giving way to him, however much he stirred her with his kisses. 'Where's Gabrielle Truteau this night?'

'Home in bed, I should hope.'

'You didn't think to bring her with you?'

'No, why should I? She doesn't know the Beauprés. They don't know her. I might ask you, where's Paddy?'

'Out with some friends, some Irish friends. Anyway it's not the same thing—not the same thing at all.'

'Isn't it, Bridget?' His hand was still at her waist.

If he would only take it away, she would breathe easier. She put her own hand out to do so.

He caught her fingers in his. 'What is Paddy to you? He came to me the other day with some scheme to set him up in business.'

'He didn't!' Bridie drew in her breath sharply. 'What did you tell him?'

'I told him I would think it over; that some of the businesses we had helped had failed.'

'Did you and your friends help other businesses?'

'No, of course not! Does he know anything, Bridie?'

'How could he know? I've not said a word.' His hand was gripping hers.

'You might be better to get rid of him. Have you thought of it?'

'Just for a bit of curiosity and a little pushiness on his part?' Bridie bit her lip. She wasn't going to tell Alphonse that she had nearly told Paddy to go. Fancy him going to Alphonse!

'More than a bit of pushiness. But two can play at his game!'

'What will you do?'

'I'll string it out for a while, then tell him the others have decided against it. Watch him, Bridget.'

'That's what Anita said only the other day, but I can't believe he means any harm. He wants to make something of himself. That's only natural.'

'Maybe you're right.' She was drawn close to him again.

This time, before his lips could weaken her resolve, she slid away and ran towards the kitchen. He followed her without a word more—no pleading, no protests. Why should that disappoint her?

Alphonse drove Mademoiselle Beaupré and Bridie

back to the cottage after the party—a very formal
Alphonse, who handed them out and then rode off in the
night without any special sort of farewell beyond a polite
'Bonsoir' and a bow to Mademoiselle.

In the morning, it was Alphonse who knocked on their
door as they were breakfasting. Mademoiselle welcomed him in.

'I've come to take Bridget snowshoeing,' he
announced, 'if you'll give your permission.'

Mademoiselle nodded. 'It will do her good to be out in
the sunshine.'

'I've snowshoes for both of us,' he went on, 'if you can
provide her with something to wear.' He looked at her
consideringly, not consulting her at all.

Mademoiselle laughed, and in a few minutes Bridie
found herself changed into a much shorter woollen skirt,
and wrapped in layers of sweaters. Still no one had asked
if she wanted to go snowshoeing! She was hurried out of
the door and the snowshoes strapped to her feet. At first
she found them completely unwieldy, but Alphonse
took her hand and showed her how to walk. Fairly soon,
she was beginning to develop a little confidence in
herself, and set off with him. He was a good teacher,
patient and encouraging, and she began to enjoy the
sensation of walking on top of the snow instead of
sinking into it. This was a different Alphonse, a nicer
man than she had seen up to now. This man was easy
with her, a grand companion.

'I'll drive you back to Montreal later on,' he said.
'Adèle's gone to visit her friend, and Anita had to be
back early this morning.'

'That'd be lovely!' Bridie agreed very readily. What
had got into him? There was no use trying to puzzle him
out; better just to enjoy this new man and the day and
the sunshine.

Alphonse stayed to lunch, and wasn't that nice, too?
Bridie wondered whether Mademoiselle had planned
for his coming, but there was more than enough onion

soup and cooked meats from the party to go round. Afterwards, she was tucked into his sleigh, kissed by Mademoiselle, and driven away, her bag safely stowed under the seat, the snowshoes packed away, too.

'The pair you wore are yours to keep,' said Alphonse. 'A present for Christmas.'

'Thank you,' said Bridie, astonished and pleased. 'I'm not sure that I should accept.'

'Don't be silly! You can't refuse—I'm a partner. We're almost relatives, as you've often pointed out. Besides, you gave me a cake, a most delicious cake. We've exchanged gifts, that's all.'

He smiled at her in such a friendly fashion that Bridie decided it would be churlish to raise any more objections. She had used the snowshoes, and accepted his help in learning to use them. She felt warm pleasure in thinking of the morning's ramble in the snow.

As they approached the city, she noticed that they were not following the usual way to the shop. 'Are we going somewhere?' she asked.

'Have you ever been to the top of Mont Royal? No, I thought not. Today is a splendid opportunity. The air is clear. We'll see the whole city laid out before us in daylight, and then, if we wait just a little, we'll see dusk claiming it and all the lights winking on.'

Bridie liked the sound of the plan. She didn't want the day to end. There was no hurry to get back. Paddy would have fed the cats and have the stoves going.

So, instead of going straight into town, Alphonse directed his horse up Côte de Neiges hill, and up the road to the top of the mount. They got out of the sleigh and walked the length of the viewpoint, Alphonse pointing out the geography of the place. The St Lawrence River gleamed frostily across the whole landscape, and it all looked clean and fresh and quiet, slumbering in the last rays of the setting sun; one minute all pinks and reds on shining steeples, then deeper mauves and purples.

'It's lovely,' sighed Bridie. 'I never thought, when I set out from Ireland, that it would look like this—I never thought how it would look at all. It was just in my mind as some place where there'd be plenty for everyone. But I have seen that there are poor people here—people living eight and ten in one room. That's the way it was when Pegeen and I were together. It's only the twins who changed that for me.'

'The twins, and your own quick thinking,' Alphonse suggested drily. 'It's strange how one action leads on to so many more, until eventually several lives are changed by it. We've all benefited: Marie-Rose, my brother, the babies themselves, you—and even myself.'

'You? How have you benefited?'

'I've met you, and been shaken out of myself.'

'Is that what I've done to you?'

He caught hold of her hand. 'I might have grown just like my brother—Frencher than the French. We tend to think we're the only ones here. We were the first, so it must belong to us solely. We don't like sharing.'

Bridie would have preferred a more personal observation, but that was not forthcoming. Alphonse seemed to have fallen into a serious mood. His face was sombre, dark like the afternoon itself was becoming. She tugged at his hand. 'It's cold! Let's walk up and down and keep warm.' They strode the length of the outlook, which they had to themselves.

'You make friends easily, don't you?'

Rosy-cheeked, laughing, Bridie faced him. 'Sure, and why not? It's a long way to travel without a bit of company on the way.'

'You've even won Adèle round. How do you do it?'

'It's no secret—I just let myself like her. Not that it wasn't hard at first, but there can't be too much that's frightening about a girl who's afraid of a mouse!'

'What did you find to like about me?' His dark eyes were dancing, his humour restored.

'I hated you at the beginning. It was when you showed me the steps of the dance in the barn in the summer that I began to trust you and like you.'

'To trust me? What an extraordinary thing to say. I haven't given you much cause to trust me.'

'You mean the kissing and that?' Bridie met his gaze. 'Isn't that the way men are? If they weren't, where would the human race be—shrivelled up, come to nothing. There's no shame in wanting.'

She couldn't understand it. Why should his shoulders be shaking with laughter when she was completely serious?

He followed her to the parapet, and put his arms round her so that she stood with her back to him, enclosed in the circle of his embrace.

'Look at the lights,' he said against her ear. 'They're all coming on in the streets and the houses—everyone building up the fires, pushing back the darkness. It's a different place, isn't it?'

'A fairy place, and us looking down on it, just outside, never getting in.' She shivered.

'You're not supposed to feel like that.' His breath was warm against her hair. 'Heavens, what am I thinking of keeping you here in the cold! We'll go back to the sleigh and find a place with a big pot of tea, bread and jam, and cakes piled high on a plate. That's what the English —and the Irish—like, isn't it?' He rushed her over to the sleigh and bundled her into it under the fur robes. Then he cracked the whip over the horse without even touching him, and the animal sprang into motion.

Paddy was pleased with himself. Things were going along nicely—very nicely indeed. The Widow Mulvaney had given him a watch for Christmas. It dangled from his waistcoat this very minute. He had better not let Adèle see that, or the fat would be in the fire. Really, she was becoming too possessive, and so was the Widow. Damn all women! They knew what a man wanted and were ready enough to provide it, but they thought that gave them some kind of rights. They longed to tie a chap down. He didn't want that; if that was what he'd had in mind, he would have made a dead set for Bridget

Langton. All he wanted from her was her little shop —and no advice about how to run it.

He cracked the whip over the horse's back. Ah, it was grand to have a bit of money—enough to hire a sleigh and go for a run. She'd be waiting for him. Of course she would. He knew the sign: the way she had run the tip of her tongue round her lips as she had hesitated. That was just to give her time to think up some excuse to get out of the house. He had known all along that she was going to agree to meet him. She leaned towards him while she was talking, and her eyes kept meeting his. Pretty little thing she was—and young. God, he liked them young! The Widow and Adèle were all right in their way, but neither of them had the freshness of a young girl. He had better go carefully with this one. She would fall into his lap as they all did, sooner or later, but in her case, it would be later. Not that she wouldn't be willing, but he would enjoy a leisurely chase. It was worth the effort. It had been a lucky sort of day for him. The Widow was off to visit her husband's family, and Adèle was in the country with hers. Yes, it had fallen out nicely.

He whistled as the sleigh took him through the streets. He had never seen anything like the snow here. A pity his brothers hadn't lived to see it. But maybe it was just as well for him; it gave him a freer hand. There was nothing like family to criticise and foretell doom. They had always poured cold water on his schemes, but they were gone, and he was here and doing quite well for himself. He felt like a king on this bright sunny afternoon. The horse and sleigh were only hired, but one of these days he would have his own. There was room for a man to better himself here, not like in the Ireland he had left, where he would always have been numbered among the poor. In Montreal there would be success and money and property. They were all within his grasp—and this little Madam he was collecting shortly was going to lead the way to all of them! He smiled in satisfaction.

As he approached the meeting-place, he thought for a

moment that she might not have come. No, he had
judged it right. She was waiting; of course she was
waiting. He was ten minutes late, exactly timed. She
would be just cold enough, just anxious enough to start
talking straight away. He would stand her scolding with
good grace, seem properly humble and then kiss her
protests away; just a gentle kiss or two and a melting
look in his eye—not to frighten her, but to take her mind
off the waiting.

He pulled the horse up with a flourish and got out, the
reins in his hand to help her in. A torrent of chatter
rolled over him as he tucked her under the fur rugs.
He held her hand and put the lightest of kisses on one
rosy cheek. Her tongue halted of its own accord. He
called out to the horse, 'Gee up, my beauty, the party's
complete.'

Bridie was content to sit back in comfort. There was
something very comforting in watching Alphonse hand-
ling the reins. He was taking her out for tea. He had been
with her all day. She didn't care how it had come about,
neither did she care where they went, so long as the day
continued.

She snuggled against him. 'Why do you like me better
today?'

'I've always liked you.'

'You had a funny way of showing it.'

He shook his head, his eyes laughing at her. 'I didn't
like you very much the first day, when you scratched me!
Now I've grown used to you, I guess.'

'You frightened me.'

'But not any more?'

'No, not any more.'

He allowed the horse to go at its own pace. 'When I
saw only your feet sticking up in the snow that Sunday
when Hartley's sleigh overturned, my heart nearly
stopped. Gabrielle thought I was a madman the way I
dug in the snow.' His hand rested on Bridie's. 'When I
found you and you were still alive, I made her keep you

awake just for the pleasure of hearing your voice, of
knowing you were there.'

Bridie's mouth opened in an O of astonishment.
She did matter to him. It wasn't just that he wanted her
in the way any man might want a girl. He liked her.
Her eyes were soft as she held on to his hand. She
didn't ask herself where the future lay, what he meant
to do about his liking. It was enough that he valued
her.

The sleigh sped through the gloom of the dusk. The
horse never hesitated in that misty white world, not
quite dark, but with the light mostly gone. Bridie nearly
told him how she had felt when she saw his face over her
when she was gasping for breath. Someday she would
tell him, but not now.

At length a sign loomed up. 'Moore's Hotel', it pro-
claimed to the silent snow. Alphonse directed the horse
round it and up a narrow path towards lights now visible.
He pulled to a stop and tethered the horse to a rack.
Then he helped her out.

She was reluctant to move. There would be people
inside, probably not anyone she knew, but Alphonse
might become different, not so exclusively hers.

'Come on, you'll want your tea and a warm fire,' he
encouraged her.

Together they mounted a few steps into the well-lit
interior, and the heat rushed out to greet them even in
the vestibule. The large room inside looked inviting.
Alphonse opened the door, and Bridie exclaimed at the
easy chairs and the large log burning in the fireplace.
There was the sound of subdued chattering as they were
conducted to an alcove with an empty low table and a big
comfortable settee. She sank into it, removing her mittens, and a waiter came over to them almost at once.
Alphonse ordered muffins and jam and a pot of tea, and
sat beside her, very close beside her.

Bridie glanced idly round the room. She gave an
exclamation of surprise as she glimpsed Paddy O'Leary
in the matching alcove on the other side of the hearth.

Her hand rose in a half wave, as Alphonse followed the direction of her eyes.

'*Diable!*' she heard him say, as she recognised Paddy's companion.

It was Gabrielle Truteau. What was she doing here with Paddy, and the two of them as guilty-looking as children who had been caught with jam on their faces?

Alphonse rose to his feet and approached the other table. 'What are you doing here, Gabrielle?' he asked. His voice wasn't pleasant. 'Do your parents know where you are?'

Bridie shivered. The day had changed altogether.

CHAPTER THIRTEEN

ADÈLE HUMMED as she unpacked. It was quite warm. She had half expected it would be icy cold when she had came in and seen that no one else was there. Somebody had kept the fires going. She had only had to add a few logs, and they had blazed into flame again. Even the little Quebec heater that heated the upstairs didn't need coaxing to throw out more welcome warmth.

She wondered where Bridie was. No matter. She rather liked having the place to herself. Now that the snow had stopped, the moon had risen and it was very bright in her little upstairs room. She blew out the candle she had used and opened the curtains wide to let in the light. Unfolding her new shawl, she put it round her shoulders. It had been a good Christmas with the family, but she had missed Paddy. She would have a lot to tell him about Bridie and Monsieur Alphonse. If he were here, they would make love in the moonlight. Where could he be? With the Widow Mulvaney?

She didn't want to think about her. She wanted only to think about him and the things she did with him. He was exciting, and he wanted her almost as much as she wanted him. She acknowledged that to herself. After all, she was a plain girl, so why should he be attracted to her at all? She felt a chill of fear. A man like Paddy could take his pick. How could she keep him? Only by becoming necessary to him. Life wasn't fair! If she had only half of Bridie's looks, she would use them to better advantage. Monsieur Alphonse wanted her: that had been very plain at the party. Really, the Irish girl had no sense. She couldn't see what he would be willing to do for her; short of marriage, of course.

Adèle was so deep in her thoughts that she was startled when she heard the shop door open and close.

There were footsteps—and whispers. She froze where she was, silent. One hand to her mouth, she waited. It wasn't until the voices were raised that she recognised them—Bridie and Paddy. What were they doing coming in together? She didn't stir.

'Why did you do it, Paddy?' Bridie must be standing in the kitchen, directly under Adèle's room, for her to make out every word.

'Wait now,' Paddy's voice was placating, wheedling. 'You don't need to take on as well. Anyone'd think I'd committed a crime! I took a girl out for a sleigh-ride and a cup of tea—where's the harm in that?'

Adèle couldn't move now. What girl? And why was Bridie angry about it? It had nothing to do with her.

Adèle strained her ears, but Bridie said nothing. It was Paddy who went on. 'Spoiled your day for you, did I? What's between you and this fine Monsieur? I've always known there must be something, so you might as well tell me about. What's a brother for if not to comfort his sister?'

'You're not my brother, and you can take your arm away from my waist.'

Adèle could picture the scene. Paddy was trying to charm Bridie, to win her round. The listener didn't like any of this. If Paddy won Bridie, he would have the shop for himself. If only she knew what had happened!

'Don't be like that, Bridie! We can help each other.'
'How?'

'You want him. I want her. We're both in the same boat—stretching out our hands to take what's within our reach. Why shouldn't we better ourselves?'

'It's not like that.'

'Isn't it? There's no need for them to think they're above us, no need at all. They just have a few more of the world's goods. But we can change that, if we work together. Think of it, Bridie. The two of us could handle the pair of them. Just the hint of a bit of scandal, and her family would soon come round to our way of thinking. You've no idea how easy it was to get her to meet me.

She's not the young innocent you probably think.'

Paddy's laugh was amused, and it made Adèle's blood boil. Was he talking about Gabrielle Truteau? The very idea that he could do such a thing! Wasn't it enough for him that she herself made him welcome? What did he want another girl for? Especially one who was young and beautiful—and rich? She almost went downstairs to rail at him, to storm at both of them. But wait, she wanted to hear what else he was up to.

Bridie was indignant. 'What is it you want? Money? You can't tell me you care for the girl.'

'Why can't I? Do you suppose I have no feelings? Didn't you see the way she looked at me—until that fine Monsieur of yours started going on about her parents and the honour of her family. You'd think I had the plague! I had typhus when I first came, but that's cured. All I suffer from now is pockets without cash in them. She could remedy that for me, if you'll help just a little.'

'How do you figure that out?'

'Her family'll be on their guard against me, but you could talk to her, arrange to meet her . . .'

Bridie didn't let him finish. 'I won't be party to anything underhand like that! Best take your ideas away with you, Paddy. I want no part in it.'

'You needn't be so high and mighty about it! You don't mind a little deception when it benefits you. I suppose your two British soldiers still think I'm your brother?'

'That's different—it's harmless. I'm not trying to get anything from them.'

'Except, perhaps, a good time, and their respect.'

Adèle could almost see the indecision on Bridie's face as, low-voiced, she replied, 'I see I'll have to tell them.'

'Ah, Bridie, you don't need to. I won't give you away. I like having a sister. Of course we could be more than brother and sister, if you weren't setting your cap at Alphonse.'

'I'm not doing anything of the kind.'

'What is he to you, Bridie? He has some sort of hold on you.'

'No, he hasn't. I'm grateful to him; that's all it is. What more could it be?'

'What more, indeed? You're the kind of girl made for marriage. You'll never get it from him—any more than I will with the little Gaby—not without trickery and a bit of cunning. But I'm forgetting, you're above all that. A pity, isn't it?' There was the hint of laughter in his words.

The listening Adèle smiled bitterly to herself. When Paddy used that tone, a woman would forgive him anything. Bridie didn't even get angry with him.

She just said, 'Go home, Paddy. I'm sure you don't mean half of what you say. The pity of it is that we should have picked on the same place this afternoon. I don't know who was more surprised, you or I.'

'It certainly was a facer! I'll be saying good night. You might do worse than give a thought to what I've said. I may just be Paddy who works for you, but I'd be as pleased as any brother to see you settled in life.'

'That's very kind of you. Good night, Paddy.'

'I was wondering . . .'

'Yes, what were you wondering?' Bridie must be on the bottom step now.

'If a brother might kiss his sister—just to make up for the hurt of the day, to soothe it away.'

Adèle strained to hear what Bridie might say, but certainly it wasn't No, for there was, after a minute, the sound of a soft kiss and a murmured Good night, and a soft whisper. Then there was silence until finally the door of the shop opened and closed and Bridie's feet ascended the stairs.

Adèle pretended to sleep. If Bridie looked in, she didn't want her to know she had heard everything. Beside, she had plenty to think about. What sort of game was Paddy playing? First Gabrielle Truteau, now Bridie herself. It was plain that Paddy considered himself a free agent: he would never be satisfied with only one.

Adèle sighed. What was she to do? She felt cold—and betrayed.

The garrison's Christmas Ball was held in Montreal's newest hotel, the Donegani, just east of the Champ de Mars. Hartley and Vivian were almost as excited as Anita and Bridie.

Anita was in red and Bridie in her new green frock, and when they arrived they found that the ballroom, too, was in green and red. There were two bands: one was in evening dress; the other in the tartans of the Scots.

The buffet table was magnificent, but she was not allowed to stand gawping at the food. She was whisked to the ballroom, and her dance-card was returned to her by Hartley almost filled with officers' names.

She had heard nothing from Alphonse since the day after Christmas, and Paddy had spoken no more about seeing Gabrielle or planning to. In fact, he had been very cheerful in the shop, and it was Adèle who worried her. She seemed so silent and strange, but Bridie put her out of her mind, for tonight at any rate.

It was with something of a shock that she spun round in Hartley's arms in the first dance to see Alphonse enter the room with Gabrielle Truteau on his arm. Bridie smiled brightly up at Hartley. It didn't matter to her what Alphonse Duvalier did.

'That's the chap who rescued you, isn't it?' Hartley waved at the newcomers. 'We must go over and speak to them.'

Bridie didn't know why they must, but he insisted, so after the music stopped she found herself led across the floor to pay her respects.

'You're looking very well, Bridget,' Alphonse greeted her.

'You can't be superstitious,' Gabrielle smiled. 'I thought all the Irish believed they tempted fate by wearing green, for then they'd wear black very shortly. I'd love to wear black. Maman says the only colour for a

young girl is white.' Her hand caressed the white satin of
her frock where it clung to her waist.

Bridie said the first thing that came into her head.
'I thought your mother said you were too young for
attending an officers' ball.'

'Alphonse persuaded her there'd be no harm in it,
since I'd be with him.' Gabrielle put her hand on her
partner's wrist.

Hartley took the dance card that dangled just within
his reach. 'May I add my name, Mademoiselle Truteau?'
At Alphonse's nod, he found a blank space to write in his
name. Alphonse could do no less than inscribe Bridie's
card. It was not what she would have called a free choice
on his part. Just the same, when he presented himself
before her at the appropriate time, she was glad to slip
into his arms and glide along in the waltz.

She was quite content to enjoy the moment, but
Alphonse began to speak. 'Bridget, I owe you an
apology.'

'What—what for?'

'For the other night. It was quite unreasonable of me
to expect you to get rid of someone who worked for you
because he made me angry.'

Bridie almost missed a step. Somehow she had never
expected him to take back the hard things he had said
about Paddy.

'I was angry with him, too,' she admitted. If he could
be honest and generous, so could she. 'Were
Mademoiselle Truteau's parents upset?'

'I didn't tell them. Gabrielle begged me not to. She
promised she wouldn't do anything so foolish ever
again.'

'And you believed her?'

'Why not? She's young, but I think she meant it.'

Gabrielle had been forgiven. She was here tonight,
and looking very much as though there were some
understanding between her and Alphonse.

'All's well that ends well,' she murmured.

'Yes. It seems to be a time for endings.' He danced her

into a corner, and although the music went on, her feet stopped moving. 'What do you mean?' She still swayed to the haunting tune.

Alphonse was standing stiff and tall, looking down at her in the shadowy corner where they had halted. The other dancers were all in the centre of the room, oblivious of them. He removed his arm from her back, though he still held one of her hands. 'I mean that it's wrong of me to keep on giving you advice. I see you're perfectly capable of managing on your own. The shop is successful. You've done everything you said you would —and more. It's time for me to bow out, to admit that I was wrong about you. You have a thriving little business and I must stop watching over you. It will only make people talk, and that can't be any kindness to you.'

It was a long speech. It should have made her happy. He was acknowledging that she was capable, hard working, shrewd, and miles away from the failure he had predicted. Her heart should have leaped, but she felt no pleasure at all. It meant that he had cut the ties that bound them. It meant he would never again come into the shop, never tell her what she was doing wrong, never demand to see the books. Her throat was so constricted with emotion that she couldn't speak. She couldn't meet his eyes. They fell before his.

He placed a finger beneath her chin and tilted her face upwards. 'What's wrong, Bridget? I thought you would be delighted.'

'I am—of course I am! I'm just—just overcome. I thought the day would never come.'

She saw him draw away, release her hand. What had he expected her to say? 'What about the twins? Now that Father Mulcahey is dead, who will tell me how they're going on?' She stretched out her hand.

He didn't take it in his, just stood before her, his expression unreadable. 'Why, I will, as you suggested in the first place.'

'Each year?' She managed to get the words out.

'Each year,' he repeated. 'I'll call on you, take you out

to tea, perhaps, and tell you all about them.'

'We can talk over old times.' She couldn't keep the pain from her voice. Let him think it was for the babies.

'If you like. Shall I tell you how they go on now?'

She nodded. 'Please.'

'They're fine infants, very healthy. Jean, he's the blond one, is already laughing and making sounds. Marie-Rose says he's trying to say "Ma-Ma", but she's the only one who recognises the word. Jacques' hair isn't blond any more. There's a red tint to it, more auburn. He was the smaller of the two. Now he's bigger, and he sings—not proper singing, but a funny tune of his own. He smiles a lot.'

'You see them often?'

'Every week. They're very engaging. I never had much to do with babies, but this pair have found a doting uncle—a whole infatuated family!'

Bridie's eyes filled with tears. She couldn't help it. She didn't weep for the twins; she was glad for them. It was the thought of Alphonse playing with them, enjoying them. She would have liked to have seen him doing it. Her hand went to her eyes. What was she thinking? Why should that matter to her?

This time his hand did take hold of hers. 'A few tears are nothing to be ashamed of! You did a wonderful thing for my brother and his wife. Be happy for them.'

'I am happy for them.' She managed to smile through her brimming tears. 'Aren't I the foolish one? Happiness always makes me cry.'

His gloved finger wiped away the tear, and for an instant he pressed her close to him in a quick hug. 'You're free, Bridget. Your life is your own. I know you'll make something of it.'

'Thanks to you.' Her words sounded stiff in her own ears.

'There's just one other thing. Don't take this the wrong way, Bridget. I'm mentioning it only because I think you should be careful. Don't put too much trust in Paddy. No, don't say anything. I'm not trying to argue

with you, only put you on your guard. You've let him slip
into the position of a brother. He isn't your brother, or
any sort of relation to you. Just remember that you
employ him.'

'Yes,' said Bridie. She didn't want to talk about
Paddy, but it was on the tip of her tongue for just that
moment to tell him about the strange interview she had
had with Paddy just two nights earlier. But Alphonse
had finished advising her. He had said so himself.

She gave him a brilliant smile. 'Let's join the dancers.'
How she controlled her tears, made them dry up, she
never knew. Pride forced her on when she would have
stayed in that dark corner with Alphonse, thrown herself
into his arms and held him tight, begged him to stay by
her. The terrible realisation had come upon her that she
would never be rid of him with his winning ways and his
handsome face. God help her, the saints preserve her!
She loved him—and he was saying goodbye to her! All
she had left was the determination that he shouldn't
know about her folly.

She danced, she laughed, she got through the rest of
the evening somehow. She even parried Vivian's questions about what she had been doing in a dark corner
with Monsieur Duvalier. 'Sure, what would we be
doing? I had something in my eye, and he was kind
enough to help me get it out.'

Over refreshments, Hartley asked her if she never
took anything seriously. 'I've never known a girl like
you,' he said earnestly. 'So happy all the time.'

Happy! That sent Bridie off into a fit of the giggles
—she couldn't stop. She had given away her sister's
babies, just said goodbye to the man she loved—would
always love. Yes, she was happy. She would never be
happy again, but her face went through the motions, her
feet danced, her lips formed themselves round words
—amusing words that made the others laugh.

Hartley kissed her when he left her at the door of the
shop, and she felt nothing—nothing at all. She went up
to bed, Anita at her heels, chattering. She must have

answered her, must have been vaguely conscious when the girl rose from the bed very early the next morning to go to work.

Bridie hadn't expected to sleep, but she had. She didn't expect that life would go on as usual, but it did. The shop seemed to get busier every day, and all three of them worked harder than ever. Paddy took over making the *patates frites*. He talked her into providing more chairs and tables for the customers. He asked her if she thought they might rent the shop next door and expand the business. None of it seemed to matter very much. She just let Paddy take more and more on himself, while Adèle appeared to withdraw more and more. She was glad there was someone to take some of the burden from her.

Paddy still maintained the pretence of being her brother, and indeed so gentle was he these days with her that she could almost believe he was. He seemed to understand something of the desolation she was experiencing. Not that he questioned her or asked what was wrong, but he did insist that she must take care of herself, must get out into the fresh air and take some exercise. He even got himself a pair of snowshoes and took her for walks in the crisp snow.

As the days slipped into weeks, the walks with Paddy and the sleigh-rides with the two officers became the bright spots of Bridie's time off from the shop. Alphonse had washed his hands of her, and she gradually began to accept that fact. Life still held some pleasures. If they were pale in comparison, at least they were something to cling to. No one had ever died of a broken heart, she told herself fiercely.

One Wednesday afternoon towards the end of March, Bridie and Paddy were out on their snowshoes. They always closed the shop on a mid-week afternoon.

'I don't suppose the snow will last much longer,' Paddy said, as they trudged along. 'Winter will soon be over.'

'I'll soon have been here a year.' Bridie halted as they

crossed the wooden bridge that spanned the still frozen stream at Little St Antoine and Craig Streets. 'It's very pretty here, cold and white. I suppose, one day, it'll be built up and the boys of the town won't be able to fish in this creek or swim in the quarry behind us.'

'Maybe not in our time, but I expect our children or our children's children will be seeing it.'

Bridie laughed outright. The thought of Paddy surrounded by grandchildren was too much. 'What nonsense you talk sometimes! What was it you wanted me to see? You were determined we must come this way.'

'Patience, me darlin', we'll just wait here a wee while and talk about life and enjoy the sunshine.' He leaned against the rail of the bridge. 'Hasn't it been a pleasant day? I can see myself settling down in Montreal and living out my days here—snowshoeing over this bridge in the winter, fishing from it in the summer. A fellow came in the other day and said he caught a trout here last summer.'

'He never did!' Bridie marvelled, not sure whether to believe him or not. You never knew with Paddy. She sat on the low rail, watching his face. There was an air of suppressed excitement about him—an air of waiting. What could he be waiting for? On such a pleasant day it was delightful to stop for a few minutes in the warmth of the winter sun. But what was Paddy up to? Whatever it was did not seem to bear too heavily on him, for he kept a steady stream of conversation about a larger shop and its possibilities. They even began to discuss what they might do with a second or a third, some time in the future.

It was so engrossing that Bridie hardly noticed that the younger children playing on their sledges in the snowy quarry had begun to trail homewards over the bridge, and that she herself felt a slight shiver as the sun came lower in the sky. She was just about to tell Paddy that it was time to go home when he stopped from his leaning-place and bent forward to help a woman pushing a high-sided sleigh with babies in it. He lifted it over the lip. The woman turned to thank him.

With a shock of absolute astonishment, Bridie couldn't move. If she had been standing, she told herself, she would have fallen to the ground. As it was, wasn't her breath coming in great gasps so that she heard it loud in her ears? Sure, it was Madame Marie-Rose Duvalier with her babies!

'Is something wrong?' The woman spoke to her, and put out a hand as she drew level, Paddy now wholly in charge of the sledge. She spoke in French.

Bridie slid from the rail and dropped to her knees beside the low carriage. Pegeen's twins—she'd know them anywhere. She put out a hand to each. 'Aren't they the lovely creatures?' she cried to the woman, only realising now how strange it must seem to Marie-Rose. 'Are they good babies?' she babbled. 'Twins are a blessing—a gift from the holy ones.' Her words were in French.

Marie-Rose Duvalier laughed, a deep, rich laugh of pleasure. 'That's what I say every day of my life.'

Bridie smiled up at her. Didn't she sound like a real mother? Delight rose in her. 'Two fine boys! What are they called?' She knew perfectly well what they were called—Sean and Sennen, she whispered to herself. Which was which? She could not take her eyes from them, and they pulling at her hands.

'They love the snow,' Marie-Rose was telling Paddy. 'I take them out in it whenever I can, even if my husband tells me I have a girl to do that for me.'

'Husbands have to be practical.' Paddy kept talking about the ways of husbands. What did he know of them?

Bridie was aware that he was charming the woman, giving herself time to touch the babies, to push Sean's fair hair back under his bonnet where it slipped round his face. He was crowing at her. Wasn't he the picture of a Prendergast—the fair ones, not the dark ones like Maling had been. And the other little lad, Sennen—he was the image of Pegeen, the same red colour of his hair and the merry blue eyes.

She rose from her knees. She was glad she had seen them for herself. She managed to tell Marie-Rose once again how lucky she was, what darling babies she had —before the realisation of the scene was brought home to her. It was as Paddy was negotiating the sled over the hump at the further end of the bridge that the truth dawned. Paddy knew. Mother of God, Paddy had found out her secret!

She waved Marie-Rose and the babies a hasty good-bye and strode off across the snow on her own. What did it mean? How had he done it? Of one thing she was absolutely certain: Paddy had been waiting there for the babies, and keeping her there as well. What did he want? Alphonse had warned her to be on her guard against him, and she should have listened. She should not have let Paddy stay and become her friend. A friend wouldn't have trapped her so. He had been watching her face all the time. He knew. Somehow, he had got to the bottom of it—he had guessed. Could it have been anything she had said or done? She was nearly crying with the enormity of him finding out.

Paddy was following her, calling after her, 'Bridget, wait for me!'

She didn't wait, but forced herself along. She wanted to get away from him, to hide, to think what to do next, what to say. Blindly she ran along the field as fast as she could.

But Paddy was faster. He caught hold of her arm, and made her come to a halt. 'Is it the first time you've seen them, since you gave them up?'

She nodded. What use was it to deny anything? He knew. She leaned against him, defeated. 'How did you find out?'

'It wasn't hard.' Paddy put his arms round her. 'I just looked into all the Duvalier family, and when I found his brother had twin boys, things fell into place. You had twin brothers. Could these twins be yours? You had worked in his brother's house. I wasn't sure of it, not any of it, till I saw your face when you saw them.

If it hadn't been today, it would have been another day. I meant you to see them—and to be there when you did.'

'It was cruel—wrong of you! I promised never to seek them out.' She withdrew herself from his clasp. She had broken her solemn promise to Alphonse. She wrung her hands.

He took her hands in his own. 'Sh-h-h, Bridie, don't upset yourself. I understand why you had to give them up, but it's different now—it's changed.'

'How is it different? How has it changed?' she demanded. 'The boys are Duvaliers. It's done.'

He didn't explain, but just looked at her. She was puzzled at the excitement she saw in his eyes.

'That woman thinks they're her own babies. That's how you got the shop. You sold them to her husband, and in return he set you up in the Hot Potato. I suppose he didn't want it ever to be tied back to him. He let his brother handle all the arrangements. Your misfortune was to fall for the brother.'

Bridie was speechless. What was there to say? He had it all. She started to turn away, but he didn't allow her to. He seized her arm and made her face him.

'It was a fine scheme to get rid of your bastards! If they were willing to pay the first time, they'll pay a second. I fancy a little shop of my own.'

'No, no!' Bridie stamped her foot. 'They won't pay. The man who's adopted them—Alphonse's brother—is very hard. He said he would give them back if anything like that happened. He would, too. He'll never give you any money.'

Bridie didn't actually know how Alphonse's brother would react, but whatever happened she must stop Paddy from carrying out his threat. The twins were loved and cared for where they were. That poor woman thought herself their mother. She was so upset at the whole idea that she made no effort to tell Paddy that Pegeen had been the mother, not herself. That didn't seem important.

Paddy looked undecided—but only for a moment.

He shrugged. 'I'm not a greedy man. I can wait a little.'

'What—what do you mean?' She paled at the way he licked his lips.

'Why, you shall set me up in a shop. Would you be willing to give me a percentage of what you make in the Hot Potato—say three-quarters of the take? That seems fair, since your secret's important to you.'

Bridie was shaken to the core of her being. 'No!' she exclaimed. 'I'd be working for you.'

Paddy smiled. 'Only for as long as it takes me to get enough cash together to begin on my own.'

She looked at him with loathing. 'How long would that be? You'd never leave me alone. Every time you wanted something new, you'd be round at my door.'

He laughed softly. 'What a low opinion you have of me, Bridget dear.' He shrugged. 'Of course, it's up to you—if you'd rather I went to the Duvaliers, you've only to say.'

Bitterness threatened to overcome her. Was she to give up everything for the sake of the twins—and the Duvaliers? She drew in her breath. She could go to Alphonse. He would think of some way out. But she couldn't, since he had washed his hands of her. Besides, he might think she had betrayed him.

She was trapped—well and truly caught with nowhere to turn. She searched Paddy's face. She shivered. He meant what he had said: it wasn't just some bad dream. He meant to have the money, but that would be only the beginning. In her heart she knew he meant to have the Hot Potato—and put her out on the street if she didn't work for him at the lowest of wages. She wanted to rant at him, revile him and hit him, but she held her tongue. Words would do her no good. They wouldn't melt the malice and greed she saw on his countenance.

'Think it over, Bridie, before you turn down my offer,' he exulted. 'You shall have till tonight to give me your answer.'

She could not bear to stay in his presence a moment

longer. Despite the unwieldiness of the snowshoes, she ran from him, ran as fast as she could.

His words echoed in her ears. She couldn't escape them—or their awful consequences. Paddy meant to have the Hot Potato. Everything she had worked for was to be taken from her. She had nothing, never would have anything: not the man she loved, not the twins, not her shop. What could she do?

CHAPTER FOURTEEN

ADÈLE KNEW THERE was something wrong. She had known it for a while, and that Paddy was at the root of it. As March slipped into April, she watched him. Oh yes, he still came to her sometimes, and she cursed herself for not being able to deny him. Where he was concerned, she was as weak as water. She let him soothe her questions away with vague promises and subtle caresses. But deep down she sensed he was holding back from her—not physically, for he seemed to need her as much as she needed him, but he no longer shared his plans.

At first she had been resentful and jealous of the time he spent with Bridie, but that seemed to have finished, and the girl looked as if she was sickening for something. She never sang any more as she worked, had refused to go out with either of the two English officers, and generally moped about the kitchen. She took orders from Paddy; she looked frightened of him.

At first, she thought it might be bad news from home that had upset her. When she asked, she was brusquely told to go about her own affairs. She didn't allow herself to be rebuffed by this, but determined to get hold of one of Bridie's letters from her brother at home. That was quite easy, it had been stuffed in her apron on the kitchen hook. Adèle read it, to find nothing alarming there. One of Bridie's brothers had married, the other wanted her to come home. A Hugh Prendergast was mentioned as doing very well financially, but doomed never to father a child. She put the letter back, no wiser about Bridie's malaise. She knew the brother had asked her before to return, so it couldn't be that.

It was not until she saw Bridie and Paddy doing the accounts, and his smug smile of satisfaction as he pocketed a wad of dollar bills that she realised Paddy had found something out about her and was forcing her to pay him. The scheming devil! They were in this together, and Paddy wasn't sharing with her. She tackled him about it as soon as Bridie was out of the way.

At first Paddy blustered. 'I don't know what you mean! You know what your trouble is, Adèle. You're jealous. It's a nasty tendency in you—one older girls often suffer from.' He put his hand on her waist.

Adèle flung it away. 'I want to know what's going on.'

'No, you don't.' He had hold of her arm and was twisting it so that she found herself forced against him. 'Much better to go on in ignorance.'

She managed to bring her knee up to strike him a blow where it would hurt him. It won her release for a moment, and she slid to the far corner of the kitchen, grabbing the poker as she went. 'I want to know what you're up to.' She raised the poker.

'Are you threatening me?' His expression was ugly.

The poker wavered in her hand. 'No, protecting myself. What have you done to Bridie?'

She thought he wasn't going to answer; then he laughed. 'You might say she's discovered how valuable I am—how necessary about the place.'

Adèle drew in her breath sharply. 'I don't believe that! I can see she loathes you. She draws away from you for fear of your touching her.'

Paddy came a step closer. 'That's the only explanation you can think of. Well, you're right! I haven't taken her—I don't want her. Don't I have you?' His eyes travelled over her figure. 'Put down the poker, Adèle. You've no cause to use it.' He took another step towards her, and this time seized her wrist in such a grip that she cried out and dropped the implement.

Then he was upon her. His mouth assaulted her, his hands ripped open the bodice of her gown, and she was flung to the floor. There was nothing of love or gentleness in his possession of her. There was strength and roughness and mastery, a brute force which he seemed to enjoy.

Adèle hated it. She hated him. She raked her finger-nails across his cheek and had the satisfaction of drawing blood. But that was small satisfaction when he used her again.

'Had enough?' he asked, as she lay under him. 'It's the last time I'll touch you.' His hand lingered on her exposed breast, and he stroked it in the first light gesture he had employed.

As the sense of what he said soaked into her exhausted body, Adèle had not even the strength to nod her head. He pulled at the nipple between thumb and forefinger. The pain made her cry out, and squirm to be free. He interpreted that as a desire for more, and gave the same treatment to the other nipple before he entered her again. If she had been able to reach one of the kitchen knives, she would have taken pleasure in sinking it deep in his back. As it was, she could only endure and listen to him, body writhing in protest and shock. Why should he treat her so?

'I don't need you any more,' he told her. 'I've found someone younger, someone prettier, someone who doesn't keep asking me questions. She looks up to me.'

'Who—who have you found?'

'Wouldn't you like to know?' His lips fastened on hers, and her traitor body welcomed him as his hands softened, caressed, where he had attacked only moments before. 'I'll not deny you're a good lay, but my ambitions go higher than a kitchen-maid—much higher! Now that I have money, I might even take a wife.'

Adèle said nothing. She felt scorn and anger. He needn't think he was going to be allowed to marry some fresh young girl. She would stop him! She didn't know how, but she would. He had as good as raped her, and cast her aside at the same time. Even when he had finished, and she lay sobbing on the floor, her clothes scattered about her, that anger throbbed in her, that cold determination to have her own back. She would find out who this girl was, and stop him. She hated him. She despised him.

By the time Bridie returned from her outing with Anita, Adèle knew what she must do. A certainty had begun to grow in her mind about the identity of the girl. He had talked about ambition and money, so she had to be of good position. What girl did he know who satisfied those conditions? Gabrielle Truteau, he must have gone on seeing her—Alphonse Duvalier would be interested to hear that. First, she had to make sure, and she knew the way to go about it. Wasn't Gabrielle's maid a friend of her dear friend Hortense? She would see what Hortense could find out.

Bridie sat on the bench in the back yard of the Hot Potato and let the afternoon sunshine of late April soak into her. Sheltered by the stone walls, it was actually warm—warm enough to have melted the last of the snow, warm enough to think that summer might come soon. It was Wednesday afternoon, and she had the place to herself. She could pretend it was still her own—that Paddy hadn't as good as taken it over. She sighed, and put it out of her mind. Today she would just enjoy the sun. She felt old and tired, washed out. But the fresh air told her that the flowers would bloom, that life would be better. She felt her spirits rise a little.

After a while, she was conscious that someone was knocking on the door of the shop. Let them knock! The Hot Potato was closed this afternoon, and whoever it was could go away. She closed her eyes, not stirring. She opened them in some astonishment when the door in the garden wall opened, and Alphonse Duvalier was framed in the entrance.

Her eyes lit up, her face smiled. 'Whatever are you doing here? Was it you at the door?' She had not seen him for months.

'May I come in?' He strode towards her without waiting for an answer. 'We must talk.' He sat down on the end of the bench. 'You're very pale, Bridie. Have you been working too hard?'

'I don't know.' She clasped her hands together. 'Can I get you something to drink?'

'No, I haven't come for that.' His hand reached out for hers.

Hers slid into it in the most natural way. He turned it over and looked in the palm, tracing the lines he saw there.

She felt alive, restored to feeling from the dull weeks of never seeing him. 'Why have you come? Is something wrong? The twins . . .'

'They're fine—but I think things aren't right with you. Do you want to tell me about it?'

There was such kindness in his eyes that she nearly cried. Ah, if only she could tell him. She licked dry lips and shook her head. 'What should be wrong?' she faltered. 'What do you mean?'

'I think you know what I mean. Better tell me about it. It's Paddy, isn't it?'

Her eyes filled with tears, and she nodded. How could he know? Her throat was so choked that she could not answer.

Alphonse continued with no trace of censure, not blaming her. 'He's found out somehow about the twins —that's it, isn't it?'

'Yes!' Her relief was enormous. 'I didn't tell him. He found out for himself. I don't know how.'

He still held her hand. 'I didn't for a minute think it was you who told him, but when Marie-Rose told me about meeting the man and the girl on the bridge, I knew something was wrong. I should have come then, but so much was happening.' He patted her hand. 'It's happened for the best. Seeing you has made Marie-Rose aware of the past. She remembered your face, and it all came back to her. Not all at once—we were quite worried over her—but over a few weeks. It was buried deep, the doctor says, hidden from herself; but now she's able to face it, to acknowledge that you gave her the babies. She's very grateful to you, and made quite a fuss about rewarding you. She was very relieved to hear about the Hot Potato and how you were prospering. My brother actually looked very guilty about the whole thing. I've never seen him so hang-dog! He thanked me for helping you.'

Bridie's hand quivered in Alphonse's, and he bent to kiss it. Her eyes overflowed—whether in sympathy with Marie-Rose or because of Alphonse's action, she wasn't quite sure. It was good to have it all out in the open at last. Secrets were hateful.

'I'm glad she knows,' she murmured. 'She still loves the twins?'

'Yes, more than ever, I think. She'll always look on them as her own. She's delighted with them.'

'Yes. Yes, I saw that. That's why I couldn't let Paddy spoil things for her.'

'So you paid him. If I'd known that . . . Bridie, you're a generous girl, a lovely girl, but you should have come to me. I shouldn't have had to hear from Adèle how you were paying Paddy for something.'

'From Adèle? Does Adèle know about the twins?'

'She does now. François and Marie-Rose have decided that the only sensible thing is to adopt them legally. They'll do it very quietly, but they'll do it. They've already spoken to a lawyer.'

'I'm glad.' Bridie felt like dancing and singing. The twins would be safe now—and she was free of Paddy! She knew a moment's shiver of apprehension. Would it be so easy to be rid of him?

As if sensing her hesitation, Alphonse said, 'I'll speak to Paddy, shall I? It will give me a great deal of pleasure to deal with that villain. Anyone who can demand money as he did needs a man to teach him a few manners.'

'Thank you, thank you!' Bridie found herself throwing her arms round Alphonse. 'I don't want ever to face him again. He frightens me.'

'I gather he frightened Adèle, too. But he won't frighten either of you any more—I'll see to that.' He kissed her on either cheek and got to his feet. 'I'll do it now, and recover some of your money—if it's not all been spent. He won't set foot in your shop again. I'll go round to where he lives and wait for him there, or if he should happen to be out, I think I know where I might find him.'

'I can't thank you enough,' Bridie faltered, facing him. 'What can I give you?' She threw her arms wide. She couldn't think how he might know where to find Paddy.

'A kiss?' he suggested. 'I've missed your kisses more than I would have suspected.' He was smiling.

She wasn't sure whether he was teasing, but she went into his arms and raised her own to twine round his neck. Her lips fastened on his, her tongue went into his mouth. It remembered the sweet taste of him as her body pressed close. She would have gone anywhere with him, given him anything he wanted. She was happy for the first time in weeks, and the most delicious sensations were rising everywhere in her. Her fingertips were tingling, so were the soles of her feet and the pit of her stomach. This moment must last for a lifetime.

He put her from him, looking almost as shaken as she was. 'Bridget Langton, you Irish witch, what am I to do about you?'

'Love me as I love you—stay with me,' she wanted to shout, but she couldn't utter the words. Instead she murmured, 'Kiss me again.' She blushed as she said it.

He shook his head, but softened his refusal by holding her hand in his and replying, 'Later—when I've done what I must—I'll come back. Never fear, Bridie, I mean to return.'

His eyes burned into hers. She was sure she saw determination there—and something else; but what that something else was, she wasn't quite sure.

He pressed her hand. 'Since Paddy will not be working here, you'll be short handed. It may take a little arranging, but I know the very person to help out . . . I'll see what I can do.' He raised her hand to his lips, and then slid through the gate.

Bridie stood with that self-same hand raised to her mouth, the imprint of his mouth still burning it. Her pulses were still racing, the excitement of seeing him was still with her. He had come—come when she needed him most. He had kissed her. He *must* care for her in some way. She pressed the back of her hand to her cheek. She did a jig round the small space. She hadn't felt like dancing in weeks. Fancy Adèle going to him; Adèle being responsible for freeing her from Paddy! She must thank her. She would be grateful to her for ever.

As the afternoon wore on and lengthened into evening, Bridie began to speculate on how Alphonse would deal with Paddy, on whether Paddy would fight him. She began to worry that Alphonse might be hurt. Why didn't he come back? Perhaps he was making arrangements for this person who was going to help in the shop. She calmed herself with that thought, not resenting at all that Alphonse was interfering in her life, that he was being high-handed even if well intentioned. After all, he had found her Adèle, and Adèle had been her saviour.

Just the same, where had Alphonse got to—and Adèle, for that matter? She was usually back by this time, and had not said anything about being late. Bridie made herself a cup of tea and forced herself to eat something, but she felt curiously on edge, unable to settle. She sat by the fire in the kitchen, for the April evening was cold, and tried to read, but it was no use. The printed page did not hold her interest, although it was a romance, and she was very fond of them since she had learned to read. The gas-lamp was alight and the room was quite cosy, but she walked up and down. When the knock came at the door, she was startled because it was so loud. It must be Alphonse, for Adèle would have come to the back.

Bridie flew to the door, and even in the dim light she could distinguish a man's figure outside. She fumbled with the bolts and then with the lock before she threw it wide. It wasn't Alphonse. She stood back in alarm and tried to shut the door. 'We're closed—come back in the morning!'

The man on the step prevented her by blocking the closure with his foot. 'Bridget, Bridie Langton, don't you recognise me?' he called to her. 'You'll not be closing your door in my face.'

It was the Irish lilt of the voice and the timbre of it that made her gasp out, 'It sounds like—no, it's never—it can't be—it's not possible! It's Hugh Prendergast.'

'So it is! Am I welcome, Bridget Langton? If I am, let me in, for it's perishing cold and I've news from your brothers.'

The door swung wide in Bridie's nerveless fingers. Hugh came in, laughing. 'I'm that glad to see you! Not that I can see much in the dark.'

Whether he could see or not, he didn't hesitate to pull her towards him and place a resounding kiss on her cheek. He hugged her so hard that he lifted her from the floor and spun her round. The door still swung open.

'Put me down!' Bridie was between laughing and crying. Were the surprises of the day never going to end? 'Hugh, where have you come from? Why are you here? Shut the door, do—the cold air is rushing in.'

When he set her down on her feet, she hurried him into the kitchen with its light and warmth, hanging on to him as if he might run away.

'There, that's better.' He held her away from him. 'Now I can see that you've grown into a handsome woman.' He made her turn round so he could look at her from every angle. 'You're not a bit like your sister Pegeen, but then you never were.' He caught hold of her hands. 'You've done well for yourself, with your own shop and all. How have you managed, Bridget Langton?'

'Sit down, Hugh, for it's a long story. I'll be mashing some tea, for there's never an Irishman but got thirsty in the telling and hearing of a tale—and I'm wanting to hear all your news.' She bustled about the kitchen, encouraging the fire to a brighter glow, setting the kettle to boil again. 'Have you eaten?'

'Yes, over in the hotel across the way. Sit down, Bridget, I don't want anything—just to talk. I've something to ask you. Just sit down and listen.'

When the tea was poured and it had been established to Bridie's satisfaction that her brothers in Ireland were in good health and good heart, Hugh began to explain the reason for his visit.

'I've never come—not the way you have, meaning to stay—I've come to right a great wrong. I've grieved and I've sorrowed—and so has the Mam—over the way we sent Maling away. I'll not have his boys crying out to strangers for their bread. I'm here to bring them home with me, raise them back in Ireland as my very own. Where are they, Bridie, for I'm longing to see them.'

Bridie gulped, and she gasped. Never in her wildest imaginings had she envisaged such a possibility. 'But you can't—no, you can't. They'd never survive across the ocean. No, no!' she cried out.

'Don't you fret yourself over that,' he told her. 'They'd not be travelling the way you did, in the hold. I'd have a cabin to myself, and I'd find a woman to look out for them. There's nothing wrong with them, is there? They're healthy boys and getting quite big now. And the apples of their Aunt Bridie's eye, I'll wager! Say they're fine, Bridie, set my mind at rest, do.'

Bridie looked at him in astonishment. This wasn't the Hugh Prendergast she remembered. He sounded genuinely concerned. He had crossed an ocean to see the twins, to take them home. Her brain was whirling. The twins *had* a home. François Duvalier was adopting them; it was a pity he hadn't done so before.

'They're fine,' she murmured. For a moment, she considered telling him that they had died. That would have stopped him, even if it wasn't the truth. But he deserved better than falsehood.

'You can't have them, Hugh,' she faltered. 'They're part of a family—grand people who love them. They've had them since the day after they were born. They think of them as their own. They're adopting them.'

'Adopting them?' He shouted the words, and pounded the table with his fist. 'I won't permit it! They're mine.'

'I don't see how you can stop it,' said Bridie. 'I've given my word.'

'You had no right to give your word! What does it mean—have you signed them away? I'll soon put a stop to that nonsense. They don't belong to you.' He was scowling at her.

'They're not yours, Hugh. They were Pegeen's and your brother's.' She wished Alphonse were here. No, she was glad he wasn't. She would have to make Hugh realise he couldn't just appear from the other side of the world and remove the boys. They were not his any more than they were hers.

'That's where you're wrong. They are mine.'

This time there was something in the way he said that they were his that made her search his face. 'What —what do you mean?'

'Just what I said. They never were Maling's. Pegeen wrote and told me after he died. She said the only thing she was happy about was that Maling had never known. She asked me to help her. At least, to help the child, for she didn't know it was twins—not then.'

Bridie wanted to deny what he said, to shout that Pegeen couldn't have done such a thing, but one look at Hugh's expression convinced her that he was the twins' father. Didn't she call to mind now how unhappy Pegeen had seemed when they had left Ireland? Some of the strange things she had said began to make sense now. She buried her face in her hands. Poor Pegeen—poor Maling! She wept for them both.

'Don't take on so.' Hugh patted her awkwardly on the back. 'It's all over and done with—God rest their souls. It's I as will carry the shame all my days.'

'Don't touch me!' Bridie raised her tear-streaked face, and shouted at him. 'Why didn't you help her when she needed your help? If she'd had a bit of money, a bit of hope, Pegeen might be alive now, and her boys with her.'

'I couldn't, not then. All the money had gone on their passage here—and yours. I didn't begin to prosper till I married. Maureen brought me the beginnings of my luck.'

Bridie wouldn't let him influence her—no, not even if he had paid for her passage. 'What does she think of you coming here? She can't want another woman's brats.'

'There you're wrong. She knows we'll never have any of our own—not since my accident. She wants children, and so do I. Where will the place go if there's no one to hand on to? Answer me that.'

Bridie had no answer. She began to see just how determined Hugh Prendergast was to have his boys. But she couldn't see that it was right that he should—father to them or not. He should have married Pegeen, even if it would have meant they'd be poor all their lives. She hardened her heart against him, and shook her head. 'You'll not have them.'

'Tell me where they are, Bridie.' He had risen to his feet, and his hand was cruel on her shoulder.

'No, I'll not.'

He shook her unmercifully. 'Tell me!'

'No, never! They're happy where they are. Why should Pegeen die for her sin and you have the boys? No, it can't be right. I can't believe it's what she'd want.'

Hugh released her abruptly, and sat down heavily. 'I wronged Pegeen. I know that.' He spoke slowly, as if the words were dragged out of him. 'I've been punished for it. Do you think I enjoy admitting that? I shouldn't have shaken you. I lost my temper. Do you want me to plead with you, beg you? I'll humble myself. Please, Bridie, where are my boys? They're my own flesh and blood.'

Bridie would have preferred him to stay angry, for then she could be angry as well, but when he showed her what his feelings were she found it almost impossible not to be sorry for him. Sadly, she shook her head. 'I can't

tell you. There are others involved.' She felt wretched,
thoroughly shaken.

'Am I not even to see them?' His words were a
whisper. 'You've grown into a hard, cold woman,
Bridget Langton, not like your sister at all.'

They struck her like a blow. She wasn't hard; she
wasn't cruel. He was tearing her apart. Did he know he
was doing it? Was it just an act to wear her down? The
old Hugh Prendergast always had his own way. Was he
any different now?

She hardened herself. 'If you saw them, you'd want
them all the more. One's blond like yourself, the other's
a red-head . . .'

'Like his mother,' Hugh finished the sentence for her.
'Look, Bridie,' he put his hand on hers, 'if I could be
seeing them—maybe talk to the people—we might
come to some arrangement.'

'What sort of arrangement?'

'Perhaps I could have one and they keep the other? I
can see they have a claim to something.'

'Tear them apart? No, that would be wrong.'

'Isn't it just as wrong for neither of them to know their
true father?'

She couldn't answer. Who was she to decide what was
right and what was wrong? She just knew in her heart
that the boys should stay together. Twins were too close
to separate. She knew that from her own brothers.

'Blood calls to blood, Bridget,' Hugh went on, his
hand still on hers. 'Help me, for your sweet sister's sake.
It was she drew me here.'

Bridie wished he could stop bringing Pegeen into it.
Pegeen was dead. She had left the twins to her. 'I—I
don't know what to say. If it's true you're their father
. . .' She left the words hanging in the air. She felt
defeated, drained, uncertain where to find guidance.

'It's true.' He released her hand. 'There is proof in the
letter.' He tapped the pocket of his jacket. 'I have it
here: I could take them to court. It'll be expensive—I
can ill afford the money on top of my fare . . .'

That sounded to Bridie more like the Hugh she had known all her life: he was counting the cost. She almost smiled.

'At least, promise me, Bridie, that you'll take me to see them, for I warn you I mean to find my boys. There'll be records somewhere of their birth. Someone will know where they are. I'll find them, so you might as well help me.'

Even then she did not give way to him completely. Perhaps if she played for time, she told herself, Alphonse would find some solution. She would go to him, tell him the whole thing.

To Hugh, she said, 'You must give me time to think it over very carefully. It's been a shock to me—I'll not deny that. I don't know what to think—what to do. Give me a day or two to get used to the idea of your being their father. It's too much for me to take in all at once.'

He looked at her, weighing her up. Whatever he saw in her face, he rose to his feet. 'I understand how you feel. Sleep on it. It's late. I'm just staying over the way. I'll come back tomorrow.'

'Yes—yes, that's the best. Come in the afternoon. The shop's very busy in the morning, and I'm short-handed for a day or so until our new help comes.' With a distinctly leaden sensation, she wondered just how she and Adèle would cope until then, for there had been no word from Alphonse about any help, and he knew it was urgent.

She showed Hugh out of the front door, the door of the shop, and was still standing, her shawl wrapped about her in the cold night air, when Adèle arrived back.

'What are you doing standing out here?' she snapped. 'You'll catch your death of cold.'

Bridie burst into tears.

'What's wrong? What's happened?' Adèle led her inside, and back to the warmth of the kitchen. She rubbed her hands and her feet, and soon had the story out of her of how Alphonse was meant to be dealing with Paddy and then coming back and he hadn't returned.

She mentioned Hugh Prendergast only as an old friend who had arrived from Ireland and taken her mind off what was happening to Alphonse.

She told Adèle that she was beside herself with worry about what might have happened. And indeed she was upset. She wanted desperately to see Alphonse. He had a right to know what Hugh had told her.

'You can put your mind at rest,' Adèle told her firmly. 'Monsieur Alphonse is quite all right. It's Paddy who's looking the worse out of their argument.'

'How—how do you know? To Bridie, there seemed a strange glitter of excitement, of triumph, in Adèle's expression. She was pleased that Paddy had suffered. At any other time, Bridie would have wanted to know why. Now all she wanted to hear concerned Alphonse. 'Did they fight?'

'You couldn't call it a fight, exactly,' Adèle laughed. 'Monsieur Alphonse caught Paddy behind the livery stable when he was returning the horse and buggy he'd hired. I don't suppose you know it, but Paddy has been seeing Gabrielle Truteau all this long time on the sly.'

Bridie had not known, and she was surprised. That was what Alphonse had meant when he had said he knew where to find Paddy. 'Go on,' she begged, knowing somehow that she didn't like hearing about Gabrielle and that there might be worse news to come. She didn't ask how Adèle came to witness the scene.

There was worse to come. 'Monsieur Alphonse took Paddy to task about corrupting an innocent girl, about meeting her without her parents' knowledge, and Paddy replied that Gaby was no innocent girl.'

That was enough for Bridie. Paddy and Alphonse had quarrelled over Gabrielle Truteau—not over the way Paddy had treated herself.

Adèle continued, with a great deal of relish, 'Monsieur Alphonse hit him then. I could hear the sound of the blow from where I was hidden at the side of one wall. When I peeked round, Paddy's nose was bleeding, and he was trying to stop it and to attack Monsieur Alphonse at the same time. He may have got in one or two blows. I was afraid they might notice me, so I didn't see it all, but the first think I knew, Paddy was on the ground and Monsieur Alphonse was standing over him and telling him what he thought of him. I heard him talk about the shop and your money.'

'But was he hurt—hurt at all?'

'Not that I could see.'

Bridie reached out her hands to Adèle. 'I know I must thank you for going to Alphonse, and I do—from the bottom of my heart.'

'It was nothing. Paddy treated you badly. I could see that.' Adèle's voice was gruff. She turned away from the outstretched hands. 'It's over now—all over.'

Bridie looked at Adèle's as she put another log on the fire. There was something here she didn't understand, some score Adèle had settled with Paddy. What could it be? There were too many other problems to unravel without adding to them. She didn't ask for information. If Adèle wanted to tell her, she would.

'Tell me what happened afterwards. Monsieur Alphonse said he'd come back here.'

'Did he?' Adèle shrugged. 'He probably will, then —tomorrow—some time soon. At the moment, I should think he has other things to attend to.'

'What other things?'

'He'll have gone to see his Gabrielle, won't he? I suppose he'll be angry with her, and she'll cry and say she was wrong, and he'll take her in his arms and comfort her. That's the way men are, isn't it?' Adèle was looking down at her, her arms folded across her breast. 'They're all fools when it comes to a pretty face.'

There was such bitterness in her voice that Bridie recoiled. She was frightened as well. Wasn't that exactly what had happened the first time Paddy and Gabrielle had been found out? Alphonse had believed Gabrielle, forgiven her, and taken her to the dance. It could happen again. Anger and grief threatened to overcome her. She couldn't bear it. Alphonse didn't want her. He wanted Gabrielle; he had meant to marry her all along. She herself was just for kissing. What a fool she had been, throwing herself into his arms in her gratitude. How he must be laughing at her! She felt shamed, degraded. Was this how Pegeen had felt when Hugh Prendergast had abandoned her?

Dear God in Heaven, what was she to do? Everything was wrong. Alphonse didn't love her. Hugh wanted the twins. She didn't know where to turn. She was alone.

She felt a tear drop on her hand, and looked up. She wasn't crying. She couldn't cry. She was too desolate.

It was Adèle who was weeping.

She stood up and held out her arms to her. This time, the French girl came into them and the two of them held close to each other.

'What fools we are—all of us women,' Adèle sobbed, shoulders heaving. 'They're not worth it—none of them is.' She said no more.

She didn't need to. Bridie understood suddenly that Adèle had cared for Paddy. She pitied her. She pitied herself. She pitied Pegeen as well. It must be the common lot of all women to weep. She let the tears flow. Perhaps that was the only comfort there was: this sharing.

CHAPTER FIFTEEN

Bridie faced the clerk in Alphonse's property office. 'I would like to see Monsieur Duvalier, please.'

He looked at her, but didn't move. 'Do you have an appointment, miss?'

She bit her lip, shook her head. 'No, but he'll see me. It's Bridget Langton—tell him that.'

The clerk looked to the door behind him. 'He said he wasn't to be disturbed.'

That was enough for her. Alphonse was in. Before the clerk realised what she was about, she had rounded the counter and was at the door. She didn't bother to knock, but just entered.

Alphonse looked up in some surprise, and his greeting was cold. 'What are you doing here, Bridget?'

After all the drama of the previous day and the tortuous decision-making that had ensued, Bridie felt as if a glass of cold water had been thrown at her. She gulped. 'Are you going to ask me to sit down?'

'If you wish.' Alphonse waved her to the chair in front of the desk. 'Was there something you wanted?'

'What's the matter?' she asked bluntly. 'You can't know about Hugh Prendergast. I didn't know anything about him and Pegeen—I swear I didn't! When he came yesterday, I was bowled over—I couldn't believe it.'

Alphonse seized on the name. 'Hugh Prendergast—is he a good friend of yours? Someone you're fond of. Is that what you're telling me? Why have you come to tell me? Am I supposed to care?'

Bridie's mouth opened in astonishment. She didn't know how to answer, but she was beginning to be angry. Had he been spying on her? The nerve of the man, the conceit of him, and him off to see Gabrielle Truteau as soon as he'd felled Paddy! 'Yesterday . . . Yesterday

. . .' she spluttered, 'you kissed me and said you'd be back. I know you dealt with Paddy—Adèle told me so. Thank you for that, and for sending me Jacqueline Dupont to help in the shop. She's a giant of a woman, and the best worker I've ever seen. I couldn't have come to see you if she hadn't been at the Hot Potato, for Adèle couldn't have managed on her own. As it was, I slipped out of the back door and ran down the lane for fear that Hugh Prendergast might see where I was going.'

This time it was Alphonse's turn to be surprised—and puzzled. 'Why would you hide from your lover?'

'I haven't got a lover!' Bridie exploded. 'Anyway, who are you to talk? You went off to see Gabrielle Truteau. I suppose it's all fixed up between the two of you now.'

'It isn't—not that it's any of your affair. I spoke to her, and to her parents. They were very upset. Gabrielle is going to stay with her grandmother in Three Rivers for a while.'

'Oh!' In spite of herself, Bridie's spirits rose just a little, then they sank with the thought of what she must try to explain to him.

'Tell me whatever it is you've come to say,' suggested Alphonse. 'I have work to do.'

She clasped her hands together. There was no easy way of leading up to it gradually, so she might just as well come straight out with it. 'It's about the twins. Hugh Prendergast says he's their father, and that he means to take them back to Ireland with him.'

'And you as well?'

Bridie looked at him blankly. Did he not understand what she had said? She was telling him about the twins, and the threat Hugh posed. 'Why would I go back with him? He's nothing to me. He has a wife of his own.'

'What's he doing here, then?'

'He's come for the boys—Sean and Sennen. Aren't you listening?'

'I'm listening, but I can't make head or tail of it. Start at the beginning and tell it properly. I saw you.'

'He told me he was the twins' father. Don't you see I grew up knowing Hugh—he was a face from home, and he has the place next to ours—but I knew nothing of him and Pegeen. It was Maling she married, Hugh's brother.'

At last, Alphonse seemed to comprehend the seriousness of what Bridie was saying. 'You mean that she married one brother and had twins by the other? It sounds an incredible story to me! Are you sure you've got it right?'

'Yes. There's nothing to smile about. He means to have the boys. It seems he can no longer father any children—he had a bad accident.'

'Do you believe he's the father?'

'I must.' She had no wish to meet his eyes. She didn't want to admit Pegeen's shame. 'It explains so much. And, besides, he has a letter from my sister which, he says, proves that he's their father. He wants them. He wants to see them, and to talk to your brother. It's horrible! He talks about parting them, about taking one back, to save himself the time and the trouble of going to the law.'

Alphonse was paying attention to her now. 'Have you come here as his messenger to plead his case?'

'No! How can you think that?'

'Don't you want him to have them?'

Bridie looked down at her hands. 'I'm torn both ways. I see he has a claim.' She raised her eyes. 'I think the twins are better where they are. Their mother—your sister-in-law—really loves them, but . . .' Bridie's voice sank to a whisper, 'will it matter to her—and to your brother—that the twins aren't who they seemed to be? Will they want to keep them, knowing that?'

'We must ask them.' Alphonse rose to his feet. 'Or, at any rate, we must ask Marie-Rose. François is away in the wilds and won't be back for a week. He's gone to look at timber for his factory.'

Alphonse took her by the arm, and with only the briefest of words to his clerk, they left. He had an open carriage waiting outside, for, of course, all the snow was gone and Montreal had reverted to wheels and put sleighs away for another year. Before Bridie would have believed possible, they had reached the Duvalier house —the place where she had worked as a skivvy—the place she had left all those months ago.

The front door was opened to them by a servant who showed no sign of recognising her, and they were ushered to a parlour. Marie-Rose was with them almost immediately.

'I'm very glad to meet you.' Marie-Rose held out her hand to Bridie. 'You've been in my thoughts a good deal. I'm glad Alphonse had brought you to see me.'

Bridie was considerably warmed by this greeting. She asked after the boys, and then let Alphonse do the talking. He quickly told her everything.

'It's unbelievable that he should travel this distance after he let this poor girl marry his brother,' Marie-Rose marvelled. 'Does he think to frighten us with a scandal? Tell this Monsieur Prendergast to go home. The boys are ours. They stay here—with us.'

'Does it matter to you who their natural father is?' Alphonse asked. 'François might draw back.'

'François isn't here. In any case, he wouldn't give them up. He's proud of them and he loves them. He looks on them as his own. If one Irishman or another fathered them—whether he was married or not to their mother—how can it matter? They are ours, our Jean and Jacques.' Madame Duvalier was very definite. 'It's a pity the adoption papers aren't through.'

Bridie felt tears welling in her eyes. She was glad, and overcome too, by Marie-Rose's stand. But how would she manage to keep the boys in the face of Hugh's determination to have them?

'Good,' said Alphonse. 'You mean to keep them. I had to be sure of that before we could make any plans at all.'

Bridie and Marie-Rose both looked at him.

'What plans?' Bridie asked. 'What can we do?'

'We must wait till François returns. He'll know how to deal with this man,' said Marie-Rose.

'Possibly he would,' Alphonse agreed, 'but I think we must act immediately.'

'How? What must we do?' Bridie was puzzled.

'Tell us,' begged Marie-Rose. 'For I shan't have a decent night's sleep till it's over.'

'I must swear you both to absolute secrecy.' Alphonse rose from his chair and began to pace the room. 'I hate secrecy, but I don't see any other way.' He came to a halt in front of Bridie. 'I know you've had enough to secrets, *ma chère*.' He stood looking down at her.

Bridie felt the colour rising in her cheeks. It was the term of endearment he had used. He had called her 'my dear one'. Despite her misgivings about secrets, she nodded. 'I promise I'll never tell.'

'And I,' Marie-Rose echoed.

'It's simple, really, but it just might succeed—and if it does, there won't be any trouble, any scandal, any gossip.'

'Tell us,' begged Marie-Rose. 'Whatever it is—just say it.'

Alphonse sat down near Marie-Rose and took her hands in his. 'There are many Irish orphans in this new St Patrick's orphanage in which you take an interest, are there not?'

Bridie had no idea what Alphonse was driving at, but Marie-Rose was quicker.

'They've been asking everywhere for people to take an Irish child—or a baby, as they can't cope with them all. That's what you mean, isn't it? I don't want some other Irish baby—I want the ones I have.' She drew back from him.

'Of course you do,' Alphonse reassured her, 'but this Hugh Prendergast has no idea what his sons look like —except that one is fair and the other red-haired. Among all those babies, couldn't we find two with a passing resemblance to Jean and Jacques?'

Bridie saw the whole beautiful scheme. Yes, yes, it

would work. It must work! 'Isn't it the Irish way out?' she exclaimed in delight. 'Oh, the slyness of it, the sheer cunning.' She clapped her hands. 'It tickles me to think of Hugh, the tightest man in Kilkenny—for that he's always been—adopting two Irish waifs, thinking he's won his own two boys. You're a genius, Alphonse.' In her enthusiasm, she'd forgotten how annoyed she had been with him only a short time before.

'I know someone who might help.' Marie-Rose's eyes were sparkling. 'But—but what about birth certificates? He'll want some proof.'

'That's the beauty of the thing,' Alphonse reassured her. 'In the Province of Quebec, we know, baptismal certificates serve as legal birth certificates. The twins happen to have two. I know, because François has shown them to me. There's the one signed by Father Mulcahey in the names of Sean and Sennen Prendergast —and the other in the names of Jean and Jacques Duvalier by the French priest in your own church. I suppose it would have been sorted out differently, except for Father Mulcahey's very sudden death after he caught typhus.'

'Yes, of course! How clever of you to think of it, Alphonse.' Marie-Rose clapped her hands together. 'I wonder how soon we can find other babies. If I start today . . .'

'It had best be very quickly.' Alphonse was decisive. He turned to Bridie. 'How long can you hold off this eager father?'

'Not very long.' She raised troubled eyes to him. 'He said if I wouldn't help him, he'd start some sort of search. He only has to go to St Patrick's church to find the records. He's bound to think of that.'

'And that will inevitably lead back to us,' Alphonse added, 'because François paid for Pegeen's funeral. Someone is bound to remember.'

'Then we must work quickly.' It was Marie-Rose who took command now. 'Tell this Monsieur Prendergast that we will see him here tomorrow evening. Alphonse will act the part of my husband. After all,' she looked to her brother-in-law, 'he knows neither of you. By that time, Jean and Jacques will be safely at my father's house in the country and the new twins will be upstairs in their cots.'

The plan was worked out between them, and Bridie was despatched back to the Hot Potato to do her part. Alphonse would have escorted her there, but Marie-Rose pointed out that the two of them must not be seen together just in case Hugh Prendergrast should catch sight of them.

Back at the Hot Potato, Bridie was greeted with the news that Paddy had appeared, had taken one look at Jacqueline Dupont, and changed his mind about whatever he had been going to say to Adèle. That made her laugh until she saw the look in Adèle's eyes.

'He might try something when I'm alone,' said Adèle. 'You don't know how violent he can be.' She shivered as she said it. 'You didn't see the way he looked.'

'You must stay close to us,' suggested Bridie. 'After all, there are usually people in the shop.' She wished Adèle looked happier. It made another worry to those already pressing on her mind.

As the day wore on, she discarded plan after plan as to how she would speak to Hugh when he came for her answer. She would give in right away—or no, better to be undecided still, and make a decision tomorrow. But then he might take things into his own hands and go directly to the Duvalier house before they were ready for him. He might already have stumbled upon their name and be watching the house or have someone watching it. He might see the true twins being spirited away and the other pair being taken in—he might speak to a servant who would give the whole thing away for a few coins . . . The possibilities were endless and terrifying. Bridie thought of them all, and doubted they could succeed. Hugh Prendergast was no fool. He'd find them out. Some small detail would give them away.

When Hugh eventually appeared, she was still undecided about what she must do.

She was unwilling to talk in front of the other two, and at least he made that easy for her. He took her across the way to the hotel on the corner, and treated her to afternoon tea with cakes and sandwiches. He attacked the food eagerly, but Bridie found she had very little appetite. He seemed to take it for granted that she was going to help him.

As she poured the tea, he asked her, 'Have you ever thought of coming back to the old place, Bridie? I'd pay your passage—first class—in exchange for your seeing to my sons—your nephews. Your brother Patrick would be glad to have you back. He asked me to mention that you'd be very welcome. Think of it, Bridget; you'd be able to watch Pegeen's boys growing up. They'd know you as their auntie.'

Bridie closed her eyes as she stirred her tea. For a moment, she was sorely tempted. To be back in Ireland, and have her nephews where she could touch them, love them—how easy and natural he made it seem. What did she owe the Duvaliers, after all?

Marie-Rose's face came before her—and Alphonse's. No, she couldn't betray them. She opened her eyes.

'I—I'll help you to see the boys,' she told Hugh, 'and to meet the people who have them. But I'll not go back with you. I have my little shop here. I'm content.' It was not entirely true. She would never be content without Alphonse beside her, but here at least she would be on the same side of the world as he was. She would surely see him sometimes.

'Ah, now you're being sensible.' Hugh smiled at her. 'You're doing what Pegeen would have wanted you to do.'

Was that really so? She could claim no knowledge of what her sister would have wanted, but Hugh appeared to have no doubts.

'We'll go and see them when you've finished your tea,' he suggested. 'The sooner it's done, the sooner I can bring them home. We'll have to sail from Quebec, for the port here won't be open for another month, so they tell me. The river still has ice in it. Ah, it's a grand country you've chosen, Bridget—but a cold one. The winters would kill me.'

The fact that he went on talking gave Bridie the opportunity to mask the fright he had given her with his proposal of going to the Duvaliers at once.

'It would be no use going this evening,' she managed to tell him calmly. 'I know for sure that Monsieur Duvalier is away looking for timber for his furniture factory. We'll go tomorrow evening, and I'll introduce you to them. They won't turn me away from their door—but they mightn't let you in on your own.'

'Duvalier—that's the name I got from the church. He's the one who paid for Pegeen's funeral. Now I know that you're telling the truth—that you really mean to help me. I shouldn't have doubted you.' He patted her hand briefly and then passed her the plate of cakes. 'Come, eat up, girl! We've something to celebrate.' He beamed at her.

Bridie took a cake and forced herself to eat it. She must seem as eager as he.

He did not seem to notice that it nearly choked her, and settled back comfortably in his chair. 'We'll do as you say, and go tomorrow evening when this Duvalier is home from his work. I hope it won't be too much of a blow to him, but no doubt he'll see reason. People generally do—just like you've done. The more they bluster, the more easily they give in. That's what I've found. What kind of a man is he, Bridie?'

This provided Bridie with a Heaven-sent opportunity to describe not François Duvalier, but Alphonse. Pray Heaven, François didn't cut short his trip for some reason!

All the next day, Bridie was on edge in spite of the way her encounter with Hugh had gone and the pleasant gossip they had had afterwards about the people they both knew back in Ireland. He had made her laugh about Michael's wedding, and the bride nearly saying No at the last minute. She didn't know whether to believe him, for Hugh had always been able to tell a good story. During her disturbed night, Pegeen was trying to tell her something. The only trouble was that she couldn't make out what Pegeen wanted. Dreams were worrying. The morning passed on leaden feet, and the afternoon was not much better. Her heart had nearly jumped out of her body when young Davey, the boy who hung around the livery stable, came in and asked if they had heard the news.

'What news?' she demanded in the same breath as Adèle and Jacqueline. She immediately thought of Hugh.

'About your Paddy.' The boy licked his lips, his eyes shining. 'Haven't you heard?'

Bridie almost turned away. He was only going to tell her about the fight with Alphonse, and she knew that already.

'Heard what?' asked Adèle, a pile of plates in her hands.

'It's said that the Widow Mulvaney's brother arrived last night from Toronto, all unexpected . . .' Davey paused, waiting for some reaction.

Bridie shrugged. 'I didn't know she had a brother.' She began counting the money in the cashbox.

'Neither did Paddy!' Davey grinned widely. 'I think I'll have some of those *patates frites* if there's any left, Mademoiselle Jacqueline. I've done well today, and they do smell good.' He took a coin from his pocket.

'Well, get on with the story.' Adèle set the dishes down on the counter as Jacqueline prepared a helping of hot potato.

'Folks say her brother found her with Paddy, and didn't like what he saw. He woke up all the neighbours with the fuss that he made.'

'What happened?' Bridie stopped counting.

Davey wouldn't be hurried. He helped himself to

one of his *patates frites*. 'He's a fine big man, is Mrs
Mulvaney's brother. A wrestler—bigger even than Miss
Jacqueline! He was all for taking Paddy apart.' Davey's
eyes laughed, and grew large in his face. 'No man could
stand up to him.'

'What did Paddy do?' Adèle leaned against the
counter.

'He told him he was making a mistake. He and the
Widow Mulvaney were promised to marry.'

That made Bridie smile, at least. 'Poor Paddy,' she
murmured, her eyes on the French girl, who had gone
very pale. She could just about find it in her heart to pity
him. The Widow Mulvaney must be at least ten years his
senior.

'He won't be so poor,' Davey was quick to tell her.
'The banns will be called this Sunday, and it's said he and
the Widow are going to buy a little shop the other side of
town. They're going to start their own *patates frites*
place. I thought you'd want to know that.

'The black-hearted villain!' Bridie exclaimed. Adèle
still stood as one turned to stone. Jacqueline picked up
the discarded dishes.

Bridie reached over the counter and put her hand on
Adèle's shoulder. 'Perhaps it's for the best,' she murmured, as Davey went to the door well pleased with the
effect his story had caused.

'Yes, he'll be away from here,' Adèle agreed. 'That's
a blessing.' She sighed as she spoke.

Hugh Prendergast called for Bridie that evening with a
buggy rented from the livery stable. 'We'll not go like
beggars,' he told her. 'Besides, we might be bringing
back one or the other with us.'

If anything was needed to stiffen Bridie's resolve, that
was enough. He was still considering parting the boys as
though they were possessions, not people in their own
right.

It was a short journey and not a particulary cold night,
but Bridie found herself shivering all the way. What if

the replacement children weren't there? What if . . . She must stop thinking like this; it was going to be all right. Alphonse and Marie-Rose would see to it.

The door was opened to them by a man-servant, and they were ushered to a study on the ground floor after Bridie had given their names.

Alphonse was seated at a desk in the centre of the room, and he looked up coldly as they entered. He did not rise, and spoke with no warmth. 'The understanding, Mademoiselle Langton, was that there would be no contact between us. Why are you here? Who is this man?'

'Something—something unexpected has come up,' Bridie stammered. 'This is Mr Prendergast. He asked me to come with him and introduce him to you.' She spoke in English, since Alphonse had started in that language. 'I'm sorry to disturb you. Monsieur Duvalier, Mr Prendergast. He's come from Ireland.'

'How interesting. Did you have a pleasant trip?' Alphonse waved them both to chairs—straight-backed ones. 'I hope this won't take too long. I'm rather busy, as you see.' He indicated the papers spread on the desk.

'That depends on you, Mr Duvalier.' Hugh leaned forward on his chair.

He was rewarded with a frown. 'In what way?'

Alphonse was so stern-looking that Bridie felt a little in awe of him. She, too, was nervous.

Hugh went on with his explanations. 'I understand that my sister-in-law here gave you twin boys some time ago. She had no right to do so.'

'Indeed?' Alphonse had picked up a pencil and had been playing with it. Now he snapped it in two with a sharp crack. 'Is this man some relation to the twins, Mademoiselle Langton? What is he after?'

'He's their uncle—at least, he's Maling's brother. He's trying to explain it to you—if you could just listen . . .' Her voice trailed off in the face of Alphonse's icy glare.

Hugh seemed quite at ease. 'I know you'll be disappointed, but they're Irish boys, after all, and my own flesh and blood. I want them.'

'Your flesh and blood? I don't understand.' Alphonse looked from Hugh to Bridie, frowning. 'Has he returned from the grave? I understood that your sister's husband was buried somewhere in Newfoundland. You assured me that your sister was a widow. Was that a lie?'

'My sister was a widow. Her husband is buried in an open grave far from Montreal. Hugh is his brother, but—but he says he is the boys' father.'

'And I'm supposed to believe this cock and bull story! I warn you, Mademoiselle, if this is some plan to extract money from me, I shall have both of you thrown from the house.' Alphonse pounded the edge of the desk in anger.

So real was the scene becoming to Bridie that she almost believed that Alphonse had turned into his brother François. She quailed before him.

Hugh was made of sterner stuff. 'You mustn't be on at Bridie, Mr Duvalier. It was as much a shock to her as it is to you—about me being the father. You see, it was like this. Pegeen was the loveliest girl in all Ireland, and Maling had courted her for years. I don't quite know how it happened. Maling was working on the Penny Road, and didn't have enough to eat and no energy, either. Pegeen was just languishing away for a bit of loving.'

'And you supplied the loving? Is that what I'm to understand? You sit there calmly telling me that you betrayed your brother—you and the twins' mother? What kind of a man are you that you could spare no bread for your brother and yet seduce his wife?'

'She wasn't his wife then.'

Alphonse threw his hands up in the air. 'I suppose you were already married. One woman wasn't enough for you.'

For the first time, Hugh was out of countenance. 'It wasn't like that,' he blustered. 'I had no wife then. I couldn't afford to marry. You don't know what it was like in the famine.'

'But you could have married this—this Pegeen—when you found out she was expecting your child.'

'I didn't know. She didn't tell me. She married my brother, and sailed for Canada with Bridget for company. My mother had paid for their fare to New York. She was the one who made me sure that the twins were mine. That was after I had the letter from Pegeen saying that Maling was dead and she needed help. I made the old woman tell me. But it was too late to come for Pegeen. I'd married Maureen O'Shaughnessy then. There wasn't any going back for either of us.'

'Yet you've come for the boys. You must be a man of some means now?'

'Ay, I've prospered, but I've not been blessed with children. We'll never have any of our own. So, thought I to myself, there's Bridget in Canada, working and struggling to care for my boys—for that's what she wrote—I knew I must right a great wrong. That's why I came, only to find that Bridget hadn't told it quite as it was. She had given the boys away. She wasn't supporting them. So I've come to you, to throw myself on your mercy—to ask you for the twins. Let me be a father to them, for that's what I am.'

Alphonse sat back. He tapped the pencil against the desk. There was no other sound in the quiet room.

Bridie found she was holding her breath. Hugh had not tried to gloss over anything. He hadn't shown himself in a good light. He hadn't excused himself. Why did she have the feeling he was holding something back? She could almost feel Pegeen at her shoulder, making her hold back her sympathy. How had it been between them, she wondered. Pegeen had married Maling, after all. Had Hugh refused her, or was it just as he had told it?

'A letter? You said something about a letter.' Alphonse broke the silence.

Hugh took a sheet of paper from his pocket and handed it across the desk.

Alphonse read it, and nodded. 'She says you are the father. I suppose I must accept that. But that doesn't mean I'll give up the boys.' He turned to Bridget. 'It was wrong of you, Mademoiselle, to let this man think you still had his sons. What did you write to him?'

'I never wrote to him at all,' Bridie protested, wringing her hands. 'I wrote to my brothers. I thought they'd grieve to hear Pegeen's boys were given away. I— I wrote that I'd placed them with a French family. They thought I was paying for them. Well, I was, in a way—there was the shop . . .'

'So that's how you did it!' Hugh's face was an angry red. 'You sold them to him. You're no better than I. You betrayed Pegeen, too, for the sake of a shop.'

'I didn't! I never!' Bridie was on the verge of tears. 'I had nothing . . . They would have died. This is the man you've to thank that they're living today.' She pointed to Alphonse.

'I do thank him.' Hugh rose from his chair and reached his hand across the desk to Alphonse. 'I can't thank him enough.' He pumped his host's hand energetically. 'Please, may I have a look at the boys? I've come a long way, and I'm longing to see them.'

Alphonse protested, but did not make a definite refusal. Hugh asked again. Alphonse rose to his feet and rang a bell. He issued some orders in French to the man-servant who came to the door. Bridie realised that he had asked for the twins to be brought. She was in a fever of impatience to find out which twins. Had they been switched?

It was Marie-Rose, wearing the garb of a servant, who carried in two baby boys. Bridie had only a glimpse of a fair head and a reddish one before Hugh had leaped to his feet and held out his arms to the pair.

For a long minute there was absolute silence. The fair-haired baby was snatched from Marie-Rose by a subdued-sounding Hugh. 'I'd know him anywhere.

Look at that, now. He's awake and smiling at me. This one is a real Prendergast!'

Marie-Rose said nothing. Alphonse was silent. Bridie rose to her feet, transfixed. She would never have expected Hugh to be so moved.

He took the second baby in his other arm and showed them to Bridie. 'Isn't this one the picture of Pegeen?' He handed her the first one. 'Try the feel of him. Don't you know him for a Prendergast?'

Bridie was overcome by his emotion. As she handled the boy, she realised it wasn't Sean or Sennen. No, these weren't the babies she had seen on Sunday. The substitution had been made, and Hugh had accepted this pair as his sons. There were tears in her eyes. She wasn't sure why it should be so, but she saw that Marie-Rose was equally affected. Passed from arm to arm, the pair began to cry, and Marie-Rose, after a little while, took them away.

There was a different atmosphere in the room when they had gone. The two men agreed to meet again the following day after Alphonse had recovered from the shock of the revelation. 'My wife will be very upset,' he said. 'I don't know how she'll react. Your story has moved me, but still . . . We've grown used to thinking the boys are our own.'

Bridie silently applauded his performance and accompanied Hugh back in the sleigh. He was confident that all would go well, but he would need to be patient.

It was surprising how quickly events moved after that. Within two days the substitute twins were in Hugh's possession, together with Sean and Sennen's legal baptismal certificates. Hugh had hired a motherly woman who longed to return to Ireland to accompany them on the voyage, and all four of them were on their way to Quebec and thence to the ship that would take them to their native land. Bridget waved them goodbye, with strict instructions to write as soon as they arrived safely. She kissed the substitute boys and gave them presents of cuddly toys and a fur wrap. She made such a fuss of them that she almost convinced herself that they were Pegeen's own twins. She stifled the feeling that somehow something wrong was being done. Hugh was delighted with his boys. Marie-Rose was able to keep hers. What better arrangement could there be?

Just the same, she would have liked to explain it somehow to Pegeen, to know if she was angry or pleased. Perhaps she would dream about her again.

But it wasn't Pegeen she dreamed about. It was Maling—a laughing Maling, who thought it a great joke. Hadn't Maling always been the one for a jape or a trick? Perhaps he would lie easier in his bit of Canada for knowing that Hugh hadn't won everything. It might take away the bitterness of the Penny Road—and Pegeen's betrayal.

At any rate, it was done. There was no going back, no way of Hugh ever finding out. Only three of them knew, and they weren't going to give the secret away. Would the other two let her see the real twins sometimes? She should have asked. She wanted them to offer. She was a fool, she told herself. They'd stay far away from her now that it was all settled. She'd given the twins up for good.

It left her with a very cold feeling, a desolate longing for someone of her own. She wished for Alphonse to come to her—but he didn't. She neither saw him nor heard from him all the rest of that endless week.

CHAPTER SIXTEEN

THE NOTE CAME from Marie-Rose on Sunday, inviting Bridie to take tea with her on Wednesday, her half-day. Bridie would rather have heard from Alphonse, but just the same she was delighted, then puzzled. What could Marie-Rose want?

She could not make up her mind what to wear: it was too warm for the blue velvet, and the rose dress was too old. Her white cotton dress with navy polka-dots, with a navy shawl, might be just the thing if the day was warm enough. Wednesday was dull, and muggy with it. She put on two layers of petticoats to make the skirt of the white cotton stand out stiffly. Adèle rolled her hair into a big loose bun at the back of her head instead of the two plaits she usually wore. She allowed kiss-curls to escape in front of either ear, and tied a green bow round the bun.

'It's perfect,' said Jacqueline, who had stayed to watch the preparations. 'What a trim figure you have, and that nice tight bodice fits so well.'

Bridie was confident that she looked her best when she stepped into the closed carriage Marie-Rose had sent for her—and just as well it was closed, because it began to rain as she stepped into it. By the time she arrived it was pouring, but an open umbrella held by a servant ensured that she was quite dry and composed as she entered the front door and was led to the morning-room.

'I thought we'd be more comfortable in here,' Marie-Rose greeted her. 'Don't you look pretty?' She took her shawl from her and draped it over a cushioned wicker chair. Marie-Rose was wearing mauve.

The room was done in shades of white and yellow, and looked cosy, but Bridie had no eyes for the décor. The twins, Jean and Jacques, were sitting by the screened-off fireplace and smiling up at her, their toys around them.

'May I?' She dropped to her knees in front of them and put out a hand to each. The red-haired Jacques took hold of her fingers and clung to them. He looked up at her, his expression so like that of Pegeen that she caught her breath. For the first time since the deception of Hugh Prendergast, she was convinced that they had done the right thing. These two babies belonged here. She told Marie-Rose so.

'I don't know what I would have done without them.' Marie-Rose picked up Jean and set him on her lap. 'As you see, they're my life—and François' too. He'll be back tomorrow and will want to thank you himself. After that, we'll say no more about it, but I hope you will visit the boys and that they will know you as their Aunt Bridget. That seems only fair.'

Bridie's eyes filled with tears. She was too moved to speak. She gathered Jacques to her and hugged him, her heart full. Marie-Rose gave Jean to her as well. 'It would be a shame not to love both equally.'

Then she did break down. But they were happy tears, healing tears, and the little boys wiped them from her cheeks. They were soon laughing and playing merrily together.

By the time Marie-Rose rang for tea, Bridie felt as if she had found a friend; in fact as though she had known her for ever, so easily did they chatter together. When they had finished and the boys had been allowed a tiny drink and the smallest crumbs of cake, Marie-Rose whisked the two cherubs away, and Bridie was left alone in the room. She had no chance even to leave her chair before there was a soft knock at the door and Alphonse stood before her.

He took her hand in his own, and kissed it. 'Have you enjoyed your afternoon, Bridget?'

'Yes. Oh yes!' she murmured. 'It was kind of Marie-Rose to invite me. It has meant so much to see Jean and Jacques.'

He still held her hand, still looked at her, and she became very conscious of his nearness, of his touch. He always had had this effect on her.

He drew her slowly to her feet so that she stood very close to him. He cupped her face in his hands. 'I never claimed that kiss you promised me, when was it—only last week? It seems a month ago.'

His lips closed on hers. She melted against him, the most delicious sensations spreading through her. She didn't care if Marie-Rose came back and discovered them. She wanted only Alphonse, and she returned his kiss with ardour. All she regretted were the two layers of stiffened petticoats between them.

He released her—but only to the circle of his arms. 'Bridget, will you marry me? I think I've loved you from the first time I held you in my arms. Could you learn to love me, just a little?'

Bridie smiled up at him. 'You must know I do already, and not just a little—but with all my heart! Oh, Alphonse, are you sure? Because I couldn't bear it if you changed your mind.'

'I'm sure. I keep loving you more all the time.' His mouth sought hers again.

It was a long, long kiss, a pledge between them. Bridie had never felt so happy in all her life. When he kissed her eyelids and cheeks and then her neck with the tenderest of light caresses, a fire of desire spread through her. Alphonse had asked her to marry him! She had never thought to see this day.

'Yes,' she whispered. 'Let's be married soon. I want to be your wife.'

'June is a good month for brides,' he whispered back, and laughing, led her to the window. 'Look, it's stopped raining. The sun is shining.'

She stood, his arm about her, radiant with love, nestling against him, rapture in her eyes and in her heart. 'How lucky we are. Do you suppose,' she murmured, more to herself than to him, 'that Pegeen and Hugh once felt like this? Let's not be parted as they were.'

'Never,' he assured her, 'I intend to keep you by me for ever. I can't live without you.'

Since this so exactly mirrored the way she felt, Bridie dispensed with words and threw her arms round him, kissing him and holding him as close as he held her. They would be married next month. The future was theirs. She relinquished her dream of returning, rich, to Ireland with a serving-girl to wait on her. That had been a child's fantasy. Alphonse was the present and the future, and her path lay here—here in Montreal with him. She would be a true Canadian—just like Pegeen's boys. This was her country now. Alphonse was her man. She was content. More than that—she was fulfilled. She was a woman, not a girl. She held him closer.

EPILOGUE

ALPHONSE AND BRIDIE were married in June. Adèle became the manager of the Hot Potato, and the following year opened another shop, with Anita in charge. By that time, Bridie had a little girl, and the Widow Mulvaney (now Mrs O'Leary) a little lad.

Gabrielle married her second cousin, and her father took him into the family business—where he never made much impact. The English lieutenants went to India, and Hartley earned his captaincy there.

Hugh Prendergast returned to Ireland and his wife, Maureen, and his mother. The old lady had a stroke, and died happy in the knowledge that her grandson, little Sean, the blond one who looked like Hugh, would inherit the property. But Maureen had other ideas. She favoured red-haired Sennen. He wasn't going to be treated as Maling had been—no, not while there was breath in her body! She would see that he got his share. None of them had any idea of what lay in store . . . But that's another story.

The 1987 Christmas Pack

Be swept off your feet this Christmas by Charlotte Lamb's WHIRLWIND, or simply curl up by the fireside with LOVE LIES SLEEPING by Catherine George.

Sit back and enjoy Penny Jordan's AN EXPERT TEACHER, but stay on your guard after reading Roberta Leigh's NO MAN'S MISTRESS.

Four new and different stories for you at Christmas from Mills and Boon.

Available in October Price £4.80